LOOKING FOR THE PATH

BACK HOME

LOOKING
FOR THE
PATH BACK
HOME

DAVID ADER

First edition

Book Design by Glen Edelstein, Hudson Valley Book Design, www.hudsonvalleybookdesign.com

Publishers Cataloging-in-Publication Data TK

978-0-578-31714-4 (Trade Paperback)
978-0-578-31715-1(ebook)

Printed in the United States of America

There are many people from my life who warrant a very specific dedication and I trust they will recognize themselves in actions, moods and their names or versions thereof in this collection.

But four men deserve special note; men who gave me respect and attention that helped me grow (up). I refer to Leo Hecker, a grand storyteller in his own right, Gustav Newman, father to my friend Eric, and Michael H. Bell who would be kicking me under the table at this very moment if he were here to read these words. And, of course, Melvin Ader who stirred my imagination with his tales of travel, adventure, history and more.

Contents

Preface

The title of the book, "Looking for the Path Back Home," may strike some readers as a nostalgic yearning for the past. It is and it isn't. The past was great in so many ways, and many of the stories you will encounter stem from real events and encounters embellished accordingly. There are times I miss terribly, things I would have done differently perhaps, but then it takes a fully lived life to recognize how things were and might have been. It takes a degree of maturity to appreciate all that was and all that will be. So, no, I'm not longing for the past; I just needed a source for my stories.

Anyway, bonds mature; I'd rather not.

When I first started to write for a large(ish) audience, I worried about getting it wrong. It, in this case, was anything having to do with the bond market. Bear in mind the bond market is filled with egos looking for an opportunity to find fault with the ideas of other people. My work was no exception. In fact, I would say that because I was such a prolific writer on the subject there were that many more opportunities to face the firing squad of critical responses. It took some getting used to.

I figured pretty early on that I was the one defining the agenda. Others, not unlike vultures circling around a kill made by some other animal, were simply there for the pickings, the pickings being my effort to come up with insights and, most impor-

tantly, the data and facts to back them up. It was a fellow Tufto-
nian, Daniel Patrick Moynihan, who said, "You are entitled to
your opinion. But you are not entitled to your own facts."

The facts I could pull out of my hat shut a lot of people up.
That, or they had stopped listening, which might be one reason I
left the industry.

Many of these stories have touches of "facts" in them.
In "Last Remains" I mention a dental implant called a sanitary pontic. My father had one after an accident when he was
in the Army Air Corps, all gold and paid for by the Army.
I didn't dive into the ocean to retrieve it however when we
dumped his ashes, and Mom's, in the water off Provincetown.
At my goddaughter Pippa Mansdorf's Bat Mitzvah, the Rabbi made note of her discovered faith when she said, "Thank
God it's over." I used that line in "Today You Are a Man."
Inspiration for "The Servant's Entrance" came from a story re-
lated to me by my neighbor Peter Cook, whose dad worked for
the phone company in Boothbay Harbor. My son Geoffrey had a
great teacher who helped with college essays and, unfortunately,
made a career mistake when he wrote a bad reference for one
of his students. You'll see glimmers of this in "Admissions Process." Eric Newman, dear friend, fishing buddy, author, and my
roommate at Columbia, once relayed a story about a black man
shouting, "Down, Lady!" in an elevator. An older woman did just
that and went to the floor. The man was talking to his dog. The
implied prejudice and misinterpretation are behind two stories
here: "Encounter in the Park" and "We Have to Move."

Mark Bitterman never did drop a phone in a river, but it's not
difficult to imagine the two of us on a boat in Montana as in "Fish
On, Phone Off." My boys Nicho and Geoffrey are the source of
"Wilce's Dream" in many ways; I wrote that with their imagina-
tions on my mind.

Then there's a story like "You're Using Too Much Water,"
about a couple preparing to hike Kilimanjaro. Any resemblance

between my composting/water-retaining/recycling and organic wife is purely coincidental. My use of the term "water-retaining" only refers to her conservation efforts. When, or if, you read "Heaven is Restricted?" bear in mind that many Jewish soldiers in World War II changed their dog tags in case they were captured by the Germans. It's estimated that several hundred graves of Jewish soldiers in European cemeteries have crosses instead of stars as a result of this oddity.

I suppose this is a warning to friends and family: be careful of what you say to me; I listen. It's also a way of saying how much those who are important to me have contributed to these stories and my happiness. What I've tried to do here is sneak in names, incidents, places, people, and times that have touched a life. If some readers recognize all that, I'll be quite pleased. If readers only take away some moments of enjoyment, I'll be totally ecstatic.

DAVID ADER

Acknowledgements

First and foremost, I want to express my love and gratitude to Pippa for her amazing tolerance, patience, support, encouragement, edits, critiques, and laughs over the years. She is the most important person in my life. I married up.

You will find a good deal of Pippa here and there in these works.

I think it's appropriate to thank your editor and in my case that's Avner Landes, who to the best of my knowledge didn't laugh behind my back, made the most appropriate comments and edits, and kept me going.

In my early days writing about bonds, Alex Tedeschi, my oldest friend in the world, was trading at Goldman Sachs. He had the patience and kindness to tolerate my questions about how the bond market worked. Mi hermano mayor Luis Curutchet still surprises and encourages me when he asks if I could send him more of my stories. I owe Peter McTeague a huge debt of gratitude for being my partner in bonds and bringing me into Greenwich Capital, which afforded me the time and confidence to put these stories together.

Eric Newman and Patrick Rafter have been with me through thick and thin, in rivers and out of them, on battlefields real and imagined. There's a bit of them in many of these stories.

And there's my sister Beverly. Bev has laughed at my writing, cried over it, and will recognize many of the things I write about more than anyone else. Thank you for being my sister. Now you can cry with a smile.

LOOKING FOR THE PATH
BACK HOME

I.

It Wasn't a Coffin

It wasn't a coffin. For starters, it was metal and vertical; coffins were made of wood and lay horizontally. He knew that much. And coffins didn't have slats at eye level, presumably for airing out sweaty gym gear, or hooks at the back. And the coffins he'd seen looked comfortable, cushioned, lined with silk or satin, to keep the occupant comfortable for eternity.

No, this was definitely not a coffin. It just felt like one.

It was locker 436B on the second floor of Our Lady of the Courageous Caucasian Prep. Colin had just been forced into it by two "things" who made up most of the school's football team when measured by bulk. They got away with this behavior especially when it came to freshmen because freshmen didn't "rate." In other words, they were the low men on the totem pole of the school's social hierarchy, and the freshman Colin proved short, skinny, and narrow enough to allow Thing One to win a bet against Thing Two.

"I told you he'd fit," said Thing One, alternatively called Karl Christensen Jr. It was said that Karl's mother had left the family either because she couldn't stand her version of Rosemary's baby or because of an abusive Karl Sr. The apple didn't fall far from that tree. Colin assumed it was a $5 bet because he overheard Thing Two counting to five outside the locker. He was tempted to say that he was impressed George Wallace Foss, aka Thing Two,

1

could count that high, but he thought better of it. The Things forgot about Colin and went off down the hall arguing about who was the better football player. He heard several "douchebag" accusations and at least one "make me" before they were out of earshot.

Had it been another part of the day, say between class periods, there would have been other students in the hall, and he could have pleaded with someone to open the locker. Small though he was, it was a tight fit. But there was no one there now, after school, and he was forced to strain his right hand at an unnatural angle to the inner workings of the clasp, nearly dislocating his pinky in the process of tipping up a lever that unlatched the locker's door. His prayers had been answered. They hadn't put the combination lock back on.

He made his escape utilizing movements he'd once seen a street performer use to wiggle out of a straitjacket. The magician had been more dramatic, writhing on the sidewalk, moaning in agony, milking the performance.

Colin's milking had taken place earlier in the day when Thing One had spilled a carton of skim—he was watching his weight for wrestling season—into his backpack. "Whoops, sorry, Miss," was the apology, accompanied by guffaws from Thing Two and uncomfortable snickers from other jocks in the vicinity. They surely aren't all brutes, thought Colin. They can't be. Hell, the quarterback, McMahon, wanted to be a priest. He could have said something like, "Knock it off."

Win Lowry did say something. He said it later when he saw Colin in the hall. Lowry was Colin's patrol leader, Troop 464. He'd just made Eagle on his trek over hill and dale to his appointment to West Point. Lowry had a speck of decency in him, maybe two specks. Colin almost liked the guy.

"You shouldn't take that from them," said Lowry.

"Lowry, he's got twelve inches and a hundred pounds on me. Exactly how do I not take it?"

"That much, huh?"

Colin once hoped that Lowry, no physical slouch himself, might step in with a good deed like beating either of the Things to a bloody pulp. Colin would have reminded him of the responsibilities of an Eagle Scout, the leadership required of someone on his way to West Point. That was before one of the Things had taken the pants off another freshman in Lowry's troop and kicked him across a playing field. Lowry did get that kid a towel, albeit a wet one, from the gym.

Lowry had said it was best to ignore them. That de-pantsed kid did not. That boy called up his parents. The parents called up the principal. The principal called up the football coach. The football coach called up the team's record: "County champs, three years in a row, and season's about to begin." The phrase "Boys will be boys" was said several times along with shrugs and grins. The victim left for a public school a week later wearing a new pair of pants. He would have gone sooner if it hadn't been in front of a three-day weekend on which the All Saints won 26 to 6 against an inner-city school the All Saints derisively called Coonskin Prep.

"Lowry," said Colin. "Do you worry about getting shot by your own troops?"

Lowry was out of earshot when Colin said that.

Colin had the dubious fortune of being placed in an advanced math class containing Things One and Two. The pair had to repeat their sophomore year of that particular class, as well as a handful of others. Twice. Passing the class was a must. A prerequisite for the Things passing a football in college, which was why colleges winked at their academic records, SAT scores, and mishaps with local police. Once again, the defense of "Boys will be boys" made up for a combined eleven years in high school.

Colin did well in the class. The Things did not. This brought about another encounter.

This time he was shoved against the locker, an improvement over being stuffed into it.

3

"Here," said Thing One, shoving a set of stapled pages into Colin's pallid face. A sharp corner flicked his eye, generating reflexive tears.

"Oh, look. Baby's crying. Baby wanna bottle?" came from Thing Two, who rolled up his pages into a solid mass and slapped Colin on the head several times with it.

The upshot of the encounter had to do with the extra homework the Things had been offered. If they completed the work, they could boost their GPA by 15 points. At the rate they were going, they'd end the term with 100 percent. That would be a combined 100 percent if you added Thing One's 49 percent to Thing Two's 51 percent. The two-point spread gave Thing Two a measure of pride.

Their anxious math teacher had explained the extra credit was to give them a boost because he was sure they could pass if they were given a chance. He left out the part about the idea stemming from a pointed conversation with the school's principal about someone's standing with the tenure committee and her strong desire to see the football players graduate. It wasn't out of any fondness for the pair but rather her self-interest in getting them out of school before she had to deal with any possible lawsuit ahead of her annual review.

There was no subtlety to the Things' demand. "We wanna pass," said one of them to Colin. He couldn't tell which was speaking as his vision was impaired by the still tearing eyeball while the other struck him with the rolled-up assignment. Thing One went on about Colin doing the homework with the intriguing idea he should make a few mistakes, "So they don't think we cheated," and the other saying, "Get it?"

Colin got it. He asked if he could offer some advice, catching the Things off guard. Thing One said he didn't want advice, explaining with a hint of humility that tutoring hadn't worked and was otherwise "stupid." But Thing Two was curious and asked Colin what he meant.

"I'll make different mistakes. If I make the same mistakes . . ."

"They'll think we copied each other!" said Thing One, his chin lifting with the pride of insight.

"I got one. You write them out and we fill in the answers in our own writing!" came from Thing Two. There was a smile when he spoke, an uncruel smile for a change, and the striking had eased to a gentle tapping. Were things looking up?

Colin readily agreed that those were clever ideas. The Things high-fived each other and then faced Colin, arms similarly raised in Seig-Heil fashion. It took him a moment to realize they were high-fiving him. He reciprocated with a jump to reach their towering arms and for a moment felt something more than relief that he wasn't being forced into the locker. Kinship? Respect? Perhaps their relationship had changed.

When Colin landed back on his feet, Thing One grabbed his still-raised arm while Thing Two pulled his pants down. The Things walked off, high-fiving again. Lifting his pants, Colin realized what he felt, albeit briefly, was akin to Stockholm syndrome, where victims feel affection for their tormenters.

His version of the syndrome lasted for 1.5 seconds, though he was grateful they hadn't pulled his underwear down like they had done to Jimmy DiBernardo, or given him a wedgie. DiBernardo had transferred after that, also to a public school.

Colin looked into his bedroom mirror that night. He saw a freckled face, not too much acne popping, the hopes of an angel-hair blond mustache if the light caught it just so, and red hair that he hated but that—so his grandfather said—had roots in the Battle of the Boyne, the Fenians, the Easter Rebellion, and any number of Saint Patrick's Day parades. "It's our beacon, boyo. It's the beacon me own father waved before those Black and Tans! Wear it with pride."

What would his grandfather say to Things One and Two? Would he do their bidding? Not likely. Not likely at all.

Colin was scribbling answers to the homework thrust upon him. Scribbling because he couldn't imagine the Things writing clearly. Scribbling because they didn't deserve better. Scribbling because they'd have to struggle when they transcribed the answers. He made mistakes, different mistakes for each of them, and added up the scores to make sure they passed if only by a hair. Each would get a 69, D+, and be done with it. He reviewed his work, as he always did, which confirmed he was right the first time. Too right maybe. A smile crossed his lips and he got out an eraser.

The math teacher was relieved after grading the homework, immediately calling the principal with the good news, who responded with an encouraging endorsement of tenure for the teacher and a happy conversation that night with the school's lawyer lying next to her in bed who crossed himself with a "Thanks be to Jesus."

Thing One was thrilled to see 69 at the top of the page with a "+15 extra credit points" and a "D+ for the semester" below that. He was actually proud he'd made it through the class, got the extra credit, passed, and would graduate. Thing Two also was thrilled, but more thrilled by an additional eight points for a 77 and a C- for the term. "Choke on this, dummy," he said to Thing One. Thing One didn't take it well. He started to yell something about not deserving it. Thing Two flung his work into Thing One's eye, causing an involuntary tear, which led him to say something about his crying that ended with a "boo hoo hoo." The teacher said that as far as he was concerned, they both managed to pass and could take it outside if they had more to say. He closed the door behind them. Forever.

Colin stared at Thing One limping down the hall. Thing One had tears dripping from his blackened eyes, which joined the rivulets of blood from his flattened nose and swollen lip. "Yo, Colin. I wanna talk to you," the Thing uttered. Colin's thoughts went to the imminent danger of a wounded animal. He backed against a

6

locker, closed tightly by someone else's lock, as the Thing loomed over him, oblivious to the blood dripping onto Collin's red hair.

"Yo, Colin," he said, his voice softer, more hurt than menacing. Colin thought about a thorn in its paw.

"Colin, why did you get Wally a better grade?"

Colin wondered what it would be like having his jaw rewired. He looked to the fluorescent lights, casting a halo behind the Thing's head. It was a message from his guardian angel, whom he didn't know he had until that moment.

"Well, because I gave him the easy answers. The ones I gave to you, well, they were real hard." He would have said "really hard" but didn't want to sound too clever. "You know, they would expect you to do better on the hard questions." It was convoluted logic, but the best he could come up with. Colin braced.

"So it's not because, you know, you like him better than me?" There was a wanting in the Thing's swollen eyes.

"More than you? Crazy. Of course not."

"Thanks, man." And with that he gave Colin a middle-five— either so Colin wouldn't have to reach or because Thing One had broken his right hand—and looked off to see the ambulance carrying Thing Two to have his jaw and two ribs reset.

2.

Staying Home

"We're done here, Mr. Goodrich!"

It was the guy in charge of the movers, Joey V, standing in the driveway. Goodrich knew something like this was coming: a yell or a voice from downstairs, saying it was all over. He took slow steps over to the bedroom window and struggled to lift it. The weather had been damp, and these old wooden windows stuck. He banged the upper rail with the palm of his hand and it stubbornly moved. He banged some more, allowing for an opening, and leaned toward it.

"Thanks, Joey! We'll see you in two days."

"Two days, yeah," said Joey V. "Oh, yeah, and Mr. Goodrich? Wicked house you have! I love these old places!" With that, he turned to squeeze himself into the moving van and then drove off.

Goodrich knocked down on either side of the window's sash, left then right, and so was able to shimmy it back down. He thought back to the time he'd removed the whole window with the notion of sanding down the edges to make it easier to open and close. Home repair was not his forte; he had to call in a carpenter to get the thing back in place.

He walked through the bedroom, sweeping dust bunnies into a bin, and pulled the crumpled punch list from his back pocket to see if anything in this room was left to do. He looked fondly at a small crack in one windowpane that he tried to convince the buyers shouldn't be fixed.

9

"SPNEA came in and said it's authentic, maybe as old as the house itself. It's really a treasure and you don't want to do anything to challenge the historic commission," he'd said. The response was a dubious "humpf." Goodrich watched the buyer trace the crack on the wavy pane with his finger. Looking at the tip of that finger, he'd asked, "What's Spinya?"

"S-P-N-E-A, the Society for the Preservation of New England Antiquities," said Goodrich. "We wanted to keep the house as authentic as possible, you know, and brought them in when we first moved in to give us a sense of what we had. Here, let me show you something."

Goodrich led the man up to the door that led into the attic. "See this?" Goodrich said. "It's the original stenciling on horsehair plaster! They were testing it. And look . . ." He went up the stairs and held his hand up against the main beam. "This is hand-hewn chestnut. You can see the adze marks, and it's as solid as the day they put it up. Look, the original pegs."

The buyer yawned out a "whatever" before turning to go back down the steps and led himself into the bathroom, where he set about turning on and off the faucets and flushing the toilet. "And you get good pressure if more than one person's got water running?"

"Yes," said Goodrich. "The pressure's fine. We upgraded the plumbing in '97."

"18 or 19?" the buyer asked he continued his poking and prodding. "Is it haunted? You have to disclose that, you know, drops the price, too. Ghosts, murders, that sort of thing."

"No, no murders or ghosts that I'm aware of," said Goodrich- Goodrich leaned over to pick up a thick flake of paint the buyer had flicked off the wainscoting in the hall outside the bathroom door.

"Needs painting," said the man, wending his way down that hall.

Goodrich turned the flake over in his fingers, counting five, maybe six layers of paint going back to long before he'd lived in the house

Goodrich continued to sweep even though the floor was clean. He went into the closet for what must have been the tenth time that day, turning the light on, looking into the built-in drawers, and brushing the inside with his hands as if trying to find something. He went as far as pulling the drawers out, looking into the dark recess. For what? For something he couldn't leave behind?

He walked into the small bedroom on the left of the hall, the one that had been Joshua's, and started sweeping once again. He pulled the broom along the wide pine floorboards, tracing the scratch marks his son had made with his toy cars. He opened the low cabinets to sweep inside those, noticing for the first time in years the chew marks their Labrador, Rafter, had made when he was a puppy. They had long since been painted over many times. With one sweep of the broom, he heard something snap against the edge of the shelf. He put his hand inside to feel for what made the sound. It was a little green plastic soldier. "Army man," his son would say, in the pose of throwing a hand grenade. His son had dozens of those at one time, lost in backyard battles or tossed as soldiers gave way to model planes and planes to guitars, guitars to books, and the books to Goodwill and the local put-and-take

Goodrich's fingers trembled a bit as he held the figure in both hands and smiled at the image of his son playing with them on the floor, and flicking marbles in the guise of cannonballs bowling through their ranks. His son would wear all manners of headgear, from an old Army helmet to a Cub Scout cap to a broad-brimmed cowboy hat, depending on the battles being fought. He put the soldier in his pocket. Leaving, he turned to look once more, closing the door and then reopening it wide, recalling the days when his son wanted the door open to the hall light.

He next went into the big room that had been Wes's, the one with the fireplace. It's where they'd all slept during the first big renovation. The boys loved sleeping near the blazing fire, espe-

11

cially when they lost electricity in a storm, which happened frequently before the generator was installed. Goodrich started to sweep again, diligently and deliberately, although sure he wasn't getting any dust. The cleaners had been quite thorough.

He went along the wide wainscoting that, like so much, was original to the house. "Chestnut," the historian from SPNEA had said. "My goodness, imagine the tree this came from. Early 1800s if not older." Wes had carved his name and birth date into it, near the floor, when he was seven. At first, Goodrich had been angry, but his wife had admonished him. "He's added some of our history, and I think that's wonderful." Afterward, Goodrich carved all their names and birthdays low on the wainscoting, imagining kids fifty, one hundred years from now finding it and wondering who these people were. Goodrich found ash in the fireplace and rubbed it between his fingers; he couldn't remember the last time there'd been a fire in it, yet he could detect the smell of old wood smoke. He put his hand on the mantle and bent over, getting on his knees to feel around, recalling the night they'd thrown some pennies into the blaze to see if they would melt. Indian head pennies they'd found in the attic. "Treasure!" Josh had exclaimed. "It's all a treasure, Josh. We live in a treasure chest!" Goodrich had told him.

Goodrich continued from room to room, moving slowly, touching the walls, the guard rails, breathing in the woody mustiness, and sensing it as if for the first time. "Why didn't I appreciate that before?" he asked himself. "I should have bottled it."

Easing down the front stairs on his aged legs, Goodrich turned to look back from the lower landing, imagining the boys barreling down early on Christmas mornings to open gifts. His eyes started to swell from the memories. He swirled his hand in the air, "I wish I could wave a wand . . ."

He walked slowly down the main hall into the living room, the formal living room, which was never to be formal, with its four large windows that faced southeast and southwest and took in the morning and evening sun. It, too, had a fireplace, a deep one with a crane that held a pot he once tried to boil maple sap in after Josh—or was it Wes—had read about maple syrup in a book. The sap had boiled but filled with ashes and covered the bricks in a sticky coating he'd spent hours cleaning. The boys loved it, however, and poured the syrup on snow to eat like pudding.

Goodrich swept this room, as well, trying to take up the old needles nestled in the wide spaces between the floorboards. He took up a pinch, about all he could get, and held them to his nose, detecting the faint hint of balsam as he crunched the dried needles in his fingers. Didn't they once make balsam tea, a scout project for Josh? It was awful.

The needles were still awful, bitter. He spit them out, sweeping the remnants into the fireplace. He looked around, thinking how empty it was. He heard scratching and thought about when they discovered a squirrel's nest behind the fireplace, but this time it was only the holly bush by the window holding a cardinal on a branch.

The bird flew off in a red flash when he approached the window, as though it had never been there. "Off to your own nest, your eminence!" he said with a smile. "Home you go!"

He went back around, one more time, and then to the kitchen, which too had a fireplace, a massive one you could walk into. It had a bread oven on the side. He opened the cabinets and doors, which were clean as a whistle. There wasn't anything left for him to do.

Looking at his watch, inevitably running too quickly, he looked out the window at the growing shadows. Time to move, the moment he once had looked forward to but now dreaded. One final walk around? Had he shut the lights off?

Goodrich eyed the built-in bench by the fireplace where they had kept Rafter's food and bowls and then Barney's after and Aretoo's later on. He lifted the seat looking for something, forgot

13

what he had in mind, and sat down, leaning his arm on the counter. He closed his eyes and thought back.

"Dad, Dad!" yelled the little boy crawling on his lap. "C'mon! We gonna open the presents." His little brother in a onesie competed with the young yellow lab to as both attempted to climb onto Goodrich's lap.

"Dada, pleasants!" The dog just licked the residual crumbs off the boy's face.

Goodrich rose as his wife came into the kitchen. "A wee bit much last night?" she asked with raised eyebrows. "Dad's already in the living room demanding another cup of coffee. I'll get you one, too. Let's go."

He grabbed the boys to him and let the dog lick his face as much as he liked. "Let's go?" he said to them. "Let's go? Not a chance. No. Never."

3.

Encounter in the Park

The senior partner raised his glass for one final toast to the departing 3L, a third-year law student who'd come in for the Christmas Party. He'd just been offered a position to start at the end of the following summer with a salary of $150,000 and a signing bonus of $40,000. It would pay for the kid's final year at Harvard and give him more than enough funds to travel in style after graduation for a trip he had talked about incessantly, and it would leave him with enough for a "kick-ass" apartment with all the accouterments, one fitting for the launch of his career in the law. "Love the law!" were the senior partner's words in that final toast. Loving the law with that kind of income at twenty-six years old, or maybe even twenty-five, didn't seem difficult.

Kick-ass. That was the term the 3L had used, wasn't it, mused the senior partner. Kick-ass. He'd thought it was somehow inappropriate. Not just the language but the boast. He wondered if the firm had misjudged the soon-to-be associate. Maybe he was too cocky, too immature. But then weren't they all that way? Overprivileged and thinking they were owed the life.

The old partner grimaced at those dollars, but who was he to complain? He'd made a fortune these last forty-odd years. He would joke at his club that it was only a small fortune, which was, he knew, another way of saying it wasn't small in the least. He earned it, surely. He was worth it. Hadn't he saved clients their millions, tens of millions, hundreds of millions, for GOD's sake? As if they needed it. Hadn't he saved reputations and all that came with them? Only on occasion did he allow himself to wonder if they deserved it.

An ex-wife—the one now living in . . . Santa Fe is it?—said he was a smug bastard who had forgotten where he came from. His alcoholic father. His now dead drug addict brother. A stint in the Army straightened him up. She was the only one of the exes that he was sorry about.

She was wrong though. He remembered. He remembered his dad coming filthy drunk to a Scout meeting shouting, "Beer's on me!" He remembered crying to himself in the backseat of the Scoutmaster's car on the way home. He remembered his father's sobbing, apologizing for you name it, losing another job, crashing the car, punching his mother. He remembered his brother in one clinic, coming out clean, then in another. And another. He remembered he couldn't do a damn thing to help. Every day he remembered. He was proud of his roots. And embarrassed. And ashamed. It was his crutch to justify most of what followed. It was on his mind when he checked that it was his name embroidered inside the coat the hat check girl just gave to him. A habit. He calculated how many billable hours that coat had cost him and double-counted. Did it really cost that much? Thirty hours?

He rolled his eyes at the sum and then reminded himself of how many hours he put in at the firm over the years, billable hours, and the goodwill hours. He deserved that coat and then some. He had ample amounts of the "and then some."

"Was it worth all the trouble?" his Santa Fe ex once asked.

"Huh," he replied. "What trouble?"

One of the firm's cars was there waiting when he left the club. It was too nice a night for a car and with winter approaching there wouldn't be many nights left when he could walk home. He'd had just the one martini, plus he wasn't at all tired. He told the driver to take the rest of the night off and walked up Fifth Avenue to the park. He'd walk through it to his apartment on Central Park West. Why not? He could use the exercise. He could use the solitude. Take the time to think. Or not to think, for a change. That would be a welcome meditation for the forty-hour weeks he was still putting in, a downshift already from the sixty plus he had been at for most of his career at Blah, Blah, Blah and Blah. He smiled to himself. Blah, Blah, Blah and Blah. He was the last Blah. He had said the firm's name so many times over the years it didn't mean anything. He didn't think of himself as one of the Blahs, not anymore.

He entered the park across from the Plaza and thought about meeting his wife, his first wife, over Mai Tai's at Trader Vic's. He looked north to one of the twin towers that was his home. He figured thirty minutes. He was in no rush and wanted to take in the night.

Inside the park, sitting in a dark section near the Dakota, sat a big young man biding his time. He was leaning over, spitting at a patch of gum that had turned black, now a permanent part of the sidewalk. The man, little more than a teenager, kept missing it and laughing at his folly. He tried curling his tongue for better aim, something his younger brother could do but he'd never been able to master. "It's genetic," his brother had told him. "It isn't your fault! You got guns, bro. Look at those arms. That's your good genes. Yo, I'd take the guns over a curling tongue anytime."

Still, he tried to curl his tongue. He sometimes worked out with his brother, trying to help him build his "guns" in the basement of their building, where years of accumulated weights had been abandoned and left to rust in the storage area near the washing machines. They had their privacy. The machines usually were broken anyway, mostly by kids trying to steal the money from inside. They stayed busted for weeks at a time, forcing everyone in the building to go to the laundromat owned by the nasty Korean who hardly spoke a word of English and kept a baseball bat behind his counter. His wife and his mother—or sister, they all looked alike to the young man—would sit in the back, working their sewing machines and occasionally looking toward the people at the washers and dryers, chattering to themselves in that chicken language of theirs.

He met an older woman from his floor there, a grandmother taking care of three or four kids—depending on who was left off at her apartment—doing laundry like him when the basement machines were down. She stared at the Koreans jabbering away and said to the young man, "Just lookee there. Right off the goddamn boat they are and got their own business. Cash business, too. How do they do it?"

The young man shrugged his massive shoulders.

"Gotta be something. Every little store here they got, selling fruits and vegetables, and charging an arm and a leg. How they do it, I wish I knew."

The young man stared at the Korean owner, wondering too. The Korean noticed the look and leaned over to put a hand below his counter.

The young man's brother was at home working hard, studying for the entrance exam to the city's select schools. He was smart, the brother, had always been. He got bullied by some of the kids in the building, but not too much. Those kids had their own dreams— basketball, hip-hop—hoping they'd make it out. A few were in gangs, it was said. They left him pretty much alone, not because they liked him but because he that very big brother and he minded his own business. He had a job, too, the brother, security at the fancy hospital near the East River, so he had a uniform and a bigass flashlight with its five-D cells. He didn't look for trouble, but he didn't run if it was in front of him. The older one knew to leave well enough alone and well enough left him alone, too.

"Boy, you always got your head in all those books. What are you reading about now?"

"Big test prep, bro. Still at it. Big test. If I do good I can get into Stuyvesant, maybe Lehman, and then, woo baby, I'll be set.

College scholarship comes next. You just wait and see."

"When's that test? I'll cook and all. You just keep your head in those books."

The brother pushed himself away from the small table in what their mother used to call their one-ass kitchen. "You'd better cook a lot! And make it chow mein." He said he was smart in his school, but all those Indians, Chinese, Jews, Catholics from the parochials, and Koreans, especially Koreans, would eat his lunch. "They've been studying for this their whole life, my man. I don't stand much of a chance. Hell, they got tutors and courses, you know."

"Koreans too, huh? What's with that all?" his big brother asked. His mind was in a laundromat.

"Oh, yeah. Money, dude. They can pay. Test practice and practice and practice and they'll pass in their sleep. Me? I just got me. And you, bro."

"So how much are these tests, the tutors, and all that?"

The little brother got up laughing and walked to the bathroom. He continued laughing as a long stream of pee hit the water.

"You laughing at what's in your hand, my man?"

"No, this Louisville Slugger would scare most folks. I'm laughing at you!"

He flushed and returned to the table. "Brother of mine, I figure it'll cost $3,000 for a sure shot. That's for a tutor who gets 90 percent in; 90 percent! Best in the city. My guidance counselor said if . . . if I could, I'd be a shoo-in. Man, I'd get in with him. For sure and for sure."

His older brother's eyes widened and he shook his head. "Three-thousand dollars? Where are we going to get that sort of cash?!? You check in the sofa. I found a quarter under the pillow last week. Maybe we got three grand in there somewhere."

"Just saying it out loud. It's off my chest. Let me get back to my books."

The alarm buzzed at 12:30 a.m. for the older boy to get up for the early shift that was usually covered by his friend Pete. Pete's wife was ill, so the young man was happy to take the shift and the extra hours. His younger brother was still at the kitchen table.

"I'm off to Pete's shift. Go get some rest."

"I'll rest when I'm done with this stupid exam."

That night the young man couldn't focus on his walk to work. He was getting honked at as he crossed the street at green lights. His brother deserved a break, like those Koreans. Imagine, Stuyvesant or the Bronx Science one. Best of the best. Man, he thought, he'd have it made; the kid who didn't have much of a chance would get one with a school like that.

Once he had been walking down First Avenue when a car, a BMW, zigged toward the sidewalk and stopped. The window went down and a young woman no older than him, looking like she'd been partying too long, yelled over, "Hey, officer . . ." He moved to the car when the young lady turned to her friend, the driver, a young man in a suit, and said, "It's just a rental cop." Turning back to the young man, she added, "Never mind." He heard them laugh as the driver zagged back into the middle lane.

He spit again at the blackened spot of gum, hitting it this time. "Bingo," he said, smiling at his achievement, deciding it was a good sign, an omen, and got up to wade deeper into the park. He walked off the paved paths, not on them, keeping to the trees and shadows, watching out for people. There were a few groups out, small, young folks laughing, giggling, swaying, and banging into each other. One guy was holding a girl's shoulders as she vomited on the path while her friends eeked, "Oooh, gross," and laughed some more.

They didn't notice him edging back deeper into the trees, his dark hoodie and black jeans blending well with the night. He kept an eye on that group as they tumbled over toward the West Side, maybe another party, and wondered who they were, how they got there. He moved back, into the shadows, and sat on a rock outcropping to ask himself what the hell he was doing there.

A fat rat ran past him, close enough that he could have kicked it. "Rats don't worry about school," he thought to himself. "Just me and the little dude is all."

The young man had never done anything really wrong. Not really. He lifted some scrubs that no one would miss from the hospital to use as pajamas. He'd taken an apple or two from the Korean grocers when he walked past, but that was when he was a kid. And, yeah, he used his mother's food stamps for a while until they caught up with what happened to her. He still felt funny about that.

This was wrong. It was wrong. It wasn't fair about the exam, all the Korean kids getting help, and the Jews, and Indians, and everyone else. No, it wasn't fair to his brother, but that didn't justify waiting in the dark for someone. People didn't bother him or his brother, so who was he to start bothering people?

He shook his head and got up to cross the park. A chilly wind came in from the north where he was heading, and he put his hood back up, bringing it low over his face. There's got to be a better way, he thought. I can maybe borrow some cash. Maybe the guys at work. Pete had some money. Maybe Pete could lend him some.

The senior partner saw a big man leave the dark of the trees and walk up the path toward him. He hadn't been concerned. This wasn't the 1970s, after all, but he didn't like how the big man pulled his hood over his head.

The older man had been mugged once before, brutally beaten, in this very park. It must have been forty years ago, and it was during a time when he was in far better shape. He fought with the mugger, thought he was capable of handling himself. But twenty-five stitches and a broken jaw and ribs proved him wrong. He should have handed over his wallet then. He wasn't going to chance it now.

The big man with the hoodie walked slowly down the path talking to himself and shaking his head. The senior partner figured he might be crazy. Or was he talking to him? Was he say-

21

ing, "Don't be stupid?" There was no one else about. All the more reason to give him what he wanted, no questions asked, and just get out of there. He reached into his jacket pocket and pulled out a large wad of cash he'd taken from the bank. It was a lot of money, a good score, as they would say. He only hoped that it would be enough, that he wouldn't have to hand over his wallet. That would be a pain, having to cancel all the credit cards and get a new license. His wallet must have been two inches thick. It contained his life. It would be worth losing the cash to keep onto that.

The big man was in the middle of the path, moving toward him, about to run him over.

He stopped short. "Hey, what's up?" said the big man, startled when he looked up to find the senior partner in front of him.

"Here," said the old man. "Here, take it. It's a lot of cash. All yours."

His arm reached forward with the bundle. The young man stared at it, and then at the old man, before looking up to the sky, the clouds now clearing away to allow the full moon to lighten some of the darkness.

"For real?" he asked.

"Just take it. It's yours. We've got no problems here. We're good."

"Thank you. Thank you so much. Thank you. God bless you, Mister. God bless you!"

He walked ahead, quickly, and started to run. He couldn't wait to get home and tell his brother.

He turned to watch the big guy run off. Had he seen tears in his eyes?

The old man patted his wallet and smiled to himself. Money well spent, he thought. Money well spent.

4.

You're Using Too Much Water

"You're using too much water."

"What?"

"I said, you're using too much water!"

"I can't hear you. I'm in the shower!"

"You've been in there for ages! You're wasting water!!"

Jack turned off the spigot, grabbed a towel, and said, "Woman, I can't hear a word you're saying. That shower is simply amazing. What's up?"

"You spend too much time in there. What are you doing? It's just a waste of water."

Jack stared at her, not so much in amazement—though he felt that—but in recognition. He wanted to say, "Jenna, you do realize we're on vacation, right?" He wanted to point out the terribly obvious given the stupendous snow-capped mountain sitting on the equator just outside their hotel door in Tanzania, the country to which they had traveled specifically to climb that stupendous mountain, the tallest in Africa, Kilimanjaro. But more than any of that, he wanted to put his hands gently around her neck—not to threaten her so much as get her attention—and say with a calm fortitude that he was confident, absolutely sure, that she knew they were in this lovely, if primitive, resort, built in the middle of a bloody rainforest!

He said none of those things. Instead, he grumbled something about it having rained a lot recently, evidenced by the small canyons in the nearly washed-out dirt roads they took to the resort.

"Still, it's a bad habit of yours. You need to be more respectful of the environment."

"They get 116 inches of rain every year. It's the wet season. And anyway, and I know you know this, the drain runs right back into the ground. And we're using that God-awful biodegradable castile soap."

This was a new argument. Not new in the sense that Jack's green sensitivities did not match Jenna's—that was always an issue—but new in that they were on an eco-tour adventure where the only eco they encountered was in the online brochures from the trip organizers and the deep dive into their investments to pay for the trip, which was more econ than eco. That, and the complimentary castile soap in the bathroom, had barely come up. There wasn't any need for guidance over the use and reuse of towels; the "rustic" resort didn't change them. Jenna did instruct the smiling, polite, and uncomprehending locals about recycling plastic bags and not just tossing them onto the road. She had gotten at least one young man to pick up a bag, add a large stone to it, and lob it deep into the surrounding forest. "Now not in your way, Memsahib," he said with a grin you could see from a mile away.

One of their tour guides tried to apologize for that. He said that, traditionally, food and things were wrapped in banana leaves, or coconut shells, and were simply thrown away after use. People were adjusting to bags and such. The country had a campaign to fight littering.

"Well, it doesn't hurt to remind them," said Jenna.

She and Jack got back at it about the shower. "Jenna, dear,

I'm all for conserving things, but water in a rainforest really isn't a problem. You don't tell people in the Sahara to stop wasting sand or Eskimos —"

"Inuit, not Eskimos . . ."

"Okay, or Inuit that they're using too much ice in their martinis."

"Well, with global warming their ice is rapidly disappearing. I went to a lecture on that. And are you being stupid or just insensitive? The Inuit, like many aboriginal peoples, have a serious alcohol problem and to use martinis . . ."

"Oh, jeez, look at the time! Cocktails in the lounge . . . I'll order something without ice."

Jenna rolled her eyes. Jack, taking sarcastic pride in his comebacks and infuriating tolerance, smiled to himself. They dressed in their best, which is to say worn, stained, and ruggedly comfortable adventure travel clothes — organic cotton — for dinner.

She was, according to Jack, a social justice warrior with a vengeance a Shiite Unitarian, he would call her teasingly until she admonished him for insulting Shiites and Unitarians. And admonish him she did. Political correctness was, for her, not merely a habit but something that had become a ritual to be followed with all the warmth, humor, and compassion of an SS storm trooper in a Russian winter.

The following day, they went on one of their pre-Kilimanjaro hikes to acclimate before the big ascent. This was on the lower slopes — 7,000 feet up to 9,000. The point was to get their red blood cells working ahead of the attempt at Kili's 19,341 feet. Neither wanted a lack of oxygen to get in the way. They'd put so much effort into getting in shape, not to mention the $23,000 cost of the climb and post-climb safari.

The stars were still twinkling when they'd gone out with the guide who went by the name of Pray Good. They were a good six miles from their lodge when it started to rain. For the first time in either of their lives, they got a sense of what torrential actually meant. Half an hour after it started, as it continued coming down in buckets, Pray Good asked if they were getting wet. Jenna was sitting on a rotting stump, pouring water out of her boots while Jack offered that his skin was soaked right through to his skin.

Pray Good smiled with a, "Yes, sahib, it gets like this."

Jack looked at him curiously and asked why he called him "sahib," an Indian word.

"Ah, they taught us that in school. I majored in tourism, and they told us that Americans like it when you incorporate local colloquialisms into the interlocution."

"Interlocution?" said Jack.

"We had a student teacher from Oxford. Anyway, I some-times will say "bwana," but a black man from Brooklyn—a thoracic surgeon at Lenox Hill—pointed out that it made white people feel uncomfortable. Unless they are from Texas."

"Call me Jack. That'll be fine."

"I've been calling you Jack, sahib, all day, but you've not re-sponded."

Jenna chimed in as she wrung out her socks, "He's like that."

"Marital bliss, Pray Good," said Jack.

Pray Good smiled slightly, knowing better than to get in-volved with arguing Western couples at elevation in a rainstorm after hiking for miles. He told them that it could get slippery in the mud, which was surely thicker on the trail back to the lodge. He also advised them to pull out their hiking poles. "And poh-lay poh-lay, slowly slowly," he added. "Hakuna-Matata, bwana!" he continued and laughed himself into a frenzy.

He was right. The mud got thicker, but he hadn't mentioned deeper, or that it would flow off the steep mountainside like lava from an erupting volcano, except that it was cold and add-ed about twenty pounds to their already heavy boots. "Haku-na-Matata!" Pray Good would say every few hundred feet "Poh-lay, poh-lay."

"Damn it, Pray Good, I couldn't go any poh-layer if I wanted. It's like swimming in, well, mud," griped Jenna.

"Take off your boots, memsahib, like me. The mud feels lovely squishing between the toes."

Jenna removed her boots, tied her laces together, and suspended the boots around her shoulders. The organic vegetable dye from her laces leeched a bright red band around her neck that resembled the traces of a failed hanging. The slimy mud from her deteriorating boots oozed into her failing waterproof and breathable rain jacket.

"This jacket of mine sucks," she said.

"I told you to buy Gore-Tex instead of"—Jack made air quotes as he spoke—"that sustainable crap."

"Polyfluorinated chemicals are in Gore-Tex. Greenpeace says so."

"I'm dry."

"You're an asshole."

They slipped and slid down the trail when Pray Good turned to smile at the boots dangling from Jenna's neck. "Memsahib," he asked, "do you have another pair of boots?"

"Why?"

"Yours seem to be melting."

"They're made from recycled tires. The others," she choked a bit as she spoke it, "are ballistic nylon."

"I made her buy those," said a contented Jack.

"Let the rain wash away your problems! Hakuna-Matata!" yelled Pray Good, who had stripped down to his shorts. "Also they can waterproof those other boots at the resort."

When they arrived back at the lodge, a grateful Jack gave a beaming Pray Good a healthy tip, as a shivering and filthy Jenna forced a smile and "thanks" and asked a clerk in the lodge for a hot cup of anything.

"Ma'am, I'll send some sweet tea to your room immediately. But I advise a very long, hot shower."

Jenna looked up at him with a resigned expression. "I'll be quick."

"No, no, ma'am. You don't want to catch a cold before the big climb! Leave those clothes outside your door. I'll have the maid wash them. Three times. We have plenty of water. They'll need it."

Jenna turned to a grinning Jack. "Don't say a bloody word." She marched off to their room, leaving a muddy puddle behind each step.

5.

Rough Sailing

Nan looked toward the west again, where the clouds seemed to be growing an even darker shade of grey. The waves had picked up too, hitting the side of the small sailboat and splashing over the coaming as it slid down into the waves.

"Don't you think?" she asked.

"No, I don't think, and I wish to hell you'd let me handle this. Unless you want to be the captain!" Harrison pushed the tiller toward her, hard into her knee, and let out the sheet. She bent down in time to keep the boom from beaning her.

"Stop it. No. Just get us back."

Harrison told her not to let the jib out, right as a strong gust took it, grabbing the line out of her hands.

"Damn it!" He pushed the tiller again, heading into the wind as she reached into the sea to get the loose sheet. She nearly fell in when a strong wave hit the opposite side, tipping the heeling boat further. "Hold onto the bloody thing, will you? For Christ's sake."

"The wind, it just took it. It's really picking up."

"Now you're a weatherman, huh? Just do what I tell you."

They were a good six miles out now. Farther than Harrison had intended, but it had been a fine breeze earlier, and he enjoyed Nan's fear.

"We should be heading back. We must be ten miles out."

He rolled his eyes, saying, "We are heading back and would be there if you would listen."

The problem was she had listened. It was going to be a brisk sail on his new boat, a fast one, and fun. Didn't she want to learn to sail? Wasn't that part of the attraction? He'd talked about his years on the Hotchkiss sailing team, then Tufts, then a chance at the Olympics. "Almost made it, too. Shortlisted." Preppy charm had given way to investment banking attitude. He hadn't sailed in years. Until, one day, late in the season, very late into the season, he decided to get this boat. So late that they were the only ones out there. She'd wanted to learn to sail., She'd taken the course over the summer. She was almost excited to go even after pointing out the red flag at the marina. And she needed to satisfy him, of course. That was more than half of it.

Nan was right. The wind had picked up. Earlier it was scary, too, but fun as the little boat skidded out from the shore, heeling over, the boom sometimes touching the water. He laughed when she leaned way out, holding on for dear life to the windward side, trying to urge the boat lower. But he just pulled the sail in, bringing the opposite gunwale right to the waterline. She squealed, and he laughed more. "Enough, Harry, enough. Please." He paid no attention to her obvious fear, loving every bit of it.

It was raining now, the wind stronger. Any pleasure of Harrison's had given way to a nasty edge, that controlling fanaticism, as the waves foamed at their peaks. The swells must have been five, six feet and the bow slipped under them as they fell into deeper troughs taking on cold seawater. "Bail! Nan. Use the bucket."

"Maybe you should slow down a bit. We'd roll over the waves better," she yelled over the wind.

"Just do it! I know what I'm doing!"

Waves were smashing on all sides as the boat got tossed about, Nan's bailing accomplishing little. She was soaked. They were both soaked and shivering from the cold autumn water and falling air temperature.

Nan took a moment from bailing to look about, peering in the water, mistaking distant white caps for another boat. A wave hit the leeward side, tumbling her into the water in the bottom of the boat.

"Wake up!" he yelled, struggling to be heard over the wind, which was whistling through the shrouds straining to hold the mast in place. "What the hell were you doing?

"Looking for a boat that could help! Tow us or something."

"I got this, goddamn it. Just bail."

Harrison was pulling hard on the sheets, trying to control the mainsail and head into the wind. He wanted to reef it, taking down the sail area, and maybe gain better control.

"Take the tiller. Head up, damn it, up!!" he yelled, moving forward.

"Huh? What do you mean up?" she yelled, pleading now against his nautical terms.

"Push it away from you until we're in the goddamn wind, you idiot!! I want to take some sail down."

Nan grabbed the tiller from him when they switched position and pushed it away. As the bow swung toward the wind, a big wave hit the side, nearly turning the boat over. Nan had to let go of the jib's sheet when Harrison fell onto the line. It flapped loudly now that it was loose in the storm—it was a storm, there was no other way to describe it—and Harrison swore at her stupidity. She held the tiller and realized that the boat would move without the sail from the sheer force of the wind on the hull. With the wind behind them, plowing on the transom, they might be able to simply head back to shore with the sails down. She said as much and Harrison threw the pail at her telling her to shut up. The pail missed her as it went over the side. "Grab it!!" he yelled, but she had ducked, and it was already behind them and quickly falling away.

"Pull the tiller. We need that pail. Pull it toward you now!!"

Nan did as she was ordered, quickly bringing the tiller to her

31

body and holding it against her stomach when the boat's stern turned into the wind and pushed them on. As they jibed, the wind caught the sail hard, driving the boom across the boat. Nan ducked. Harrison had been moving back, looking the other way to find the pail, when the wooden boom hit him on the side of the head and continued to move over toward the starboard side taking him into the water with it.

Nan screamed when he went in, but she dutifully held the tiller, like he told her to do, as he bobbed behind. He waved, she was sure of it, and tried to swim, as the waves broke over his head. She thought she heard him, telling her to push the tiller away, turn the boat into the wind. That might stop the boat, certainly slow it, she knew. She could do it. She looked back at him, now forty yards behind. Was he trying to swim to her? The waves kept on crashing over him as the wind on the stern and in the flopping sails pushed the little boat on.

Nan looked at the shore, directly downwind, fighting to hold the tiller straight. She turned around to see if there were other boats out, but she was alone. She looked back again, finally losing sight of Harrison, and surfed the waves until the boat smashed into the rocky shore.

It took some time for the police to get to their boat and search for Harrison, but they didn't find anything that day. "We're so sorry," said the man in charge. "We're still looking and we alerted the other stations. It's possible he might have come ashore, you know, what with this current. But without a life preserver, in this storm, I don't know what to say. I'm so sorry."

The boat was a total loss, they told her later. She almost smiled but held back.

6.

Allagash Sentimentalism

I'm going to cut down my Christmas tree today. I don't think there's much of a story in that for your paper.

It's that scraggly little bit of a thing, no taller 'an me, out in that open patch, over there, in the middle of these woods. "Wilderness" like you called it. The trees 'round it, big old balsams and pines, and spruce, don't forget the spruce, tower over that pup. Sits in their shadow, you know, won't let sun touch it. No wonder the little guy can't grow. Won't make it either, not for long. I can almost hear those big old pines looking down and laughing at him. Bullies they are, just big sticks. But that one, hell, tough little sucker making it this far out there all alone.

I seen it in the grove a lot, when I go over the trapline and all. Kept an eye on it. First noticed him three years back and didn't think he'd make it. Snow covered him 'til March. Then there he was popping up over the top. Felt bad, I did. Crazy if you ask me. Too much time out here. I mean, looky round. There are trees and then some. Must be a thousand like him. More, don't you think? More than a thousand. Ten thousand. Don't know why I noticed that one.

Here, feel that? Solid cabin and lordy lord it took me a bunch of trees to build it and didn't think about them other than wood. That stove over there must have burned I don't know how many cords, but plenty over the years. Plenty, believe me. It gets cold up here, ayuh. So cold some nights they explode on you, the trees. I been hit with wood shrapnel. Almost took my out eye once. Got me thinking, you know. Got me remembering things from away, what I came here to forget.

Yes, chiefy, things to forget. Won't let me though. Nope. You don't need to write that in that book of yours. Not a book, you say? Column, huh? "Down East Originals." Okay, in that column of yours.

I do admit I like the birches. They make good tools, handles for knives when they crack, and the bark burns like they been doused with kerosene! Handy to get a fire going if I'm stuck out there in a blizzard, and that's happened, I can tell you. Fact is the bark peels like a banana. Make a lean-to out of it, kept the rain off, sheds water like the back of a duck. Between that and the fire, saved my bacon plenty. Wet and in that cold, phew, wouldn't have made it.

Course there's the canoe. Not a nail in it. Just birch, cedar, and spruce. Made it with that old fellow, Jethro Cook, years back. A real Indian he was, Abenaki and Wampanoag. Claimed his real name was Pennacook and great-great-great-grandson or something of King Philip, but Jethro was a teaser, so who knows? Showed me how. Sewed the birch bark up with spruce roots, split, and soaked. Fixed it with spruce gum melted down for resin. You want some? It's spruce gum. Nah? Kind of an acquired taste, eh?

That canoe's gotta be, oh, forty years old, maybe more. Maybe fifty. Jethro got himself killed. Run down by a bull moose in the rut. Not funny a'tall, but he'd have laughed about it. Jethro was old then, eighty, eighty-five, something like that. Listen to me saying that's old! Bad leg he limped on. Don't think he'd 'av outrun a bull moose on his best day.

That little tree won't make it. Nope. Scrawny pipsqueak. Just look at it. Those aren't branches, they're twigs. Sorry thing, really. Needs sun. Needs breathing room to spread its root out.

Those bigger trees won't let it though. Bullies, if you ask me. Not sure how he took in the first place. Could be just a small patch of sun hit the right spot and the squirrels didn't eat the seed out of his mama's cone. Squirrels do like them, the red ones. Don't be numb! Yes, red squirrels! The chatty ones. Speaking of chatty, ain't I just the chatterbox? I don't get a lot of visitors, so I'm making up for lost time. Talk to myself, though. And the squirrels. And the trees. Hell, I'll talk to anything that'll listen. Don't you worry now. They don't talk back. Much.

You wonder if trees know things? I do. In the wind, they move like they're laughing sometimes. That gets me laughing. When I cut 'em down, I wonder if they don't know. Never used to think that way. Some'll call it cabin fever, but I don't think so. No, I think I've got a feel for things nowadays, different from when I was younger. Maybe that ESP thing. Or could be cabin fever is about right after all!

What's that? Well yeah, I feel bad hunting, even fishing. More'n I used to, that's for sure. They don't want to die neither, get caught, get eaten. Would you? But it's the trees I wonder on. Like that one, the little one. All alone out there. Crazy talk is what it is. Hell, when I cut it down, I don't even need an ax; bend it over and get it with a knife. Quick and done. It's just a tree. Won't make it anyways. Just won't. Poor little fella.

That's the one, yep. Sort of stands out. Pipsqueak it is. Cold out here, isn't it. Let's head in. I got two bottles I'll put under it. When I cut him down. A gift to myself. Know what it is, in them bottles?

Whiskey? Hell no. Calvados! Yes, sir. Straight from France. Had it there, you know, in the war. Calvados and mademoiselles! Get a bottle every year. Have to order it special. Oh heck, let Christmas come early. If you're still planning on staying the night, we open it.

No, I don't mind. Welcome the company. You can write about that in that paper of yours! Still can't figure anyone would be interested, but that's your business. Tell 'em this crazy old coot likes apple brandy. That's what it is, you know. Apple brandy.

Yeah, I guess so. Time waits for no man. You want to do it, cut him down? No? Sad thing, huh. Hand me that ax, will ya? Thing's made in Sweden, says right on it. You could shave with it if you had a mind to. See this bald patch? I test the blade with the hair on my arm. Keeps me sharp too!

Ah, the hell with it.

No, you lummox! Course I know it's the wrong tree. This one's, oh, thirty, forty feet maybe. See that up there? White pine blister rust they call it. Just noticed. It'll kill the tree in time. But it's blocking the sun for the little one. If it comes down, it'll give the fella a chance. Plus, I'll burn it in the stove. Kills the blight, you know. Figure if I cut that one there it'll give the guy more sun and root space. Hell, we'll use a branch for the Christmas tree. Now put that in your story and let's get to cutting.

7.

The Feast

Leaving the market, Mabel constantly adjusted her heavy grocery bags to maintain a hold. It was a struggle, but she managed to find them a resting place against the soft protrusion of her ample belly. She also held an ear-to-ear grin anyone would see if it weren't for those overflowing bags largely hiding her face. She was going to have a feast: crab-cakes, a lobster roll, a bottle of Sauvignon Blanc chosen because of its pretty label, coleslaw, fried-up sweet potatoes, and, why not, an ear or two of fresh corn with sweet butter. She could already see herself licking her fingers. It had been years since she had feasted on such a meal. And Mabel had many years on her.

The cinder-block steps leading up to her trailer home were getting even looser, forcing Mabel to hold the groceries that much more tightly. She'd complain, again, as if complaining might get them fixed. It wasn't quite her trailer; she rented it from Simon Legree. Simon Legree was not his real name. However, she felt it appropriate having read about the sadistic slave overseer in a Classic Comics version of Uncle Tom's Cabin she picked up at the local dump's put-and-take.

"Woman, are you soft in the head? You know my name. Why do you keep calling me Mister Legree? If you're trying to stall on that rent again . . ."

"No, sir, nuh-uh. I know your name. It's just that you remind me of somebody, and when I see you he just pops into mind. It's not soft, sir, that's for sure. If anything, this old head of mine is hard as a rock. Been told that enough times."

The comic would have been worth something if it had had a cover. She made some under-the-table income picking up things at the dump and selling them. She used to do that off the sidewalk but now had graduated to local flea markets, which were long on fleas but short on cash. She kept this comic and read it again and again until the pages had grown fuzzy, and the images faded from the constant fingering.

She had lots of throwaway things in that trailer. Not things she threw away; she rarely threw anything out if it still had some use. What she had was the flotsam and jetsam of other people. She wasn't a bag lady or a hoarder. She simply had an extremely frugal temperament. You never knew when something might come in handy.

It suited her even when it didn't need to. When it didn't was a long time ago, when she was with Lucius, or Luscious, as she called him. He called her Maybelline because she hated the name Mabel and had once tried her hand at selling Lucky Heart Cosmetics door-to-door. The job hadn't worked out; Lucius didn't want her knocking on strangers' doors at night. So she went back to what came naturally to her, which was cleaning houses.

Mable and Lucius were what educated folk would call the working poor. They wouldn't have agreed. Proud, perhaps, yes. Content for sure. Content even without the children they so wanted but couldn't have. Content together.

Lucius died way too young and for no good reason. He had a temp job over the Christmas rush at the Post Office. Coming off the very late shift he missed the bus and went to walk home. Crossing an unlit intersection, he looked left, a driver turned right. The driver was drunk, uninsured, and lost his license. Mabel lost the only love of her life.

That was twenty-five years ago. After Lucius left, Mabel picked up some more work from her clients to help make ends meet. Dog walking, cleaning up after them, was demeaning, and she never cared much for dogs, having been bitten by a nasty old cuss of a bloodhound when she was a little girl. That was one reason Uncle Tom's Cabin meant so much. The image of bloodhounds chasing down runaway slaves resonated.

As time went on, most of her clients died or moved to some old-age home, and the new folks wanted highfalutin maid services. "Are you bonded?" one fancy lady asked, holding an iPhone in one hand and sipping from a latte held in the other. She stared at Mabel over the granite kitchen top waiting for an answer, a vague smile on her lips but a face that shined discouragement. Mabel didn't even know what bonded meant. Those jobs mostly went to younger women, much younger, whom Mabel suspected weren't even born here.

"They all speak that Spanish," she'd say, conceding without a hint of jealousy that they looked more energetic than she did anyway. "Must be that spicy food," she'd say with a happy laugh to her girlfriends at church. "Oh, Lord, and do those girls have figures!" And she'd laugh even more.

In short, Mabel scrambled to get any job she could find. And a scramble it was. She tried babysitting, but families preferred teenagers. She did a week at a coffee shop as a waitress and was grateful when the owner fired her, the stress on her feet too much. "Carrying a bit too much of myself," she joked to him. He slipped her $40 from the cash register, calling it severance. She wasn't too worried. She wasn't depressed. "Child, things work out the way they do for a purpose I can't even try to figure on," she'd say. She just wanted to keep busy and earn a little.

She'd gone to the final day of her town's library book sale when they gave away the books that didn't sell, usually for good reason. She'd picked up a few that were not in the best of shape, but thought maybe she could sell them on eBay using an account she'd opened on the library's public computer. Mabel talked with one of the librarians, asking about Classic Comics Illustrated, and one thing led to another. The librarian lived with a social worker and volunteered at a local shelter. Sensing Mabel was a heavy woman on thin ice, she suggested that maybe she could help with some "things."

"Mabel, at your age you might be able to get some assistance, perhaps food stamps, at least until you get back on your feet."

Mabel laughed it off at first, joking that no one would want to get back on her feet. Her mind went back to the jobs she'd once had and lost, to efforts she'd made that didn't pan out, realized the money she had in that old cigar box—she always was paid in cash and never trusted banks—wouldn't last forever.

She got public assistance and food stamps. It wasn't much, but it wasn't much less than she earned on her own in the best years and rather more than she'd been making recently. At social services, they talked to her about job searches and employment assistance. They asked about her experience and skills. Mabel listed her profession as "housemaid." The aide at the social services raised her eyebrow at the term but said nothing. Mable left out dog walker and waitress.

She was able to pay rent on the trailer more or less on time and buy groceries. With that cushion could still find some work now and then under the table. Over the table was rather rare. Stops at Goodwill and the Faith Farm Thrift Store were her treats when she was in an indulgent mood. That, too, was rare.

This day would be an exception.

The clerk at the grocery store had tallied up her purchases and looked down on the array of food stamps Mabel had given to her. "Ma'am, you can't buy lobster with food stamps." Mabel said, "Oh, yes I can," and handed over a printout she'd made at the library from a USDA website that showed allowable foods. "If it doesn't say no, child, it surely means yes." She said that in a cheerful voice. "I checked twice!"

The clerk shook her head, looking around to see if anyone else had seen the exchange. "Welfare queen," she said to the next person in line.

Then Mabel picked up the wine. "I'd like a white wine, please. No, I don't know a Chardonnay from a pussy fussy, you can imagine. I once had a glass of wine, oh, maybe it was two glasses; it tasted a bit like a pineapple. Oh my, that was wonderful."

The man at the liquor store put Mabel's bags on the counter and walked her over to the New Zealand aisle. She liked the picture on a $10.99 bottle of Sauvignon Blanc. Wine is not paid for under the SNAP program, he advised when she handed over more food stamps. "Oh my, ten dollars and ninety-nine cents? I could fly over to New Zealand for that sort of money. It must be dee-licious!" The man smiled, leaned in, and whispered that it was on sale for just $3.99.

Her eyes sparkled. "It must be my lucky day!"

As the man watched Mabel slowly waddle off, holding her bags for dear life, he took $7 out of his pocket and slipped it into the register.

She walked the distance to her home, resting every time she encountered a bench. She always walked to save money, even though as a senior she could get a discount on the town buses and even taxis. Such luxuries were just not her nature.

Except today. Today she indulged as she had done only once before. That was what the lobster, the wine and crab-cakes, coleslaw, and Jersey corn were all about.

It was their fiftieth wedding anniversary and, as best as she recalled, that was pretty much what they had, just the two of them, to celebrate their marriage on an out-of-season weekend on the coast of Maine. It was the last time Mabel had lobster. It was the only time she had lobster. They laughed at the idea that they were eating at a lobster pound.

"You'd think they'd keep dogs in a pound," she told Lucius. "Maybelline, I just as soon keep on eating lobster!" he said. And they loved it, licking the butter from each other's fingers as they shared one, then another, and then a third. They'd had sworn an oath they would save up and do it again to celebrate their fiftieth.

That month she was two weeks late with the rent and didn't feel the least bit bad about it.

8.

Fish On, Phone Off

"Fish on!"

His rod doubled over as the rainbow tore line off the reel right down to the backing. The guide, Hank, was rowing the boat around, yelling at Alex to keep the rod up. "Use the rod, use the rod. You got something serious on that line. HOLD IT UP!"

Alex did as he was told. When the fish slowed for a moment, he reeled in, the hook pricking the trout, driving it to run again. "ROD UP!" said the guide. "I got it, I got it," yelled back Alex from the front of the little drift boat. "Rod UP! I hear you! Rod up."

Hank spat a stream of tobacco juice into the water and shifted the boat onto a rocky sandbar in the middle of the river. "Easy on the reel. If he runs, let 'em go. He'll tire out. Whoa, see that flash? He's gotta be twenty-six inches. That's not much less than the record for this river. "

"What's the record?"

"Thirty-two inches."

"Six inches is a huge difference!"

"That's what most guys like to believe. Twenty-six is big enough to satisfy this guide."

It was a back-and-forth tussle with the fish. After a dozen fights already, Alex's arm felt tired, a good tired, a tired from doing a man's job, catching fish off the front of a boat out in Montana with a guide and his best friend. When he'd brought the fish to the boat, Hank, the guide, told him to get out of the boat, wet his hands, and get ready for an awesome picture. "Man, he's heavy!" said a smiling Alex.

"You got him? Hold him out over the water. If he jumps I want him to land at home. Hold him way out, like that. Yeah, this will look like a monster! Well done. Perfect."

Hank snapped several shots with Alex's phone, and instructed him to put the fish in the water and sway him back and forth until it revived. Alex already had the fish in the current. "I know, I know, I've been doing it all day. I'm almost an expert at it."

"Just want to make sure. When you come back he'll have added those eight inches. He'll be a trophy."

"You said six inches, no?"

"Yeah, but like I said, most guys exaggerate. Call it a fish story." He held his hands out facing each other and moved them inch by inch wider.

A voice came from the front of the boat. "You have any bars?" It was Max, Alex's college pal, best friend, his kids' guardian, God forbid, in the event. He was leaning against a casting brace. He wasn't casting though. Max's eyes were cast down to his agitated hands.

The guide shifted the oars into the boat and rummaged around in the cooler that served as his seat. He held up a plastic bag. "I got Power Bars, cookies, maybe some Snickers. Couple of Zagnuts I think. Chips. " Alex reached for an oatmeal Clif bar and an apple. And a banana. "Don't go crazy, Ahab. We'll be stopping for lunch soon. Got roast beef, turkey, and you, Alex, wanted veggies, right? There's hummus, red peppers, sprouts, the works. No one starves with me. What can I get for you, Max?"

Max was bent over, his face in his other hand. His mouth was moving but nothing was coming out. "Max, you okay? Seasick?" asked Hank. "You want a bar or something?"

"Yes, please. I can't get any . . . I had a signal a while back, but nothing here."

Max was fingering his cell phone, playing with the settings for some connection. He looked up, a pained expression on his face, and admitted he was trying to send a message.

"No, sir," the guide said. "That's right. You won't get a signal out here. That's a good thing. It's why we're out in the great beyond! Freedom from all that binds you."

"Isn't the great beyond about what's after death? It was in that REM song I think," said Alex.

"I need to send a message," whined Max again. "Hank, when do you think we'll be in a better location?"

Hank shook his head and put on a contented smile. "There is no location better than this. Look around you." Hank pointed his cleft chin to the mountains, sagebrush, and a herd of elk on the slope of a nearby hill. "Maybe the lodge has Wi-Fi. But we have all this." He let the oars fall as he spread his arms to take it all in.

Alex mentioned that it was the Sunday of a three-day weekend and chances were whomever he was sending the message to wouldn't get it anyway. "C'mon, Maximilliano, learn to relax. Who's so important it can't wait?"

Max held his cell phone up in an attempt to get a better connection, squinting in apparent pain into the big blue skies of Montana and damning the Rocky Mountains for blocking a signal. "I got a negative feedback report on eBay," said Max. "I can't have that. It'll ruin my reputation. I make a lot of money on eBay."

Alex rolled his eyes when Hank looked over. Hank just smiled as if to say, *I get all kinds on the river.* But Alex didn't share his western patience. "Max, your reputation is deteriorating before my eyes. Look at the river, for God's sake. There's a hatch on! Fish, dammit, fish."

Max turned about to see what appeared to be a blizzard as thousands, maybe tens of thousands, of caddis came out of the water chased by a score of trout. The fish, big ones, jumped out of the water, some close enough to splash water into the drift boat. Hank pulled two rods out of the holders. Alex grabbed one and cast. Hank had to force the other into Max's hands. "This is what's important, Max," said a still smiling Hank.

Max still had his phone in his hand when he made a disinterested cast. A rainbow rose like a missile shot from a submarine, straight up, and took the fly in its leap as another rainbow, larger still, jumped over it. The two reeled in a pair of trout, a good twenty inches each, and continued until the hatch subsided. They'd caught six between them in the space of fifteen minutes.

Hank ushered the two back into the boat, saying they'd go for another thirty minutes and have lunch at a spot where they could find teepee circles and a closer view of the mountains. "You think it'll have bars?" asked Max.

"Bars, Max? A saloon is more likely. But I'd say the odds of either are kind of low; we'll be right up against the range. You'll love it. And you'll get more fish. That I'd bet on. "

Hank rowed against the current to a steep bank and suggested his clients walk onto the flat plains and look around for those teepee circles. "Keep an eye on the ground. You might find an arrowhead. And stomp your feet. It'll scare the rattlers away. Seriously. Max, did you get that?"

Max stopped typing into his phone and looked up. "Sorry, Hank. No bars. Were you saying something?" Alex kicked Max in the seat of his waders, which, given their weight and constriction, was at best a modest encouragement. "C'mon. There's teepee circles up there. "

"What are teepee circles?" asked Max.

"Umm. You know, circles. Made by teepees, I guess. Hank, what are teepee circles?" said Alex.

"The Indians put up their teepees just over that bank. Used rocks to hold down the sides and left them. The rocks, I mean. When you find a circle you find where they were. "

"Ah," said Alex. "Like old foundations back east. Cool. I should have brought my metal detector!"

"Rocks, Alex," said Hank. "I don't think a detector picks up rocks. Look around, though. Arrowheads and such. Like there. "He pointed to Max's feet and, sure enough, a small white arrowhead was there on the ground. Max took a picture with his camera. Alex pocketed it.

"If I had bars, I could send this to Carla," said Max.

"If you had bars, I'd flatten you!" said Alex. "C'mon. "

"I'm just trying to look at my messages," said Max, as he held the phone in one hand and struggled up the embankment with the other.

They encountered no rattlesnakes but found the circles, half a dozen of them, protruding from the flat grass that separated the river from the rock edge of the mountain cliffs maybe a mile away. A screech came from overhead and Alex looked up right as he heard Hank shout, "Bald Eagle!" from the beach. Hank also yelled that lunch was ready. Alex continued to look up as the eagle swooped low to the river and grabbed a trout in its talons.

"Whoa, Max! Did you see that?"

"See what?" he replied, looking up.

"That group of naked girls! Just over there, you blithering idiot. "

"Girls? What are you talking about?"

"Lunch. Let's eat. "

The eagle flew with its catch to a huge nest in a grove of cottonwoods on the far side of the river then took off flying west towards the range. "There's a great river over those mountains. Filled with trout. It would take us, oh, two or three days to get there. He's, hell, he's probably there already," said Hank. His gaze followed the eagle out of sight.

Hank chewed on tobacco and in between expectorations commented on just how lucky he was, how lucky they were, to be

47

out here. Alex readily agreed as he lay back on the sandy beach and closed his eyes. Max munched on Alex's sandwich—hummus, sprouts and red pepper with tahini—which he held with his one free hand. His other waved the phone in the air.

"Max, you might want to put that thing away. It'll be a while before it'll get anything. Drink in this beauty," said Hank.

Alex listened, impressed with Hank's patience. It was the sort of patience that made him a good guide, especially with clients whose minds were elsewhere. He grabbed his sandwich from Max's hand while Max clutched the phone to his chest.

"Hank, out of curiosity, so if we don't have cell coverage, what do you do if we have an accident or something?" The question was from Alex.

"Well, I'm an EMT, and have gear on board. EpiPen, defibrillator, decent first aid kit. We're trained for emergencies. And there's the satellite phone if we have to call in the cavalry."

Max perked up. "Satellite phone! Does that get . . ."

"Sorry, Max. No. Only connects to the search and rescue fellows. For emergencies. And I've only had to use it once, thank God."

"What for?" asked Max.

"He had a client who got a bad review on eBay and was so upset his fishing buddy tried to kill him," said Alex.

Hank smirked, trying to hold in a laugh.

"What exactly did you sell that got you in so much hot water?" asked Alex.

Max tried to ignore the question, but when Alex pressed, Hank asked as well. "Nothing really," mumbled Max, arousing their interest even more. They wouldn't let it go and Max gave in. "An iPhone."

"You are kidding," said Alex.

"It was a 6. I wanted the better camera on the 7plus."

"So, what's the problem?" Hank was curious.

"Nothing," groused Max.

"Must be something," countered Hank

"He claims it doesn't get Internet," said Max.

The swig of iced tea Hank was in the middle of swallowing was shoved up by a gush of air and ran out his nose. Alex's mouth was wide open as he shook his head slowly back and forth. "There must be some form of justice in that," he said.

"It worked fine. I think it's his carrier. Has to be. I have Verizon and it's fine. Maybe he's just in a bad zone. Alex, you have ATT, check your . . . "

"Not on your life, buddy boy. Not a chance. "

The three got back into the boat and drifted downriver. Grasshoppers jumping from bushes off the banks fell into the river, presenting a big meal for the hungry fish. They were aggressive about it, too, splashing down on the hoppers and returning for more. Alex, the better caster, was able to land his hopper fly within a couple of feet of the shore and, bang, hooked three before Max could get his line in the water. It was a hat trick: a fat brown, a long rainbow, and a nice brookie with orange spots on its side. Max finally wrestled a good-sized rainbow to the boat and seemed, at long last, focused on the achievement.

"Twenty-three inches, Max! Nice, nice, nice. Want a photo?" said Hank.

Sure," said Max.

"Okay. Wet your hands and hold her up from the net. Over the water. Same drill as with Alex. "

"Why wet my hands?"

"Trout have this mucus covering over their skin. It protects them from fungus and infection, and I think it makes them slicker in the water. Easier to swim. If your hands are dry, the mucus might come off."

Max gave a hand a deep soaking, dipping it again and again into the clear water. He held up the trout in front of him and smiled into the camera.

"Nice! It looks huge. Look at that hump.

Max smiled again, and Hank offered, "Kind of takes your mind off your cell phone, doesn't it?"

The smile disappeared, replaced by more furrowed eyebrows and a worried look. "Did you hear that?" Hank and Alex shook their heads, but Max dug into his pocket, fumbled the phone into his wet and slimy hands, and, with a leap that would have made a feeding trout proud, launched it into the Yellowstone River.

He had one leg over the side when Hank yanked on the suspenders that held up his waders and pulled him back. "Stay in the boat!" he grunted as he rowed backward with his left oar, forward with his right, to turn the boat over the spot where the phone presumably was entertaining curious trout.

"It's there. Can you see it?" pleaded Max.

Hank let the anchor drop from the stern, holding them in the current, and peered over the side. "It could be here, or the current could have taken it downstream. Guys, look down."

They looked over the port side, tipping the boat enough to get Hank to yell, "In the middle! Keep balanced! Max, you take that side. Alex, the right."

"Anything?" asked Hank.

"No, just rocks," said Alex. "Some look like phones, though."

"Not funny," said Hank.

Max had his hands over his eyebrows, silent and worried.

"It was in a case, right? An Otterbox?" said Hank. "It'll be waterproof."

Max slumped to his seat. "It was sort of an Otterbox."

"Sort of?" asked Alex.

"Well, it was a Chinese version. From eBay. I paid $7 for it. Including shipping."

"China?" said, Alex. It wasn't a question so much as a statement.

"Seven bucks," said Hank. That, too, was a statement.

"The seller said I could return it, so it must be okay," said Max with a less-than-confident tone. "They had an okay rating.

Ninety-five percent, I think. I'm almost sure they said it floats."
They looked downstream over the rushing water.

"If it does, it's gone," said Alex, tsk tsk tsking in the process.

"Maybe someone will find it?" whimpered Max.

"I kind of saw it sink," said Hank. "Pretty sure, in fact."

"Did you have your name on it? ID?" asked Alex.

"I was going to put it on," said Max. "Call it!"

"What?" came from Alex.

"Call it! If it's here, it'll ring! We can get it with the net!"

"I don't think you'll hear it through the water, pal," Alex responded.

"It'll light up!" brightened Max. "We'll see it go on!"

Alex indulged Max, while Hank leaned forward, hands on knees.

"Uh-uh. No signal," said Alex.

"Figured," said Hank.

"Wait!" said Max. "Call the emergency guys! They can call the phone and . . ." He stopped himself. "My phone has no signal."

They fished for the rest of the afternoon, landing at the lodge near dinnertime. They caught a dozen more. Even Max caught one, a brown that weighed six pounds if it weighed an ounce. The photo showed a depressed man in late middle age, mouth twisted as if it had a hook in it, with a fish that could have made the cover of a magazine.

While Alex helped Hank tie up the boat and collect their gear, Max waddled up to the lodge. He had said something about using the bathroom. Moments later he came back flapping like a duck in his one-size-fits-all waders. He had on his biggest smile of the day.

"Good news?" asked Hank.

Max was doubled over trying to catch his breath, his palms pushing up against the air as if he found Jesus in a tent revival. "All well, all well!"

"Someone found your phone?" asked a dubious Alex.

"Better!" he gasped. "Buyer wrote. Had bad reception! Has

ATT. Says it works fine. Retracted the bad feedback!!"

If his flopping waders had fit better, he might have caught up with a fleeing Max, who couldn't understand why Alex was chasing him with the net.

9.

No One Wanted to Be a Hero

No one wanted to be a hero. No one.

Not now, anyway. It was over, pretty much, or would be soon enough. That's what everyone was saying. That's what newspapers were saying; the last one most of them saw was yesterday's news two weeks ago. It was true. You could taste it. You could see it in the slouch of prisoners marching back, mostly kids and old men. They looked more relieved than depressed, more exhausted than anything else. And all those white sheets hanging out of windows? Everyone knew.

The Army was so sure it was over, they assigned one GI for every twenty, thirty Germans. Think on it. One GI with eight rounds in his M1 for thirty prisoners. That's confidence for you. Or stupidity.

The hunt, if you could call it that, wasn't for the enemy. Not in the minds of the guys who actually carried guns. Let the fighters hit 'em. Hell, they got paid enough and it wasn't like there was anything left of the Luftwaffe. Let the tanks roll over them. Ditto on the Panzers if there were any of those that weren't already burning.

The hunt was for two things: a safe end to it all and souvenirs. Souvenirs to go with a story when the grandkids asked what Gramps did in the big war. Souvenirs to sell to some goldbrick in the rear who wanted to prove something to the folks back home.

Talk about grandkids was new, a good thing. It started back in February, just after the Bulge. They stayed in a convent for a night. The kids, orphans, sat in their laps, giving kisses for chocolate, brushing their soft cheeks on rough beards. That's when it started, talk about what they'd tell their grandchildren. It was a sign of hope. It was a sign that maybe they'd make it after all.

The time for heroes was long gone.

The sergeant told Hart and Abrams to check out the road ahead. He might have winked too, or it might have been a twitch after he suggested to the rosy-cheeked 2nd lieutenant that they might as well wait for the tanks to catch up. The tanks were just a couple of miles back. The lieutenant, a West Pointer class of '44, must have been taught that yelling enough would compensate for a lack of traits an officer should have. Like experience. He screamed, "That's an order!"

The GIs standing nearby instinctively dropped to the ground. They'd learned many things in their time in the service, and one of the most important was not to draw attention to yourself in a combat zone. The sergeant pushed the young officer against a wall with a stern warning to keep his voice down as it wasn't a secure area. He said a sniper had shot the officer in the platoon they'd passed that very morning.

It wasn't true, but it quieted the young lieutenant down. He got even quieter when the sergeant suggested that "the lieutenant" join the patrol, in the rear of course, for the slim chance at some real combat experience. The lieutenant demurred, saying something about a report due at battalion HQ. The sergeant concluded with a "Yessir" and a flip of his fingers that could have been confused for a salute, then returned to his diminished platoon.

They were on the front steps of a damaged home, bullet pockmarks dotting the exterior. It was too nice to be a farmhouse, but then most of the houses in Germany were better than what they'd seen in France and Belgium. White sheets flapped from windows that once waved swastikas. The GIs were trading loot and sharing a green bottle of something, Schnapps maybe, liberated no doubt from the owners who were nowhere to be seen. The sergeant didn't ask for volunteers. He just shrugged in front of Hart and Abrams and gave them a look that said, "Your turn," pointing his chin down the road.

"You heard him. Just don't listen too much," he whispered. "Walk slow, stick to the ditches, and stop after a couple hundred yards. Little Lord Fauntleroy didn't say how far now, did he?"

Abrams returned a gesture that said, "And the horse you rode in on." Hart's smiling Irish eyes rolled back with a resigned shake of his head. They gave each other a knowing nod that spoke to three seasons of frontline experience that had left them almost unscathed. Physically, at least. The nod said "We get the joke."

Hart checked his M1, Abrams his Thompson. The two headed off on either side of the road leading east. Every so often, they glanced back to make sure no one was behind them. They were more concerned about that officer than any Germans. A German probably would just want to give up. What they wanted was to hear the rumble of tanks that would let them step into the narrow ditch bordering the road and wave goodbye to this assignment. Hart said he wouldn't mind taking some more prisoners. Maybe he'd get a Luger. He had one back in Luxembourg, complete with a holster and a belt with a buckle that read "Gott Mit Uns." He lost it in a poker game he knew he shouldn't have played because it was on a Sunday and he still retained an iota of parochial school guilt. His mother would have certainly disapproved. More to the point, he was lousy at poker. The guys from the other unit promised they wouldn't let him lose too much. Yeah, right.

Ah, but a Luger. Better than a medal. A Luger said you'd been here, counted coup, seen the elephant. A Luger had value. A Luger was status. There had to be one out there somewhere what with all the Germans surrendering, and Austrians. The whole lot.

One lousy Luger. Sure, there had to be one amongst the hundreds—no, thousands—of prisoners. Hadn't there been everything else that needed liberation? Nazi flags, daggers, patches, Iron Crosses, for God's sake. And cameras. Give an officer a Leica and you'd get a three-day pass. Dirty pictures, too. One fellow gave a limping sergeant, old enough to have fought in the last war, two packs of Luckys for a gold cigarette case. That sergeant sucked in the tobacco scent so long you'd think he'd pass out. He must have been happy with the trade.

But as for Lugers? None.

Hart and Abrams looked down the empty road. All they saw was mud, and that was good. They didn't want to see anything, but if they did it would probably be more of those ragged arms high above unshaved faces bearing scared-shitless smiles. Hart was thinking about dead bodies. They'd been told to rifle through them in case they carried any useful intel. They never did. The dead were just regular soldiers nobody would ever have given a map to. Or a Luger for that matter. Lugers were officer guns.

Maybe they'd capture a grateful officer who'd give over his Luger grip first, his hand over the barrel, with an accented "I am your prisoner" followed by a crisp salute. A real salute, too, not a "Heil Hitler." That would be one for the grandchildren.

"DOWN!"

Hart dropped into the muddy ditch, willing himself deeper into the ground. Abrams had crawled into a puddle ahead of him and kicked back at Hart's helmet. He used hand signals to say there was a soldier, enemy soldier, with a rifle, to their left. Hart didn't understand hand signals. "Just say it, you idiot. Sonofabitch must have seen us."

They peered over their ditch to see someone, a hundred yards up a wooded hill, peeking out from behind a massive tree, his rifle nervously pointing left and right. He wore a grey uniform. He wasn't a sniper. A sniper would have taken them out already. And thank God he wasn't SS. He was just one guy on a hill. Alone.

They watched. He shifted around on that spot, crouching too little for good cover, pointing his gun all over the place, looking for Hart and Abrams lying low in their cover. Hart looked down the barrel of his rifle, adjusted the sights, but the German was partially blocked by the tree and he had lousy aim anyway even if better than Abrams's.

"Get help?" said Abrams.

"Naw, just scare him off," said Hart, who fired off a few rounds in the direction of the tree. The German ducked behind it and fired a couple of rounds back, kicking up dirt no closer than twenty feet from where they hid. He was nervous and a bad shot to boot. They waited a few minutes, hoping the shots would bring up their unit. No one came.

Abrams pointed to the right of the hill and said he was going up and told Hart he should creep up on the left. "You shoot, covering fire. He'll move to the right and I'll get him. Stay the fuck down, right?"

Hart readily agreed to the 'stay the fuck down' concept. They started their ascent, Abrams crawling up on the right, Hart on the left keeping the German, who was still pointing all over the place, in doubt.

Hart had it easy. It was April. The ground was soft, the leaves and debris moist, and he didn't make a sound as he moved from the cover of a boulder to a stump to a tree, with the German in sight all the while. Abrams was more exposed. The German fired a few rounds down the hill at nothing in particular. The effort seemed half-hearted. Abrams thought maybe the German, too, was trying to scare them off. He wanted the German to just walk away or give up. That he didn't, that he wouldn't, pissed him off, angering Abrams more than any fight he'd been in.

He crept closer, staying low, making no effort to surprise the German. That was Hart's job. Abrams had the Thompson. When the Kraut bastard moved—Abrams was thinking of him as a Kraut now—he'd open up. He double-checked the safety and lifted the Thompson. He was ready.

Hart was ready too. He'd moved closer. There weren't thirty yards between him and the German. There he was, half his body behind the tree, the rest exposed, and the Kraut still scanning with his rifle left and right, up and down. Hart stepped on a branch—the German must have heard—and he flattened himself waiting for a shot that never came. The German just kept moving his rifle around, pointing at nothing. He wasn't very threatening. To Hart, he acted more confused, or maybe he didn't care. Or maybe he'd gone out hunting, like for deer, and didn't expect to run into anyone, least of all Americans. Hart almost felt sorry for him, a hungry soldier looking for food in the wrong place at the wrong time.

There was no need to aim. Hart would fire off some rounds, the German would move to the other side of the tree, and Abrams would let loose. From where he was, he could see Abrams looking back, and he gave him a thumbs-up. Hart rose from behind a tree and moved out to get off his shots. The German picked that moment to come out from his tree. They stared at each other. Hart noticed a white flower on the German's collar and, in a split second, thought that any guy wearing a flower in his lapel would be a gentle guy, someone who didn't want to fight, someone who'd want to surrender.

Or maybe it was more like a scene out of the Wild West. The German would sniff the flower, take his time, and come up shooting.

Someone fired. A couple of shots followed and then nothing. The German was on the ground, still. Hart felt something in his side, but whatever it was wasn't bad. He fired another round into the German. Abrams, who'd run up the hill, let go a brief volley into him as well. The body jerked under the unnecessary assault. Hart had got him with his first shot.

"You okay?" asked Abrams, pointing to Hart's side with the barrel of the Thompson.

Hart looked down to see the stock of his M1 shattered where the bullet had hit, blood trickling from the splinters that had entered his hip. He pulled the splinters. "Yeah, I'm fine."

They went to the body and kicked it over. He was not a young man, not one of the kids they'd seen, but a guy in his thirties, younger maybe. A pistol case dangled from the man's belt. Abrams gestured with his chin. "Your Luger."

There was no Luger. The case held letters and a photograph. The picture was of a blonde woman, pretty, smiling, kneeling. Her arms wrapped around two little girls, maybe three or four years old, not more than five. They wore exaggerated grins that said "Give a big smile for Daddy." The girls wore matching white dresses and had identical white hair ribbons. Their hair glowed whiter than the mom's, if that was possible. Hart thought they looked like little angels. He crossed himself.

On the back was a name, Gretl, in an adult's handwriting and one other written in a child's scrawl, maybe Hanna. And there was a doodle of a dog, with a smile, the sort of drawing a child would do to make a father smile when he was far from home.

They didn't look for souvenirs after that. Anyway, the war was over, pretty much, or soon would be.

10.

The Last Cast

When Charlie Calisher was shoved into early retirement, he made a promise to himself; he'd fish until he got bored. Boredom was not the goal. Boredom was a worry, an admonishment, a sentence that he was beside the point.

He'd been at it since May and was still not bored. He'd had exceptionally good days when he'd land twenty-three fish, hook, and lose, another seven, and extraordinarily bad days, like when he caught nothing but a chill after slipping on a slimy moss-covered boulder, filling his waders with icy river water, and losing his rod, a $750 Winston, in the process. That was hours earlier on this the final day of the season.

Fortunately, on this occasion, he'd managed to keep his head above the current—fast but only three feet deep—and was helped to his feet by a pair of young anglers who had rudely invaded the run he was fishing. Charlie had tried to tell them as much.

"Hey, young fellows. I'm still fishing this spot. And see that sign, 'Trout Management Area'? It means fly fishing only."

They had looked at him as if he was speaking another language before casting their spinning rods right into the run. They also were drinking beer, tossing the cans onto the bank. Charlie had thought to say something but couldn't be bothered; he just picked up the cans himself. "Massholes," he muttered as he glanced at their Red Sox hats and couldn't help but hear their townie accents.

But when he fell, they were quick to run in—without waders—to get him up and over to the bank. "You okay, old-timer? You took a wicked fall." Charlie was more embarrassed than hurt and brushed them off with a couple of thank-yous as he dropped his chest waders and lay down in the gravel just over the bank, his legs awkwardly kicking in the air to let the water drain out. He felt as foolish as he looked.

Old-timer, he thought. Christ.

He was cold but could warm up. He'd told the Massholes a thing or two and made it clear he wasn't happy about their littering his river. He still had it in him. A temper to display, a sense of responsibility, something other than just an old man falling. Yeah, he'd told them a thing or two.

If beauty is in the eye of the beholder, then age can be a relative thing. At sixty-three, Charlie would be younger than his father, who lived to ninety-four, and younger than his best friend from high school, Gus O'Rourke, who got pancreatic cancer two years ago. He went, snap, just like that.

His dad has been an old ninety-four, unable to walk, on oxygen, anxious, and depressed. He was in a steady state of deterioration after his heart attack at sixty-seven, a month after retiring, and a stroke a few years later. So much for the golden years.

Still, "old-timer." Seriously?

It said over the hill, needing assistance. It said you were feeble, you required help, reading glasses, and hearing aids. That you could be ignored by some low-class Massholes with their Walmart made-in-China spinning rods in a flyfishing-only stretch. And it implied, as if the labored lumbering to your car wasn't enough of a reminder, that you were once in better shape.

Charlie's feet sloshed in the booties of his still soaked waders as he stopped short. He shook his head in disappointment in front of a late model Toyota Avalon. Of course he knew what car he drove, but it struck him especially hard that it was a Toyota Avalon. A Google search once revealed it as being at the top of a list of "top 10 cars for retirees," aka an old man's car. He asked himself why he didn't buy the red BMW 330i, which he liked so much, and why he bothered to look up "old man's cars" in the first place.

He got out of his wet things. Once the car was on he put the heat at full blast, turned the seat warmers up all the way—he'd bought the winter package. He put the seat back, closed his eyes, and enjoyed the toasting sensation on his ample rump. Charlie poured himself a mug of sweet hot coffee from the thermos he'd had the foresight to bring, took long sips, and closed his eyes. What to do? Go home? Warm up? Get back to fishing? Read the book he'd brought along—The *100-Year-Old* Man Who Climbed Out the Window and Disappeared? Maybe he'd put together a resume and test the waters. Then he thought about friends his age who worked at Whole Foods under the bosomy gaze of assistant managers young enough to be their granddaughters.

Fishing it would be, and thank goodness for those heated seats. Charlie changed clothes. Ever prepared, he got into the extra clothes, grabbed his spare rod out of the trunk, and put on his mostly drained waders, toasting his mood with a final cup of coffee. He wasn't lumbering now; he was marching upstream. After all, he may have gotten wet, but he hadn't gotten bored yet. That was the unwanted goal, a dead end. Besides, the sun was out. Perhaps it had gotten warm enough; there might be a hatch going on.

A few yards in he'd forgotten if he'd locked the car, so he took the keys from a waterproof case (which also housed a cell phone, wallet, and fishing license), pushed the button, and realized he had already locked the car. "A mind's a terrible thing to waste," he said, trying to remember where he'd heard that phrase. The United Negro College Fund came to him.

"That old TV ad. Does that organization still exist? They should have changed the name to the African American College fund. Yeah, but what if something else comes into fashion, like 'the People of Color College Fund'? Is there a word that would transcend the changing words of political politeness? Why am I talking to myself?"

Now that he had so much less interaction with people, lonely conversations with himself had become more frequent. It was one more thing he missed about his old job.

Charlie trampled through the underbrush, scrambling over collapsed stone walls, to get to a pool he knew held fish. It was a hike, to be sure. Despite the cool air, he was sweating. "Can't sweat," he huffed to himself. "Slow down. Don't want to catch a chill." He stopped a lot to catch his breath and settle his racing heart. But the struggle raised the hope he'd have it to himself.

Two others had the same thing in mind. He broke through the brush only to see the Massholes splashing their lines through the pool with their industrial-strength lures that might catch a shark, but never a trout. Their loud stomping would spook any trout into the depths where they would not be feeding. Of course, it could be nature at work, too; the hatch had run its course. But Charlie preferred to blame the Massholes. The anger made him feel less like a curmudgeon and more like a serious fisherman, more like a real man.

"Hey, buddy. You hit the right place. They were coming up like crazy but went quiet like," one yelled, a cigarette dangling from his mouth.

I'll just bet, thought Charlie. I'll just bet.

Now what? It took enough out of him to get here, but he'd read about a section in a narrow ravine a good mile or two upstream, straddled on both sides by a national forest. That section, word had it, saw few people. That section, so it was said, held wild brookies, twelve inches and more, and big rainbows. That section, rumor had it, was a mystical place if you could find it.

Charlie stared into his pool in the vain hope that maybe fish would rise again. He tore his gaze away, looking upstream toward the steep hills that cradled the legendary ravine. It would be a trek, yes, but he wasn't bored yet. Besides, he could use the exercise.

The path that followed along the river narrowed into a barely trod track before giving way to an obstacle course of more brambles, thorny bushes, and downed trees. Charlie was huffing it, starting to sweat again, and started slowing to retain his stamina. He edged over to the river and decided to walk upstream against the current. It was easier than pushing through the vines and getting stuck, but swimming upstream was still a workout.

Charlie sat down more than a few times to rest and to slow his breathing and heart. Sufficiently rested, he looked up and down the river, trying to match his breathing to the splashing of the current against the rocks while scouting for the rippled circle of a rising trout. But this wasn't the ravine, not yet, and he was determined to reach it.

After a good hour, the banks started to steepen on both sides as the river curved toward the east. The afternoon sun was hitting one stretch at a near-perfect angle, providing just enough warmth and inspiration for a big hatch, possibly a massive hatch, of blue-winged olives, size 16, a perfect size for Charlie: easy to see on the water and easy to tie onto a thin tippet. And beneath those BWOs were trout popping to the surface, lots of them.

Charlie's heart was beating hard again. Now, though, it was for the beautiful sight on the river. One trout jumped out of the water a few feet from him; it must have been eighteen inches.

His hand shook as he tied on a matching fly and cast over a rise. Nothing. He cast again. Nothing. The fish were popping up but not for his fly. He took it off and tied on another—identical in theory, but fish can be finicky. Again, nothing. He took it off and added some lighter tippet along with some grease to help the fly float. "Eat it," he said to no one but the fish. "Eat it."

BAM! He had one on and it was fighting. Charlie's rod was light, a three-weight, which should have been ideal for this river, but this fish was big, really big. It took line out, and Charlie kept the rod high — "Let the rod take the pressure, protect the tippet," he told himself. He reeled in, the hook biting the fish, and the fish tore downstream. Charlie followed. "Go easy," he said out loud. "Let it run. Easy."

Charlie followed the fish, sensing its exhaustion, holding his rod way up and slowly reeling in just as he stepped backwards into a hole that took him to his knees. Freezing water poured over his waders and he didn't care. The rod was nearly doubled over, vibrating with life. Charlie was vibrating too, shivering. It wasn't the cold doing that; it was the monster at the end of the line.

The fish was tired but fought all the way into the waiting net. By God, he had never seen anything like this on a New England river. A male rainbow, hooked jaw, twenty-six inches, fattened up for a winter that felt like it was already here. The fly came out easily — all his hooks had the barbs pressed down. Charlie swayed the monster back and forth in the current, water flowing over its pulsing gills, until it swam off, revived, alive, to be caught another day.

He reckoned he caught over a dozen more but stopped counting after six. All were returned to the river. Freezing on the outside, he was warm on the inside. It had been a good day, a great day, the best day. Charlie also felt revived, alive. He smiled as he closed his eyes for a moment. It was getting dark anyway. He'd had enough.

Jack O'Brien and Pat McHale were tossing the final cans of their original six-pack into the woods when they saw the Avalon with its engine running. They half expected the old guy, the one who'd fallen in the river, to give them grief. Instead, they saw him with his head resting on the steering wheel. Charlie didn't rouse when they tapped on the window. McHale, an EMT, tried to find a pulse, attempted CPR, then looked to Jack. "Dial 911."

Neither Pat nor Jack, nor the EMTs that finally showed, nor the doctor who pronounced him dead, noticed that gently hooked to the tip of his left forefinger, as if to admire it, was a size 16 blue-winged olive. It was barbless, of course, so fell out easily.

II.

Found Money

If Harry hadn't turned around from the urinal, he wouldn't have noticed the envelope, but then the guy had come in and stood at the one right next to him. There were three urinals, and he should have taken the empty one at the other end. Everyone knows the drill. But not this guy, apparently. This guy chose the middle one against all unspoken protocol. Granted, Harry thought, it was a hotel that catered to foreigners. Maybe the guy was French or something and didn't know how things were handled in men's rooms in the US of A.

It was weird, and the guy was wearing Capri pants and a tight, gaudy shirt. He smiled at Harry before turning to stare at the newspapers the hotel conveniently posted over the urinals so pissers could do two things at the same time. But Harry was uncomfortable with both his proximity and the outfit. He finished his business in a stall, zipped up, and turned away.

That's when he saw it. Harry looked at the envelope. It was so thick he couldn't miss it. Then he looked to see if anyone was watching. No, no one else was there but Pierre or Mario or whatever his name was emptying his bladder while humming to himself with his eyes closed. He was peeing with both hands on his hips. It was a habit that usually annoyed Harry, but his mind was elsewhere. He entered the stall, closed the door, and, using his toe, moved the envelope closer. There was some writing on the

67

front, the ink smudged from some liquid that Harry didn't want to think to about. The bulge appeared to him to be in the shape of bills, a lot of bills given the thickness.

Harry heard the urinal flush. There was no sound of water running in the sink or the hand dryer at work. The guy left without washing his hands! Must be European, thought Harry. He opened the stall door, walked to the sinks, and took a handful of paper towels back to the stall. Using them, he picked up the envelope and put the bundle in his jacket pocket.

He took a long time washing his hands in hot, soapy water, half hoping someone would barge in, in a panic, looking for his lost envelope. The other half of him hoped no one would claim it. The few men who came in didn't do anything more unusual than what you would usually do in such a place, though Harry's lingering at the sink did cause some sideways glances and quicker exits than usual.

Harry bent over the sink and splashed his face, twice with cold water. He patted himself dry, balled the paper towels up, and tossed them into the bin, missing it twice, but getting it on the third time. He looked at himself in the mirror, adjusted his tie, and brushed back his hair, though he had nothing special to comport himself for. He had time on his hands. That's not a good thing for someone trying to earn his commission this month. But then this month wasn't so different from last month, or the month before, or probably the next month.

Ah, but he was at his hotel, where he could fall into his dreams, unharried, anonymous. This was his Midtown oasis, the place he went between meetings if he had meetings, or when he needed a break. It had a men's room on the quiet mezzanine floor where the lounge chairs were perfect for a nap, to read, to escape. The day he discovered it, he'd taken an exploratory stroll around the mezzanine, outside one of the meeting rooms where some seminar was being held. A table with coffee and pastries sat outside, and Harry, looking around, helped himself and tiptoed away.

A voice stopped him. "Ah, you've discovered the salesman's secret."

Harry turned to see a chunky older fellow with a knowing smile and dancing Irish eyes looking at him. Caught red-handed. He apologized and went to return the pastry.

"Take a seat."

Harry sunk guiltily into the deep cushion of the chair across from the man who had a coffee and three pastries in front of him.

"Are you with the convention?" Harry asked.

"Is there a convention? If there is, those cakes are sitting by their lonesome selves, and the coffee's getting cold. Don't you agree?"

Harry stuttered an agreement, apologizing again for taking them.

"Don't apologize to me! I've had plenty of sustenance here over the years. It's like I said, the salesman's secret."

The man explained that the city was filled with salesmen scrambling about from customer to customer and needing a rest once in a while, and as they got older, more than once in a while.

"We find places. Hotels, mostly. To put down our feet. No one bothers to ask if you belong, just act like you do. And if there's a meeting, or convention, well, voila, free food. Sometimes you can sneak into the conventions and load up on things—premiums, they call them—you know, giveaway stuff."

He opened up a shopping bag with a "Pfizer" logo to reveal a mass of pens, notepads, a box of cigars, a Slinky, penknives, and fishing lures. A mass of useless things with the names of various drug companies on them. "They're having a dermatology convention at the Hilton. They give out great stuff. Dentists get good things, too."

"Isn't that stealing?" asked the younger Harry.

"Hmmm, I don't think so. I open the bag and they toss things in. I don't even ask."

In the years that followed that first encounter, Harry took a more subdued approach. He'd steal a few minutes' rest, a coffee, a sandwich, but sneaking into meetings or loading up on convention souvenirs were not his thing. He was honest. And, besides, drug companies had stopped giving out such goodies.

Leaving the men's room, he patted his suit jacket twice to feel the bulge of the envelope. His eyes darted around, seeking a man—who else would drop anything in a men's room?—one who was maybe in distress, anxiously looking around for something he lost. But people were acting the way they normally do in hotels: walking, talking, minding their own business.

Harry walked around the mezzanine that overlooked the main lobby, strategically placing himself in a seat that would enable him to observe the men's room's entrance and the staircase that led up to it. On the way, he picked up a coffee and a bagel, with lox, a rare treat, from a table outside a meeting hall where a sign read "Actuarial Club Continuing Education." A door opened into a room loaded with pale men and some pale women, mostly in blue suits and white shirts, wearing thicker than average glasses, and scribbling notes while a similarly dressed man droned on about a bell-shaped graph. Harry overheard the word "asymptote" and took a second bagel.

He again checked his pocket and kept an eye on the men's room door. A man, heavyish, sweaty, bounded up the stairwell and rushed into the room. Harry stood up, ready to walk over and return the bundle, but the man exited at a calm pace, a relieved look covering his face. He, too, took a bagel and lox before entering the stairwell. Harry watched him as he came out on the main floor below and, leisurely, walked out to the street.

The comings and goings were all abysmally dull. There was no sense of urgency beyond the normal needs of a bathroom; certainly, no one appeared to be wandering around looking for something. Harry again touched the bulge in his pocket, sensing a weight he hadn't felt when he first put it there. With his fingers, he felt the shape of the contents, confident that it held cash.

Who lost it? Was it a drop-off for some espionage plot? The hotel did do all that foreigner business; Harry had just overheard a conversation in some language that sounded suspiciously like Russian at a table nearby. The pair of speakers then got up, and each took a bagel—though the ones with lox were gone—and entered the room of actuaries.

Or maybe it belonged to a drug dealer who lost it in the stall, the envelope dropping out of his pocket. Even dealers needed to use a toilet, right? Would he return with a vengeance? Harry considered dropping the envelope back where he found it. He'd seen *Scarface*. Twice. Harry looked around for Hispanic-looking faces. He saw plenty, mostly the hotel's staff.

Maybe it belonged to one of them. Maybe some poor employee was holding it to send back to his family in Mexico, or for a down payment on his daughter's wedding. Maybe he was trying to pay for his kids to join him. Harry suddenly felt guilty and scanned the hotel staff to see if anyone was upset. But it was business as usual as far as he could tell.

It could be ransom for a kidnapping! But then the floor of a stall would be an odd place to leave it and surely someone, FBI or undercover cops at least, would have been watching. Or one of the kidnappers. He, again, tapped the envelope. If someone was watching, he couldn't tell.

Harry got up to leave, to find a quiet place to see exactly what was inside the envelope, but he sat down quickly when he saw two burly men in ill-fitting suits brush aside a cleaning lady and barge into the men's room. He slunk deep in his chair to spy on this development. One of the men came out, turned back to the door, and looked around the mezzanine. Harry pushed himself down deeper and put his hand in his pocket. If they came to him, he'd put it to the table and walk away. It hadn't been opened. He'd merely found it, he would say. The man started to walk toward Harry at a quick pace, and then, like lightning, grabbed a napkin off a table and took one of the remaining bagels, pumpernickel, and ate it in three bites. His companion came out of the men's room to join him but took just a petit pain au chocolat, which he ate in two bites, brushing the crumbs off his plaid jacket.

A woman looking suspiciously like an accountant approached them and spoke. They looked around, eyes down, more like teenagers caught smoking than criminals. They shook their heads, replaced the napkins, and hurried away. The woman's gaze followed them and then she, too, took a pastry and sat down at the table labeled "Registration."

There were very few pastries or bagels left.

He relaxed as no person showed up in a panic, as if they'd just lost a small fortune. By now, whatever lay in that envelope had grown in Harry's mind. At first, he imagined a few dollars, perhaps a couple of hundred. Now, as he fingered it, the width seemed to grow. If it were 100s, it could be tens of thousands of dollars! Enough, Harry imagined, for, well, big stuff . . . a car, an apartment. Retirement?

His fingers played more with the envelope, continuing to look around. The actuaries, on a break, formed a line at the men's room and grabbed snacks off trays being brought over by hotel staff. None of them seem more harried than an actuary would normally appear. In other words, if one of them had just lost a packet of money, he didn't show it. And it would be a "he"; the money had been in the men's room, after all.

Nonchalantly looking about, trying his best to appear a simply bored patron in between meetings, he made a small tear in the envelope in his pocket. He feigned a yawn for effect then lifted the edge, just a bit, for a glance.

There was the green, the green of bills. He lifted the envelope some more and the first one he saw was a 20. Twenty was good. It wasn't $100 but it wasn't a single either. The next one was, however, then more 20s, some 10s, there was 100, a C-note, and another, and then some 5s. It wasn't a car, let alone retirement, but it undoubtedly was more than he got in his biweekly paycheck. The amounts were so random and rather light in total, he realized. It couldn't be the stash of some criminal episode. He relaxed on that thought when he saw two men rush through the mezzanine on their way to the men's room.

"Calmate, Mr. Rodriquez, calmate," said a tall, thin, dapper man in a black suit with a gold hotel badge on his pocket. He was speaking to a short, dark man, wearing a blue jumpsuit, with the name of the hotel stitched across the back. Sweat was pouring down his face.

"Eet must be here, Meester Swenson. Eet must be here."

They went to the top of the line, entered the room, and returned. "I apologize, gentlemen," said Swenson. "Did anyone find an envelope here?"

It struck Harry as odd that Swenson would ask men waiting outside the men's room if the envelope was lost inside. Perhaps it was a different envelope from the one Harry's fingers held in his jacket. The small crowd looked up and down at each other, shook their heads, and returned to their conversations. Swenson, followed by a hand-wringing Rodriquez, went down the stairwell.

Harry sighed and took out the envelope. $3,653 in total. A lot, he thought. A lot for a Hispanic hotel employee who, from the look of things, was probably a janitor, maintenance man at best. Still, Harry felt a twinge of responsibility. Of guilt. He fantasized for a moment about what he'd do with the money, sighed again, and went to the hotel's management office.

A large artificially blond woman sat at a desk. Over the top of half-rimmed glasses, she glared at him. "Yes?" she asked. Not, "May I help you?" Not a greeting smile, just a "yes" as if he'd disturbed her doing something important. Nice service, Harry thought.

"Is there a Mr. Swenson here? I, err, found, umm, an envelope. Upstairs." He was quick to add that it was torn open when he found it. "It looks like it has some money in it and I was wondering if, if, anyone lost something."

The large woman leaned forward, her second and third chins jiggling in the process. "How do you know Swenson?"

Harry felt himself get flushed, surprised by her question, then unsure how to answer. "Oh, I heard a man calling his name. I assume he's the manager."

"Assistant manager. One of many. I've seen you before. Are you a guest or what?"

A guest or what?

"I'm a 'or what' with the"—Harry thought quickly—"with the actuarial meeting. First time here."

She raised her drawn-on eyebrows, a tad suspiciously, Harry thought, and said, "Just give me the envelope. I'll make sure Swenson gets it."

Now it was Harry's turn to turn off the charm. "No doubt you would, but I'd like to hand it over to him directly. It's, um, my company's policy. I'll need him to sign a receipt. We are a regulated industry." Harry smiled slightly, blinking slowly at the woman. That was a good answer, he told himself.

"I'll find him," she said, rising with an effort. "Take a seat if you're going to wait."

Harry remained standing and took out the envelope, stealing a rubber band from the woman's desk to wrap around it. One of the 100s was sticking out. He took it, glancing about to make sure there were no cameras on him. Then he took one more.

Swenson entered, followed by Rodriquez, followed by the large woman a slow distance behind.

"Hi, this was in the men's room, in a stall. One of my colleagues said a Mr. Swenson was looking for an envelope."

"I thought you said you heard someone call his name," said the woman.

Before Harry could speak, Rodriquez came forward with tears in his eyes. Harry was about to go into his pocket and say two 100s had slipped out when Rodriquez grabbed onto Harry's hands. "Thank you, thank you, thank you," he said, tears dripping down his cheeks. "My numbers came in 632! I never win. Until today!"

Rodriquez reached into the envelope and pulled out two 10s, looked at Harry, then put one back. "For you, Meester. For reward!"

"Numbers? You play the numbers?" asked Harry.

"Never win. Until today."

Swenson thanked Harry, shook his hand, and left, pushing Rodriquez back to work. The woman plopped down into her pneumatic chair, which sank a good four inches under her bulk. "We done here?" she said.

"We're done," said Harry. "Yes, we're done."

On his way out he went back to the mezzanine and grabbed a pastry off the actuaries' table. Just because.

12.

Man's Best Friend

Willis stumbled again. He hadn't seen the slick root of the spruce. Anyway, he had given up trying to avoid them. He grabbed at a wet pine branch, smearing his already raw hand with its glue-like sap, but managed to keep standing this time. Maybe the sap would help heal his cuts. He'd read about that somewhere. A wilderness survival book, maybe.

He swore out loud and then shouted, although there was no one to hear him. Catching his breath, he wiped his hands on his wool-sheathed thighs to rid himself of the sap, but only managed to get bits of pine needles and dirt to adhere to his filthy, burning, palms.

"Enjoy the trip?"

He turned and made a half-hearted kick in the direction of the immense Newfoundland that had leapt over the same root.

"Easy, cowboy," said the dog. "Don't kill the messenger."

Willis sat down on a log, head in his hands, shivering, and looked up when he felt the warm, moist breath of the Newfie sitting inches from his face. He scratched the dog's ears. "A Saint Bernard carries whiskey, you know. What do you have for me?"

"Brandy. I believe they carry brandy. Not whiskey. Maybe a Scotty carries whiskey, but it couldn't be much. The poor thing would trip over the barrel like you're tripping over those roots. If it's any consolation, at least you look drunk doing so."

Willis went to slap the dog's rump, but it had moved just out of reach, tail wagging. His arms went flying in the air, paddling away, missing the dog, and he fell face down on the cold ground.

He scrambled onto his hands and knees, finally standing, and continued to walk down a slope, looking to find a stream, then a river, and then follow that to something—a trail, a road, a house, a barn, a trading post, anything to get him out of the North Woods and the rain. Rain for now until it turned to sleet or snow. And it would do that, had done, every day, ever since the plane went down. And sunk. Sunk before he could get anything useful from it. Like food. He had a bag of BBQ chips and a chicken parmesan sandwich wrapped in foil between him and the co-pilot's seat. His stomach was in agony just thinking about that. It was there, shining, when he broke through the shattered windscreen. Why hadn't he grabbed it? It would be delicious now even cold.

Even frozen.

It was ice on the wings that took it down, ice that ringed the lake he'd crashed into. He managed to get out of the plane, swim to shore, and there was the dog, dry as a bone, just waiting for him. Warm as toast, the dog was. Warm like a blanket that Willis clung to getting sloppy kisses in return.

The dog led now, glancing over his shoulder every so often to make sure Willis was close enough. At one point he stopped, crouched, wagged his tail, and whispered a shush. Willis crouched as well, hand on the dog's shoulder to keep himself steady. The dog was so very warm, and Will so very cold. He plunged both hands into the thick coat.

A family of deer was in a clearing just ahead. They froze for a moment, staring at him as if to suggest he must be some sort of an idiot to be hiking in the woods at this time of year without gear. The dog barked and they scattered, their white tails lifting straight into the air over their rear ends mooning the intruders in their territory.

"Rude," said his companion. "These are the cute brown-eyed animals people don't want to hunt anymore?"

"They're hunted. They just don't want to hunt them back home. Too suburban."

"I say bring back mountain lions."

"They'll eat dogs too, you know."

"Only the slow ones."

They argued over why the dog didn't go after the slow one, the youngster that still had spots on it. Willis was starving. Surely the dog was hungry, too. Willis went on a rant about the brandy, but the dog just stared at him and moved on. Willis followed as best he could, calling for the dog to stop. The dog looked behind, shook his head, and continued. He took slower steps, deliberate steps. It was a conscious effort to keep Willis moving, his arms flying about as he tried to keep balance.

"Wait up. Please. I need a break." Gulping air, Willis plopped himself down on the forest floor, head cradled in his hands, elbows on his knees. "I'm not sure I can go on much further. I'm freezing." He wanted to grab his belly, now cramped in pain like he'd been punched with a cold fist. But his arms couldn't cooperate, wouldn't listen. They were flailing like he'd fallen into a hornet's nest.

The Newfie sat before him, dignified, his eyes judging Willis, not without concern.

"You don't have much choice if you think about it," the Newfie said. "You've got no real food. Not much in the way of supplies; just the lighter. At least get to some water. Get a drink. Did you know a human survives in threes? He can go without air for only three minutes, without water for only three days, and without food for three weeks. You've got the air. Now get the water. It's just down there." The Newfie pointed his muzzle further down the slope and nudged Willis's face.

"C'mon, hold onto me."

"Wait. A lighter. You just said I have a lighter?" Willis patted himself to find he had one in an inside pocket. He didn't even smoke but craved a cigarette now. It might warm up his lungs.

"You found it on the floor of the hangar before you got in the plane. Remember? You were worried it might spark or something."

"Oh, yeah. Yeah. What a memory." A thousand things passed through his mind: that damn chicken parm, the thermos of coffee, the parka. And his boots. At least he was wearing his hiking boots. He kicked to make sure they were still there. They were so heavy. His kicks were so feeble; it was like kicking through oatmeal.

Willis grabbed the dog's coat and lifted himself. He was amazed at how solid the dog was, how its massive shoulders were able to take his weight. It was like pressing on a rock.

"Thanks," he said.

"Better than whiskey," replied the Newfie.

"Or brandy!" They laughed, then moved downhill. With his hand on the dog, Willis found the walk easier. The dog would call out, "Watch it!" when crossing over thick roots. That woke Willis from his state, and he'd kick the root away.

Ahead was a stream splashing over rocks. Willis was sure he saw fish rising in the pools and wondered how to catch them. He was desperately hungry now, weaker from it. Half dreaming, he thought back to something he'd read in a survival manual: you can trap fish by closing them off with sticks, holding them in a funnel-like pen, and catching them from behind. With your hands. He didn't know if he had the strength for it. Bears caught salmon. The dog looked like a bear. He nodded to the pool, and the dog shook his head.

"You've got hooks and that fishing line," said the Newfie.

"Huh?"

"In your outer pocket, Willis. You've got that little survival kit. There's a candy bar there, too."

Willis didn't think he was that dazed, that forgetful, that confused. But sure enough, there was a small box, no bigger than an Altoids tin, filled with treasure: hooks, line, bobbers, weight, lures, and a small knife. And a Snickers, smooshed but edible. He couldn't bring himself to eat it yet and didn't know why. Keep that for later. Spirits revived, Willis moved a little quicker to the stream, which now, he was sure, was filled with fish. The dog edged off to the side, staring at Willis, his image fading as Willis rushed into the water.

He took in long gulps of the ice-cold water. Too many gulps. He couldn't control it. He tried to get out but found he was thrashing about, stronger at that moment, but unable to do more than splash as he sank again and again below the surface. In those final moments, his mind cleared. He remembered the crash, his scrambling out the front as the water rushed in, and the exhausting attempt to swim to the shore he never was able to complete.

13.

Wilce's Dream

At the persistence of his father, Cliff Skinner, his mother attempted a breathing technique to slow her labor enough to push her soon-to-be-born baby out at midnight. Clifford had heard that the first child of the new year would get all sorts of prizes, including a front-page photo in The Banner. Wilce was born on December 31 at 11:56 p.m.

Cliff also contrived that the local Chevrolet dealer, the largest in this part of Vermont, would give the family a new pickup, something he wanted more than a newborn when he couldn't afford the three kids he had, or the alimony to their different mothers, two of them ex-wives and one of whom the court said he couldn't see even if he wanted to. Which he didn't.

There were no awards for the last baby of the year. The mother screamed bloody murder, gave a long and piercing moan, and out came Wilce, eight pounds four ounces, blue and wet, until the midwife swaddled him in a cotton blanket so white it seemed to shimmer off the overhead light, and he let out a wail to rival his mother's.

In the unknowable way of a newborn, his eyes were unfocused, unaccustomed to this world. For a brief moment, however, the bright lights of the room comforted him, his crying suspended as he squeezed his mother's finger with a surprisingly firm grip, only to rise again as he shut his eyes tight and let the world know he'd arrived.

Cliff made vain attempts to change the time on the birth certificate, going so far as to wind his Timex ahead three minutes, only to be advised by the formidable head nurse that the attending had a "plenty accurate" watch that was synchronized every day to hers. His disappointment came as a gruff "Ah, crap," which he swallowed as he spoke it. Anyway, another baby, a girl, was born precisely as the ball in Times Square on the black-and-white set the nurse had been watching fell, coinciding with cheers of "Happy New Year" elsewhere in the maternity ward.

Wilce never got to know his father. In what later years struck him as a cliché, Cliff had taken what remained of a cold case of Genesee Cream Ale on a hunting trip on a too warm October morning, tied a rope around it, and fallen out of the tree stand as he tried to haul it up. The fall didn't kill him; he landed on an arrow he'd left leaning on the beer. His mother told him the story, again and again, trying to assure her son the father was not one worth missing, but Wilce, in the way of fatherless boys, would make up fantasies that he was on a secret government mission somewhere, still alive, or wandering the woods with a deep secret, living off the land, waiting for his chance to see his son.

Too often, Wilce would look out his bedroom window to the forested hills beyond, half imagining he saw a wisp of smoke from a campfire that could be a sign his father was out there hiding out from the "bad" guys—spies, robbers, aliens, Indians, Krauts, Redcoats—who were after him. At eight, Wilce himself was wandering the woods behind his home, really more of an overgrown lot that had once been part of a dairy farm, when he saw a figure, an old man, sitting on one of those old stone walls, the type that are so common but, when you think on it, seem out of place in the middle of New England woods. The man was sitting on one that bordered the property, looking up. Wilce followed his gaze to a bright set of high silvery blue clouds, nothing more than that, and realized that a stranger was nearby.

The man turned his gaze to Wilce, smiled with a nod, and turned back to the clouds. It was a kind smile, the sort Wilce imagined his father would have, the smile that the pharmacist, Mr. Bates, had when Wilce and his mother would go to get advice and medication. Cheaper than a doctor, she'd say. Bates would always come around the counter, bend down, and give him a box of Cracker Jacks. "Don't eat it all at once. And don't eat the prize inside."

Wilce said he would never do that; he kept those prizes in the old cigar box Bates once gave him for what he called "treasure." Inside the box, Bates had taped a Ben Franklin half-dollar.

The old man waved again and called out, "Yahoo!" Wilce knew enough not to speak to strangers, but the man was on the edge of his woods, where no one ever was, just sitting, and seemed unthreatening enough. Wilce answered back, "I'm not supposed to speak with strangers, and I won't, and if I yell our dog will come, and he's really mean and bites."

"Well, then I'll stay put. I don't mind dogs that don't bite. But, oh my, if they do, then no-sir-ree, buster, no-sir-ree, indeed."

Wilce tightened his lips, trying to look serious, and nodded with a sense of confidence, as if he actually had a dog. "Who are you?" asked Wilce.

The old man looked back to the sky, then to Wilce's home. "Well, I can tell you who I'm not. I'm not the painter your house wants. Nor am I a roofer, for that matter."

"You're staring at clouds."

"I am and plan to stay that way a bit longer if your dog doesn't come after me."

Wilce blushed at that remark.

"There's a lot of stories in clouds. A lot of stories. Like when the sun shines through them. See those rays of light? Makes you think there's a pathway to heaven or some such place. Me anyway. It's like reading a book. Do you like to read, Wilce?"

Wilce was surprised. If the man knew his name he must know Wilce loved to read. Reading was better than a lot of things, better than friends even. The late school bus would drop him at the library, where he stayed until his mother picked him up. He spent those hours in a nook under a rear staircase, a stack of adventure books beside him. To dream.

Miss Delucia, the librarian, was a stern-looking woman, but Wilce knew better. "I will tolerate little boys here only if they are quiet as church mice and don't draw in the books. Understood?"

"Yes, Mrs. Delucia."

"It's Miss Delucia, young Mister, and I plan to keep it that way. Now come along." She took him by the hand to the stacks of the picture books, which he dove into, never noticing when she poked her head around to see how he was doing. If she caught his eye, he just smiled and went back to reading. And she'd smile, too.

It was Miss Delucia who in her very few spare moments taught him to use the children's dictionary. It was Miss Delucia who would sneak a cookie, wrapped in a napkin, into his hand. "Now, shhh about that, and don't leave crumbs." And it was Miss Delucia who recognized that Wilce could read far beyond his years.

That's what he wanted to tell the old man, to let him in on this secret. Wilce put his thumb under his chin, his fingers curled in front of his mouth, a look he made when he was thinking, trying his best to look serious. "Yeah, I like to read a lot. I'm not supposed to boast or anything, but I'm the best reader in class. Maybe the best in the school. Teachers tell me that, but I'm not supposed to say anything. Older kids don't like when a younger kid is better than them at something."

"Well, that makes perfect sense. Perfect sense. Some things are best kept secret. Or to just a few, like your teachers or family, and sometimes not even them."

"What are you doing here?"

"Me? Oh, just looking at the stories, just looking. I'd like to be the wind, blowing clouds here and there, helping them make stories. Some days I feel like I am, too." He picked up a dandelion and blew onto the seed head and followed with a raspberry, making Wilce laugh.

He took a deep breath. "Now think about that. By my blowing, those seeds will end someplace they might not have if left to their own devices. Maybe a squirrel would eat them. But they'll get a new story to tell just because I blew on them. Could end up miles from here. Who knows? I bet you've got stories."

"I like stories, too! I used to like picture books but now read chapter books, long ones too, so I can think about the pictures and change them if I want."

"Like blowing on clouds?"

"Maybe like that."

"Keep on blowing them. Me, I should be moseying along. Glad I ran into you. Just wanted to check up and see how you were doing."

"You know me?"

"Suppose I do, a bit. Or it could be just a story I dreamed up. Hard to know. And when I'm off, you might think you know me a bit. Or it might be a story. Oh, I nearly forgot. When you get a chance, take a look at the secret hideout, you might enjoy it."

"Where's the secret hideout?"

"Anywhere. It could be in a corner of some library. Under your bed. It could be right here." With that, the man tapped his finger to the side of his head. "I gotta be on my way, son. See ya."

He took some time getting up. Wilce cringed at the creaks and cracks he made, but the man simply gave a smile that said, "Getting on in years." He looked to the sky once more, meandered toward the far side of the lot, pushed through brush, and disappeared into the trees.

"See ya," shouted Wilce. He considered following, to see where the man went. Instead, he watched the quivering leaves that had closed behind the man. They seemed to wave goodbye.

Wilce bent down for a dandelion, held it just over his lips, and blew the seeds away. They caught a breeze that carried them, perhaps, miles away, where they would settle. Wilce imagined another boy picking up those dandelions and blowing them on. It could go like that forever. A seed, a great-grandson of one he just blew away, might come back to this very spot.

He did it again, following the seeds over the wall. Sitting there was a brown paper package. Had the man left it by mistake? Or maybe it was a trap, and if Wilce grabbed it, the man would sneak up and kidnap him. But there was no one, no one at all. Wilce went to the package. He stood up on top of the wall looking about and yelled, "Hey, Mister, you forgot this." No one appeared. He tried again, "HEY, MISTER!" Still, he was alone.

He weighed the package in his hands, feeling the edges, knowing that what was inside was a book. Turning the package over he read in broad cursive script, "For Wilce." That was all. He ripped off the wrapping, inspecting for some words of insight. There were none.

The book's title was "The Secret Hideout."

It was a dog-eared paperback. The only thing holding the binding together was some black cloth tape. There was the childish scrawl on the front that maybe once read Clifford, but it was unreadable and the last name was smudged away.

And inside the cover page were two $100 bills, more money than Wilce had ever seen, enough for a bike. For a rifle! Wilce counted it three times and looked around four times. The man really was gone; this wasn't some trick like they warned about in school, like if someone offered you candy or asked if you wanted to see a puppy. This man was gone for sure and had left this for Wilce. He was the only Wilce he knew, and his name was right there on the wrapping. He double-checked that, too.

The story in the book was about a boy who, too, found a book, a secret book about a secret club. And it was about the very town where Wilce lived. Though it had been written years before, there were drawings of places he knew well, like Bates' Pharmacy, his school, this very forest. There was a story, an adventure sort of mystery. It wasn't a great story, not even a very good one. But the story was beside the point. The point was the club.

The book was full of club rules, initiation rites, instructions on building shelters, and how to hunt and fish like Indians. The secret stuff included how to write in code, even how to follow people without being seen, and how to disguise yourself. Wilce read how you could put a pebble in your shoe to walk differently and throw trackers off your trail.

At the end, when the boy and some friends had created the club, the Sachem Club it was called, the truth was revealed, that the book had been written by his father about a club he had started when he was a child. And now they were in the club together. Wilce thought it was just an okay ending, but he didn't care. He cared about the pebble in his shoe and the odd tracks he was leaving in the mud.

And the money. With that money, he would start a club. He could get everything: wood for tree forts, tents and camping stuff, knives and axes, bows and arrows. Maybe he could buy a BB gun and not some cheap Red Ryder thing that couldn't shoot straight. A good one. No, he'd get a Henry. He'd get a .22, the Henry Pump Action. The one with the octagon barrel. And he'd hide it under his bed where no one ever went. It had to be a Henry. A Henry was a Scout's gun. He'd been in the hardware store next to Bates' staring at the knives on display when a teenager in a Boy Scout uniform got one from his father. The boy had just made Eagle.

He smiled at Wilce. "Hey, kid, you want to hold it?"

After checking to see it was unloaded, he held it out for

Wilce. The Henry was heavy for Wilce, but he didn't want to let it go. "Jeez, you're the luckiest kid in the entire world," was all he could say handing it back. The clerk, the father, and a few others standing by laughed. The Eagle Scout just smiled.

"Join the Scouts. When you become an Eagle, maybe your dad will get you one."

Wilce didn't know why that made him sad. But, anyway, now he could buy that Henry. He wouldn't need the Scouts. He'd have his own scouts. He wrote down the names of nine people who could join him, then crossed out seven. Ten was too many, too many to keep a secret and, maybe, they wouldn't vote for Wilce to be the club's leader, the Sachem, who was like an Algonquin chief, and that wouldn't be fair because it was his club and he started it and it was his idea. No, four people would be perfect. They would be his best friends. He went over the list, adding names, erasing some, trying to decide who would be worthy of being in his club, the club where he was Sachem.

"What's a sachem?"

Wilce struggled to open his eyes. He recognized the voice, but it was out of place. It didn't belong in his head, at least, not at that moment. It came again, louder and unwelcome, as startling as the sun pouring through the roll-up shade that wouldn't stay closed. As startling as the creaky fan blowing into his opening eyes.

It was his mother calling for him from the kitchen.

"What's a sachem? You were talking some nonsense about a sachem."

Something wasn't right. Wilce felt around for the book, knowing that the book wouldn't be there or anywhere. The panic rose as he tore at the sheets searching, hoping he was wrong, that it would be there, fallen under his bed, the place he'd use as a hidey-hole, the place he'd read by flashlight, the place where he'd hidden his Henry .22.

"Go get your own breakfast. I'm on shift, and they pay time and a half on Saturday. Yeah, and TV is broke, so go play outside."

Wilce just said, "Yeah," giving the bed and under the bed and his whole room another look. But he knew, he knew all along; there'd never been a book or the cash or an old man looking at clouds.

He didn't eat the cereal. He wasn't hungry and there was a hurt in his stomach like he'd been punched. He knew that because he had been punched once by Billy Egan, who was just goofing around. Billy was going to be in the club.

A couple of squirrels were chasing each other along the stone wall out in the back until one took off up a tree. Wilce followed it up until it was lost in the branches. He looked past those to see clouds sweep by. In those clouds, he saw things, animals. A lion roared. A horse bucked. Was that a buffalo turning to look at him? People, too. George Washington for a moment, then he was a dog. An angel was following, but it wasn't an angel after a moment but a ship, a huge sailing ship, and then a wave. The wind picked up and he saw a dinosaur, jaws gaped open about to devour a huge fish. They changed and changed yet again. In those clouds he found stories.

Wilce picked up a dandelion and blew hard on it watching the seeds catch the wind.

14.

We Have to Move

Phillip turned the car into the gravel driveway, comforted by the grassy hump down its middle, the part that car tires hadn't trampled down. The hump had grown since he was a child. He'd always thought it looked like something you'd find at an English country home. Maybe in the Cotswolds, though he hadn't ever been there.

The old man sat on the porch staring out at him, a curious look that might have been mistaken for anxious, slowly pumping his legs to rock back and forth in the shade. When Phillip opened his car door the old man stopped rocking, put his hands on the sides of the chair and lifted himself a few inches, sat back down, tried again, and with a grunt managed to stand up. It took him an eternity. Phillip wanted to run up and help but knew better; the old man was serious about his dignity. When he was almost fully erect, he offered a limp wave, maybe a smile, and said, "Been waiting out here a while. A real scorcher."

Phillip smiled back and retrieved his bag from the back along with the groceries his mother had asked him to pick up. "Leave those be," said the old man. "They're not going anywhere. Come and rest up after that trip."

"Too hot, Dad."

Phillip put the bags on the porch steps. He looked up to the yoo-hooing as his mother, looking very much the part of the wizened old woman, jogged to him drying her hands on her flowered apron, and gave her son a hug. "Here now. Give those to me. I'll put them away. AC's on. And I'll bet you're hungry, precious thing."

"I'll keep an eye on the bags," said his old man.

"Those old eyes aren't even good for a girly magazine. Besides, they'd melt out here. I'll bring out some iced tea and lunch, so just sit yourself down and chill out."

She went back inside, juggling the bags in her arms and trying to push the door open with her foot. It was quite the balancing act. Her son was about to ask if she needed help, but he knew she'd say no so he just held the door and watched her go in. Where on earth did she pick up the expression "Chill out"? She was still strong, his mom; still had her marbles. Most of them.

He pulled up a chair next to the rocker, moving it deeper into the shade. He looked out over the property. The garden looked a bit seedy but not too bad, and his father's Volvo 240 wagon needed a wash.

"Jeez, Dad, how old is that thing? Christ, it's got a McGovern sticker."

"Old enough to know better, and I picked up the McGovern sticker at a yard sale. The car drives fine and it's paid off. Hell, I paid cash for her, come to think. Same time I paid off the mortgage. Same year I retired, for that matter. It's been a while. A hundred years, maybe."

The old man sat back and pumped his legs to get the rocker going. He again mentioned it was a scorcher, fanning himself with a previous year's edition of the New Yorker he'd picked up at a doctor's office. He had a pile of magazines he'd picked up at one of his many doctor's offices, and his son asked if he had any on fishing.

"There's a Gray's Sporting Journal in here somewhere. God, I used to love that magazine." His father rummaged through a stack and handed the journal to his son.

"This'll do you."

"2007? Dad, have you thought about a subscription, for God's sake. Forget that. I'll get you one."

His father stopped moving his legs and looked at him. Through the wrinkles, it was hard to tell if it was a frown or a smirk. "Money. Why spend money when I can get them for free? Used. That's recycling, right? You're into that. And I got to tell you, it's about perspective."

"Perspective?"

"Per-spec-tive." He sounded out each syllable. "Per-spec-tive." He explained that fishing doesn't change from season to season, and those New Yorker cartoons from last year are just as funny as the new ones. "Old ones are even better. I don't always get the new ones." The old man continued on about how they taught American history in his day. How the facts were the facts and he never could see much reason for changing textbooks other than newly minted PhDs needing to publish. "Publish or perish." He lost his thoughts in the life of an academic and started talking about political correctness before he returned to "per-spec-tive."

He went on about saving money, and how when he was young people did things; it wasn't all about status. He banged his fist softly on the side of the rocker and he spoke of the linoleum countertop they had in the kitchen for, at least, thirty years, being as good as "marble or granite or that plastic corium stuff, right? And a boatload cheaper."

"I had a camera," he went on. "A Honeywell Pentax. Got it in 1963. Still was using it when we went on that Italy trip. Only stopped because you couldn't get Kodachrome anymore. Nowadays, people buy cameras with a change in season. Crazy waste if you ask me."

"I didn't ask."

"Well, you should. I must have learned something over all these years."

His mother opened the door and came out with a tray of

glasses half-filled with ice, a pitcher of iced tea, and a bowl of sugar. She set it down on the small table between the two men.

"Mom, do you have any Equal or Stevia?"

"Oh, I don't think so. Daddy usually steals it from the coffee shop, but we haven't been there in a while. Your sister had it last."

"Figures."

He poured glasses for himself and his father, and the old man put a heaping teaspoon of sugar into both.

"Whoa, Dad, I don't want sugar."

"That other stuff will kill you. Chemicals. All chemicals. Artificial sweetener means just that. No harm in a little sugar. Better than those chemicals."

His son acquiesced with a smile and sipped the tea, enjoying the sweet granules that refused to melt in the cold liquid.

The old man leaned back, took his own sip, and looked to the trees, whose leaves were drooping in the heat. A hummingbird sipped at a red feeder that hung from the porch. He pointed to it with some effort.

"I love those little birds. Always have." He tried to follow it as it buzzed away. "I don't like to say this. We have to move."

The son sat upright, a rush of heat hitting his face, not from the weather but from those words.

It was inevitable but still a shock. Dad was in his nineties, and the place needed constant work. They had talked about "when we'd have to move," and his father always said he planned to die peacefully in his sleep like his father did—"and not like the screaming passengers in the car he was driving!" He meant it. He was an independent man of a different generation. The idea of staying put had been a source of stubborn pride for years. Hadn't the old man tapped into his savings to build a bathroom on the first floor, one with a walk-in tub? Phillip couldn't believe his father would spend that kind of money until the old man showed him it was cheaper than a year in a nursing home.

Moving had come up when he broke his hip a few years back, but, miraculously, the old man recovered fully and then some. He talked about hip replacements and knee replacements and said at this rate he'd be brand new before he'd have to move, which would never happen anyway, "not over my dead body."

As it turned out, he was all too serious about the "dead body." It was last fall when Phillip found a bottle of Oxycontin in the guest bathroom's medicine cabinet. The old man had been spending more and more nights in that guestroom, tossing and turning, in his own words, so as not to keep his mother awake. He brought the pills down to his father's den, shaking the container, weighing its contents, trying to guess how many were in there. Phillip had made it a habit of cleaning up expired cans and medicines when he came over.

"Dad, you shouldn't have these around. They're too powerful for you. At your age, I mean. If you don't need them, throw them out."

"Leave them be. They're there for a reason."

"What, you're dealing now?"

His father squinted, turned away for a second, and then turned back to his son. "It's not always easy, you know. Getting old. I'm happy, led a good life. Hell, still lead a good one. But I see where it's going. The destination's fine, it's the journey."

The old man looked away again, staring out the window. Phillip's eyes followed, but he only saw the lawn and thought it could do with a watering.

"You remember Bill Webster?" It wasn't a question. The old man recalled how Bill Webster had coached Little League for forty years — "Had a team, not yours, make it to state championships once." Bill Webster — "That handsome sonofabitch" — was a paratrooper on D-Day. Bill Webster was the local dermatologist — "cleaned up more zits for the senior prom than all the lies Nixon told." A good guy was what his father called him, which was high praise from the old man. "He was losing it. Alzheimer's,

I guess. Goes into a nursing home — a memory facility — all locked up like some criminal. I went to visit. Bill didn't know me at first but came around. Know what he told me? He said he'd rather be dead than there. 'My advice to you, my friend,' he said to me, 'is to do what you can, anything, to stay out of this urine-stinking place.' He was dead two weeks later."

"I'm sorry."

"I'm not. Know why? His wife, against the rules of the place, brought him a bottle of single malt, and he drank it with a handful of some pills. She found him dead as a doornail, in bed, dressed in real clothes with a smile on his face." And that's why I have the pills. Just in case. Which is also why all my papers, all my affairs, are well in order. Bottom drawer on the right side of my desk. File says 'When I'm dead.' I don't like mincing words."

With amazing speed for a man his age, he leaned over toward his son, eyes looking teary, and grabbed the bottle of pills. They didn't discuss the matter again. Until now, it seemed.

He looked at his father pumping his legs to get the rocker moving, then stared over the property, at the garden, weedier than it used to be, crabgrass on the once-proud lawn. Phillip's eyes shifted to the porch, which could use a new paint job. He looked over the brown grass imagining snow forts when a storm would close the schools. He had to wait for the Ws to hear his town mentioned on the old radio in the kitchen and would yell, "Yee hah." He'd be undressed by halfway up the stairs running to change into his play clothes.

His home. The home he grew up in. His old room hadn't changed since he left for college. He could almost smell the combination of sweat and the marijuana he'd smoke with the window wide open. For the first time in years, he realized how much he loved the place. It was home, more his home than where he lived now. His mind flooded with parties his parents held, he and his sister spying on the adults from the top of stairs until his father would catch them and bring them downstairs. Had he really let them sip whiskey sours?

He was ten during that dry summer when he and Billy Egan were burning ants with magnifying glasses and making small fires on yellowed grass. The fire had gotten out of control and spread to the woods behind them. He cried the whole time, even as the fire department put it out, imagining how he could have been hurt or hurt someone, and fearing he'd go to hell, or at least catch hell. He had singed his hair and looked like a Beatle, which was, he thought, kind of cool and just made him feel worse.

But his father had only asked if he was okay and then taught him how to make a safe campfire. To make sure it was out, they'd peed on it.

His mind raced back to friends coming over and playing in the old attic, and finding trunks of old clothes, his father's moth-eaten uniform, a pistol he'd had during the war, which his father then threw away. And, he'd forgotten about this, a wedding photo of him with a woman who wasn't his mother, a first wife he said had died, but whom he'd actually divorced. No kids, but he used to dream of a brother somewhere looking for him.

He recalled carrying Jack up the steps when he was born, and now he was visiting with his grandson, who would never get to know this house, this wonderful house with its nooks and crannies and hiding places and old, good smells of fireplaces and baking. And how he wouldn't know his great-grandfather from more than stories.

So, the stubborn, proud old guy was finally giving in. Where to? He didn't need a nursing home. Smaller house on one level? Apartment? Assisted living? They had looked at options in the last few years but wouldn't discuss them. No, those were contingencies. And now, now they were real. He wondered if his father had a sense of urgency. Well, it's time, inevitable, he thought.

His father's rocking had slowed and his eyes were starting to shut. He took the glass of iced tea from his father's hand so he wouldn't drop it, but he roused the old man.

"Hey, I'm not done. Get your own."

99

"You were nodding off."

"I was closing my eyes, not nodding off. Anyway, give that back. I'm parched."

He handed the tea back and the old man took a long swallow, finishing with a satisfying "ahhhh," followed by a "fill 'er up."

He poured some more, and his father added two hefty spoonfuls of sugar and stirred, licking the spoon when he was done and adding a third with a wink to his son.

"Dad, what do you have in mind?"

"Huh, what do you mean?"

Phillip tried to smile. Had the old man forgotten what they were talking about? Maybe he just didn't want to discuss it anymore. Still, as difficult as it was, Phillip felt he had to push the issue. Before he spoke again, he took a sip of iced tea, added a spoonful of sugar to help the medicine he was about to bring up go down—his father was right about the sugar—and clear any sadness he was sure his voice would reveal.

"You said it was 'time to move.' I know that's hard, I know. But it'll be fine. Better. What do you have in mind? What does Mom say?"

His father looked at him, bemused, a sparkle in his eyes that made him look a decade younger. He put down the tea and leaned forward.

"I don't know what Mom has in her mind, but whatever it is, it's a sound mind. I'm not so sure about yours. Me? Jesus H. Christ. Boy, it's hot as hell out here. It's time to move, alright . . . inside. AC's on and the Red Sox are playing the Yankees . . . Go Sox! You coming?"

15.

One Restraining Order Too Many

Two things happened at once. First, there was the scream. Then the late-night commuters were jolted forward, then backward, hard, as the air brakes screeched the train to a sudden halt. There were the requisite female screams like you hear in old movies. The ex–football player fifty pounds ago, who'd been snoring in the row of seats he'd taken up, was on the aisle floor swearing. He must have hit the floor face-first if his bleeding nose was any indication. The older woman in the tailored Dior suit, not a screamer, tried to help, held his arm, asked if he was okay. He pulled back his arm and brought her to the floor. "Fine. Don't I look just fine?"

The fat conductor jogged down the aisle, bobbing his head to look into the next car. He paid zero attention to the passengers, who were asking what had happened. He held a walkie-talkie to his elephantine ear: "Yeah . . . No . . . Can't tell," he said, before telling everyone to sit and remain calm. No one did. Everyone was talking, speculating about why they stopped. A woman toward the front of the car yelled for a first aid kit. That caught everyone's attention. Then the other screams started.

They came from the next car down. With the door between the cars wide open, the screams came through clearly. The off-peak passengers were streaming in from that car, pushing the people in front, looking back from where they'd been. "Call the cops!" said a tall man clutching a briefcase to his chest. "She's insane."

The conductor squeezed his way through, parting the crowd aside, still trying to see ahead. He yelled into his walkie-talkie, "Need cops pronto." He then turned to the passengers and said, "Folks, just move ahead. Please. Just move ahead." The last people rushed in, forcing their way past the people in front of the door. They were in a panic and splattered with blood.

The woman who tried to help the guy with the bloody nose was right there offering to assist the people running in. "Are you hurt? Do you need help?" Those from the other car stared at her. A couple shook their heads. A thin man, pale green, looked like he was about to pass out. She took him by the arm and sat him down. "I was a nurse," was all she needed to say.

One of the refugees from the other car turned to look back and started pushing forward again. "She's coming!" he said. Then everyone started to move up. The big guy from the floor elbowed aside a smaller guy into a seat. The conductor continued urging, "Calm down. For God's sake, calm down," while hearing only static on his walkie-talkie.

Everything got quiet when she came into the car.

She wasn't quite a bombshell, but close enough if you could ignore the black eye and broken nose. If everyone else was in a panic, she was the opposite. She placed a bloodied chef's knife on an empty seat and straightened it so the tip pointed to the back of the seat. "Be careful," she warned. "That's sharp." Her voice was calm. She was looking at the knife, moving it just so with her fingertips when she spoke again. "Well, I suppose that's that, after all. He'll never violate a restraining order again."

She may not have been a bombshell, but she did have a lovely smile.

16.

The Hobby Shop

"I won't be too long," said his wife. "I'll meet you back in . . . say . . . forty-five minutes. Tops. Don't be late again. Not in this weather."

"Sure, sure," he replied, edging back toward the car with three bundles of groceries in his arms.

"What did I say?" she asked.

He leaned over to put the bags on the hood, hugging them to keep them from toppling over. Had she just said something? He was sure he'd heard her voice behind him. His arms still man-handling the groceries, he twisted around, feeling the twinge of a pulled muscle, to look over his shoulder. There she hovered, arms crossed, a hand tapping an elbow. He had a vision of a rolling pin.

"I'm sorry, what?"

"What did I just say?"

"When?"

"Just now."

"Oh, umm." He furrowed his brow for a second, thinking of her last words, trying to remember why they were even at this grocery store. "That the Van Daalens are coming over!" he said. The broad smile on his face was a function of relief that he could answer his wife's question and because he rather liked the Van Daalens.

"Don't you ever pay attention? I said, get me in forty-five minutes. I'm just having my hair done."

"Oh, yeah, well, of course, that goes without saying. I thought we were still talking about the other thing. Thirty minutes. I'll be back."

"What other thing? Anyway, pick up some wine. Decent. Ask the guy in the store; the one who wears those ridiculous bowties. He'll know. Cabernet. California. Spend $30, at least. No, $50. The Van Daalens are very sophisticated. Oh, and he likes his martinis, so get some . . ."

"Gin.. . . ."

"Vodka. He likes vodka martinis, as do I. Vodka. Get Ketel One. Do I need to write this down?"

"Couldn't hurt."

"You drive then."

She wrote down a long list of instructions, shaking her head as she put it under the clip that held many comparable notes on the wagon's dashboard. He glanced over toward the notes and wondered how the stack got so thick. He was reading the first word, Ketel One, underscored three times, when a pounding noise caught his attention. He looked outside to see a belly with a municipal worker behind it manning a jackhammer, his entire body bucking with its loud reverberations. Cool, he thought, nodding his head in sync with it. A jackhammer.

"There!"

"Where?"

"There. The salon. For goodness' sake. We've only been there a hundred times."

"Right."

"I sometimes think you're half off, " she said as she got out of the car, tapping the note stack with the middle finger of her left hand as she did so.

"Thirty—no, forty-five minutes. Right?" he said.

She shook her head and entered the salon. He noticed an exotic black woman, maybe Ethiopian, open the door and offer his wife a colorful mug of something equally exotic, or so he imagined. Maybe a cappuccino, something European that ended in a vowel and spilled foamy milk. Or it could be some dark, mysterious, Ethiopian coffee—he thought they grew coffee in Ethiopia. Is she Ethiopian? She could be Mexican and that cup could hold spicy hot chocolate like they'd had in San Miguel a few years before. His tongue almost swirled the chocolaty ooze and tasted cinnamon and hot peppers. A model, he thought. I'll bet she's a model. His wife spoke to the woman, who looked back at him, curious, giggling to herself before closing the door behind them. Maybe I'm too old for models, he thought.

He waved toward the door and drove off, looking forward to the forty-five minutes he'd have to himself with nothing to do. No, now just forty-three minutes according to the clock. Nothing to do. Maybe the library, to catch a nap? It was raining too hard for a walk.

More roadwork was underway on the main street toward the library, slowing the traffic to a standstill, forcing him to take several turns around the edge of town. He slowed down, rubbernecking at the bulldozers and backhoes, hardly hearing the honking behind him. He drove on. Why so many banks? he wondered before checking to see if he had cash in his wallet.

At one more jam, he took a right turn onto a street called Maple Avenue, recalling that was where his Boy Scout Troop had met. Without a thought, he knew exactly where he was, where an elementary school, now an assisted living facility, once stood. He knew the people who lived in this house and that, which family gave good candy on Halloween, and where the old biddy lived who gave out apples they searched for pins. They never found any.

The homes that hadn't been torn down, replaced by homes too large for the lots, looked surprisingly fresh. He passed a few for sale signs, hoping to find an open house to explore. He hadn't been in this part of town in a hundred years, certainly not since he cleared out his parent's home; maybe that would have an open house today. He could find his way around blindfolded.

Alas, his old home wasn't for sale and, anyway, an extension had been added, making it look lopsided. There was a tire swing hanging from the old maple in front; he thought the tree was huge then, but it didn't look so very different now. There were the remains of a snowman next to it. He wondered what the children who built it were like.

He took an instinctive right at the end of the street. He didn't know why; he was just driving around. He passed the old pharmacy where he bought comics when he was a kid. And occasionally stole candy.

It was the source of some family tension. His mother hated comics; his father attributed such disdain to her English literature degree. "From Smith, no less," he'd say. Mother complained about the violence and scantily dressed women and the ads for things like X-ray vision glasses and sea monkeys, which she insisted were just dried-up bugs that would "stink to high heaven."

He liked—no, loved—Classic Comics Illustrated. His dad would argue for him. "They're educating the lad," he'd say again and again. "They're not merely comics, but the great works of all time. History without all the fuss and bother. They'll encourage him to go on learning, but in a fun way."

His mother would raise her eyebrows and point out that "Father" read those comics more than any great classics sitting around the house, and they would both laugh at that. His dad would sneak a quarter or two into his pocket when he was going out, whispering to bring a new one home. And, once in a while, his mom did the same thing.

On the next block, a ratty sporting goods shop had a permanent "Big Sale" sign painted on its window with all sorts of detritus lined up outside: wooden snowshoes, a toboggan, plastic flying saucers, a target with a bow leaning on it.

A bow, he thought. Perhaps they'd have a BB gun inside. He'd bought his first baseball glove there. The memory brought a smile to his face. A driver behind him sitting on the horn snapped him from his reverie. "Alright, alright, keep your shirt on," he said to no one.

And on the corner, with a decidedly worrisome wooden porch, stood the store where he spent most of his time and any money he had in his youth. The simple name said it all: The Hobby Shop. He pulled into an open parking spot as soon as he saw it, getting yet another loud and steady honking from an angry-looking man behind him who made a rude gesture as he passed. His eyes, however, quickly went back to the dusty old window of the shop and the treasures that lay behind it.

Through the rippled glass, he saw boats, tanks, cars, monsters, planes, and rockets and, well, models upon models, some of which he thought had been there since he was a kid.

He had to force open the door, swollen from the rain. A bell suspended from the door rang and brought out the manager. "Need a hand, son?" Son. The man called him son.

"No, sir. No, just looking. Haven't been here in, God, a hundred years."

"Hundred years, huh? Quite a while, quite a while. You look good for your age. Can't say I do. Can't say I ever did, come to think," the older man said. "Well, welcome home. Holler if you need anything."

"Will do," he said.

"Oh, and half off."

"Come again? "

"Half off everything. Closing shop, son. Store going, too. Moving to, heck, moving somewhere warm is all I care about. When it goes."

"Oh, no. Why?"

"Well, put it this way. You'd be the twentieth customer today if nineteen others had come in before you. Anyway, look about."

The old floors creaked as he went down the narrow aisles that had once made his eyes go wide and his heart pound. There on the shelves were the balsa-wood planes he'd made with his father, the glow-in-the-dark Frankenstein, Dracula, and Wolfman. They still made them, or maybe they never sold. The PT-109, Sherman tanks. He picked up a scrimshaw kit with the faded words "genuine sperm whale tooth" printed on the dusty box cover. It was marked $5.95.

The man peeked his head around the aisle corner. "Finding everything?"

"Yes, and more. Some of this stuff was here when I was a kid."

"Models and such. They do take you back, you know. And, well, yes, that's sort of the problem. That scrimshaw thing's been here since Ismael brought it in. He leaned closer, "Illegal these days, I suspect."

"I'll take it."

"Half off."

"And this," he said, grabbing the PT-109 along with a Tiger Panzer tank kit. "Hold on a sec."

He went up and down the aisles grabbing more and more and bringing them to the front. "Paints, I'll need paints and glue and X-Acto knives. Do you have those?"

"Well, yes. How about a complete set? I don't think they make them anymore here. In the US, I mean. This one's the real McCoy."

"Yes, I'll need that."

"I got a Dremel, you know. One of the old ones. Made in the good old US of A. Which is funny if you're going to build that tank model. Yankee tool making a Panzer tank. Half off, and that's half off the price I've had on it for a hundred years."

"Do you have the drills, sanding stuff?"

"I'll put them up front for you."

He went back to the aisle and reached up for the big kits, the wooden ships that he couldn't get to when he was a youngster.

"Are these really hard?"

"Not easy, not easy. Why don't you start with something easier and build up? Like this." It was a skiff: a simple wooden skiff. "It's a Peapod Dory. A real classic, that one."

"Yes, and after that?"

"Well, there's the lobster boat. That's a bit more challenging. Then, maybe, the Pequod. Ismael brought that one in, too." He chuckled at his joke and fell into a mild coughing fit. "Too much sawdust on the lungs. When they cremate me, I'll burn for days."

"I'll take it all."

"And a deal you'll have. These'll keep you busy for a while."

"No, I mean everything."

"Everything?"

"Everything!!"

Everything was on his mind when he put down two 100s, four 20s, a 10, a 5, three 1s, and a credit card. The old man pointed to a handwritten sign on the counter: "Cash or Checks. ONLY!" A check was extracted from the now empty wallet.

"This should get the ball rolling," he said.

The old man leaned back on his stool behind the counter, finger to his cheek, and chuckled. "You just might want to ask how much I want for the place."

"Right. How much?"

A check was written for a substantial down payment.

"You're serious?" said the old man. He held the check to the light bulb dangling over the register, scratched his head, and squinted at the grinning face looking around the shop. He wrote down the number of a lawyer.

"Give young Rubinstein a call. He'll handle the sale. You're not joshing now, are you?"

"Not in the least," he said, handing over his business card. "I don't imagine I'll be needing many of those anymore."

The old man started counting out bills from the register.

"Keep that for the down payment. I'll be back."

The old man stood on the sagging porch watching his final customer make half a dozen trips to the wagon. He insisted he carry all the treasure by himself, breathing in the smell of dust, balsa, and shellac, and the memories they held. Even with the backseat down, he couldn't fit it all in. "I'll be back," he said, waving to the old man leaning on a porch post. The old man was nodding back and thinking he might just build something too. It had been a while.

The sun had come out when he stepped into his car. The clouds had dispersed and the sky was blue. The air felt crisp. He looked back at the boxes and recognized the grocery bags shoved between them. A question popped into his head: "What on earth was that woman talking about?" He then remembered he had to pick her up at the hair salon and hoped the Ethiopian model would be at the door. Maybe he'd ask for a cup of whatever it was she was offering. Maybe it would be hot chocolate.

He was thirty minutes late. His wife let him have it before she sneezed harshly as the dust rose from his accumulations after she slammed the car door shut.

"What the hell is all this crap? I'll bet you didn't make it to the liquor store. Are you even listening to me?"

He turned with a smile and said, no, he hadn't heard a word.

17.

The Servants' Entrance

Clifford Danforth couldn't have cared less.

There'd been the rumors for a while now; the President would be coming and it was all the town talked about. "Honestly?" asked the headline of an editorial in The Boothbay Register, the town's one and only paper, which went on to fret about traffic jams. It was August, griped the editor. The summer folk were overly abundant. Why here, he asked, when that Kennedy clan had the big place down on Cape Cod?

This part of Maine, this part of New England, was Yankee territory—Republicans back to the Civil War, which Asa Saltonstall, age 103, claimed he could still remember. "Two hundred and sixty-three men voted in the 1864 election," he had told a dozen reporters every February 12 for the last twelve years. "Women didn't vote in those days, you know. This township had 262 ballots for Lincoln and the 263rd had a rude word printed over McClellan's face so they tossed it out, but, ayuh, the voter's intention was clear." The paper always included an "ayuh" even if Asa didn't say it.

Ike came to Maine in '55. He'd gone fishing all the Christly way up at Lake Parmachenee, which might just as well have been in Quebec for all it mattered to Mainers. And before him, it was General Ulysses S. Grant. Both Republicans, at least.

But JFK was popular, even if he was a rich Masshole Democrat and a Catholic to boot, especially with the women of Boothbay Harbor. The young folk and the vacationers liked him, too, and the place was thick with vacationers in August. He was, after all, almost a local, certainly more than that Nixon fellow and a damn sight better looking if the ladies had anything to say about it. And just about everyone was readying a celebration, a parade, even. The fellows at the Legion Hall talked about an honorary plaque.

"He's got more of those plaques than he knows what to do with," Danforth told the boys at the hall. "Probably just throw the goddamn thing in the rubbish," he'd said, "where it rightly belongs." He was a workingman, proud of it, and a lifelong Republican who didn't like to see a fuss made over much of anything, ever. Strapped up high on the telephone pole, fixing the line after yesterday's unseasonable nor'easter blew a tree across the wires, he only cared about getting the phones working.

"An ill wind blows nobody no good," he told his wife that morning.

"Are you griping about that JFK visit?"

"Not particularly. Just griping."

"Business as usual, Danforth," she said. "Business as usual."

"Hello? Pick up, for Christ's sake?" he yelled into the handset after tying in his wires to the main switch. "Can you hear me good? Hello? Hello?!? Goddamn it, Peter, what the hell are you doing?"

It was Peter Mather, Clifford's boss, friend, and manager of this branch of the Down East Phone Company. "Hiya, Clifford, how are you? I hear you loud and clear. Static's gone."

"What the hell are you doing there? I connected thirty minutes ago. Got four lines to fix up Damariscotta ways!"

"Been five minutes, at most, so keep your shirt on. Anyway, just got the news. Official. President's coming. Got the Secret Service here already. Just talking to those boys."

"Ayuh. Is that Jackie coming? I wouldn't mind seeing her."

"Heck, they don't say and I don't ask. Anyway, we have work

to do. The President is staying at the Bishops', you know, down Spruce Point."

"What a surprise, the Bishops down la dee dah Spruce Point. Didn't think he'd stop by me for a 'Gansett."

"I mean, Mr. Personality, that you gotta get lines installed there pronto. 'Parently, he needs to be in touch with everyone. Maybe they'll want that red phone, you know, that goes to the Russians. We may even have a red phone somewhere in the back."

"How many they want?"

"Six."

"I'll pick 'em up after I've done Damariscotta."

"Clifford! It's the goddamned President. To hell with Damariscotta. You get over here now and pick up those phones.

"Oh, trust me. I'll walk as fast as I can."

Danforth took off his New York Yankees cap and wiped his salt-and-pepper flat top. His was the only such hat in Boothbay Harbor, maybe the only one on the coast of Maine, it was said. When he first met the man who would be his father-in-law, he looked at Clifford through an assessing squint and asked if he was a Yankees fan.

"Me? Not particularly."

"Then why in heck would you wear such a thing?" his aggravated future father-in-law demanded from beneath a worn blue baseball hat with bright red B emblazoned on it. Without a moment's hesitation, Clifford replied, "Because it pisses people off."

"It would do," said the man. "And I'll trust you don't wear it in this house." And Danforth didn't. He mostly stayed on the porch—summer, spring, fall, and winter.

He inched his way down, enjoying the sound of his spikes kicking into the wooden pole. He breathed in extra heavily, taking in the tar pitch smell of the pine pole that the summer heat brought out. The phones were his life, his responsibility, and he was committed to them. "Phones don't talk back," he would say and turn away with a smile when folks didn't get the joke.

Peter Mather wasn't surprised when Clifford came to the office three hours later.

"Where have you been?"

"Damariscotta. My goodness, Peter, are you wearing your Legion hat? Honestly. Going to rent a tuxedo for his and her majesty?"

Mather sighed deeply, shook his head, and lit a Camel. "Never you mind. Just get yourself over to Spruce Point, would you? Pretty please? With sugar on top? I've got to get over to the Hall, you know, clean up the yard a bit with the fellows."

"You're not going to have time to make up one of those plaques. Waste of good money anyway."

"No, too right there, but figured we'd paint the fence, mow the lawn. He's gotta drive right by it, you know. From the airport. We're going to arrange something. Stand and salute. Get the kids to wave flags."

"Oh, jeez, why don't you kiss him on the lips, for goodness' sake. Honestly, I'd kiss that Jackie though. You bet."

"Just get the hell over to Spruce Point."

"Won't get six phones installed before five o'clock."

"Overtime pay, Clifford. Union rules."

"My rules, Peter. I'll stop by after for a 'Gansett.'"

Danforth put a box of phones in the back of his truck, including a red one that no one wanted, and drove off to Spruce Point, to the Bishops' cottage. They called it the Cottage, to the amusement of the locals, since objectively it was a massive turn-of-the-century mansion built on the rocky peninsula. The original Bishops were from Boston, of course, and had made their money off French-Canadian immigrants sweating in one of their woolen mills until they moved them to Georgia.

Any remaining Bishops were rarely at the cottage aside from a few weeks during the summer, but they kept it open, keeping the locals employed, which was good enough to make them local celebrities. James Bishop would come to the Whale's Tale, loudly order 'Gansetts for the house, and whisper for a Courvoisier VSOP; the Tale kept a bottle under the counter especially for him. He insisted everyone call him Jim, but no one did. If you were born in Lincoln County, it was Mister Bishop and always said with a slight sneer. Bishop was now ambassador to somewhere because he'd made a big contribution to JFK's campaign.

"Probably Quebec," Frank Pelletier would say at the Tale.

"She ain't a country," came from Ron Belliveau.

"Well, she should be," Frank would counter, and they'd both lift a glass to that.

Danforth drove his truck up the long drive, circled the fountain with the "pissing angels," and parked at the front doors. He looked up at the house and, as he'd done since he was a child, wondered why they needed so many rooms if they didn't plan to use it as a hotel, or asylum as he once suggested to James Bishop, who laughed too loudly even for the Tale and slapped him on the shoulder. "Droll, Cliff, very droll." No one called him Cliff.

The drive had a number of black Ford Galaxies wagging long radio antennas that he thought were rather much for the FBI agent who approached him, dressed immaculately in a dark blue/black suit with a gold tie clip that had a shield on it.

"Sir, can I help you?" asked the agent.

"Nice cars you have. My tax dollars at work, no doubt. You with the FBI?"

"Sir, do you have business here?"

"Phone company, like it says on the truck. You FBI guys asked for phones. I'm here to install them for, you know who." He gave an in-your-face wink. "Where do you want them?"

"We're Secret Service, not FBI. We protect the President. They, the FBI, also do investigations. Just a moment." The agent waved over two of his colleagues, dressed identically, down to the gold tie clips, instructed them to stay with "this phone man," and knocked on the front door. Another agent, looking like one of those new Ken dolls his daughter wanted, answered, looked over at Clifford, and motioned him forward.

"I'm Agent Woodcock. You were scheduled to be here three—no, four—hours ago."

"Had some lines down up Damariscotta, don't you know. Regular customers, taxpayers and all."

"Anyway, take the truck around back, and I'll meet you at the servants' entrance."

Danforth looked at the agent, leaned forward with his head cocked to one side, and said, "Come again? I got an ear infuck-tion and cunt hear you. Bad ear. From a Jap plane. Exploded right in front of me." He added, "During the war."

Woodcock bent his head forward, his eyes rising in their sockets, and pointed to nothing in particular. "Go around the back and I'll meet you at the servants' entrance in the back."

"Servants' entrance, huh? Do I look like a servant? No, chiefy, I'm with the phone company."

"That's right, Mac. You're with the phone company. I'm with the Secret Service. You must have missed that. Now go around back to the servants' entrance. I'll meet you there and escort you to your work. Get it?"

"If I wanted to be a servant, I'd put on a monkey suit like you and look at you just like this." Cliff leaned his head back as far as he could and looked down his nose. "I'm no servant. I walk in the front or I don't walk in at all."

"Look, Mac, if you want to install those phones, you'll go around back!"

"If you want 'em installed, you can do it yourself . . . Mac!"

And with that, Clifford Danforth turned around, threw the box in his truck, and peeled off. First, he went to Legion Hall, had two 'Gansetts, relayed his story, and told the guys there painting the rocks that bordered the walkway they were wasting their time.

"What's a matter, Clifford . . . he a Sox fan?" said Wen Bark-er, Commandant of the Post. "Or just a Democrat?"

"One's as bad as the next," offered Clifford. "And both worse than two times each the other."

The guys painting the rocks looked at each other in confusion but didn't comment on Danforth's math, not when he was in a mood. "But that Jackie's a looker," said Will Harris, who'd had his license lifted for the season for selling undersized lobsters, not that that stopped him from throwing out his pots.

"I didn't say he has bad taste, now did I?" countered Clifford.

"No, that you didn't," said Will.

Danforth parked the phone truck in front of his newly painted Cape, which he painted himself on his week break earlier that summer. He went into the breezeway from the back door, removed his dirty clothes, and tossed them into the hamper.

"Anyone here? I could eat a whale."

"Why, you're home early," came the voice of his wife, Kate, who greeted him wearing a frilly apron she'd won in a Betty Crocker contest and handed him another Narragansett. "Jenn Mather stopped over, said you were up at the Bishops' installing all the phones for Jack Kennedy. I figured you'd be there all night."

"Christ, does every busybody on this coast know my business?"

"Peter told her when he heard that Jack Kennedy was coming. I think that's the berries. Jack Kennedy here and you getting him his phones and all. Did you see him?"

"Not here yet, and I don't care if I see him or not. See if he can install a goddamn phone line though. Bet they didn't teach him that at Harvard!"

Kate's smile evaporated as she grabbed the bottle of beer from Clifford's hand.

"What on God's green earth did you do now, Danforth?"

"I didn't do a thing."

"I don't believe that for a moment. Not one minute. No, sir. What do you mean Jack Kennedy can install those phones?" She took a long sip of the beer, glaring down her nose at her husband.

117

"Well, it's just that . . ."

"Just what?"

"Well, who do they think they are, those FBI agents telling me to go round back to the servants' entrance. Goddamn arrogant bunch of SOBs, I tell you. I've never walked in the servants' entrance of anybody's home, mansion or no. I was in the Navy too, you know. And my boat also got sunk too after that . . ."

"Yes, after that Jap kamikaze crashed into it . . . I know, heard it before once or twice every day since I've known you."

"Well, I've never gone in through some servants' door, and I am not about to start now."

"Jesus H. Christ, Danforth, that's because no one here has a goddamn servants' entrance."

"Apparently, Mr. James I'm-too-good-for-beer-Bishop does."

"Danforth, this is the President of the United States. He needs phones. What if the Reds attacked? Oh, I can see the headlines now . . . Russkies Win, JFK Phone Not Hooked Up. Maine moron gets the blame."

"You'd think I'd get into the papers, do you?!"

"Don't get smart with me. What about your job? You can't refuse. I mean . . . Danforth . . . John Fitzgerald Kennedy!"

Clifford took a long pull from his beer, wiped his mouth with his sleeve, and his wife took another apron that read "Don't argue with an idiot" and hit him with it. "Don't use your sleeve for crying out loud, Danforth! Let people think you're low class; don't prove it!"

Clifford put his beer down, took the apron, and wiped his mouth, then wiped the wet circle left by the beer.

"Danforth! The President!"

"Well, they can stuff those phones up their back entrance as far as I'm concerned. The Russians aren't going to bomb Boothbay Harbor anyway."

"If you lose your job over your stubborn pride, you'd better hope they don't!"

"It's not pride, Kate, it's principle."

"It's your job. That's the principle part. Now get in that truck, get to Bishop's and say something . . ." Kate sat down hard in the metal chair at their kitchen table, tears forming in her eyes. "You can't get fired, Clifford. Who cares how you get into someone's house? You came in the backdoor just now . . ."

"That's because we got that new rug in the hall and my boots are all dirty and I don't want you yelling at me for mucking up the floor."

"Well, imagine that brilliant degree of insight. Maybe Mister James Bishop wouldn't want you to muck up those Chinese rugs he's got in his foyer either!"

Clifford finished the beer and said, "Ayuh," turning to leave.

"I'll drop off dinner. Maybe I'll bring something for the FBI."

"Secret Service. They protect the President while treating real Americans like second-class citizens, so don't bother. I'll be at the Legion Hall . . . painting rocks."

Danforth turned fast into the Legion's parking lot, spraying pebbles over the guys painting there. "Jeezus H., Clifford, this ain't the Indy 500," said Simon Wilcox, also called Swill by his friends. "Say, Cliff, did you change parties?" Will Harris asked.

Danforth took a spare brush and started swiping the round stones surrounding the driveway. Kate drove by in the Rambler, leaned over to roll down the window, and yelled, "You boys hungry? I've got aplenty."

"Katherine," shouted Peter Mather. "Why didn't you marry me?"

"Because you were married to my second cousin and stink to high heaven! If you want these goodies, get me a beer, and shove my husband into his truck and get him off to the blasted goddamn Bishops' before he loses his job."

The paintbrushes were put down and all eyes turned to Clifford Danforth, who paid no attention. "Clifford, what's Kate on about?"

"Servants' entrance."

"How's that?"

"They told me I'm only good enough for the servants' entrance."

"Well, I'll be goddamned. Servants' entrance."

"Who the hell has a servants' entrance?"

"Bishops do."

"You mean where Jackie's gonna be?"

"Her hubby anyway."

"He's the President, Clifford."

"You don't say? So Harold Stassen lost. I'll be."

"You gotta put in the phones, Clifford. What if Jackie wants to speak to those kids of hers?"

"Then Jackie Kennedy can ask me in the front door like everyone else."

"Goddamn, was she there?"

"No, just the FB . . . I mean Secret Service."

"Why not the FBI?

"They don't . . . never mind. If they want phones all they need to do is ask and open the goddamn Christly front door."

"Well, I'll be damned, Clifford. You refused to install the goddamn phone for the goddamn President of the entire goddamn United States?!?!"

"I did no such thing, and stop spreading rumors. I'll install every phone in Lincoln County so long as I go in the front door like everyone else!"

"Well, not the servants, Clifford. They don't go in the front door, it appears," said Will. A chorus ensued.

"Ayuh, goddamn."

"Sonuvabitch, goddamn."

Danforth downed his beer and tossed the bottle at the garbage bin just as Katherine threw hers. They collided and shattered. "For the love of Pete, Kate," said Danforth.

"You get yourself over to the Bishops', get the phones in, and I'll clean up."

"I won't."

"Then you clean up. I'm going home."

She sprayed pebbles over the lawn of the Legion Hall when she drove out, did a wide U-turn, and wound down the window. "Danforth, you're a stubborn moron of an idiot and if you lose this job you can sleep up at that rat-infested deer camp for all I care."

"She angry, Clifford?" asked Swill.

"No. That's her way of saying how much she loves me."

Clifford spent the next couple of hours painting the rocks but stopped when he cut himself on a piece of a beer bottle.

"That'll be a nickel, Danforth," said Wen Barker.

"How's that?"

"Deposit on those bottles. For the hall."

"For cryin' out loud." Clifford reached into his trousers and pulled out a dime and put it in the jar marked "Tipping ain't a city in China."

Back home, he sat in the very worn Barcalounger he picked up at the town dump, slurped another beer, and read a Life with Janet Leigh on the cover. "Jeez Marie," he said out loud.

"What's that?" said Kate, knitting on the couch.

"Thalidomide. The medicine that gives kids those short arms."

"Horrible, just horrible," she said. "Those poor kids."

"Oh no, for the love of . . ."

"What now?"

"Your boyfriend's writing about Navy Art that Roosevelt owned. I bet the guy didn't write a word of it. Paid a real writer, I bet."

"Who are you talking about?"

Clifford folded the magazine and shoved it toward Kate, poking with his finger at the page. There it was on page 83, right after the Canadian Club ad showing a guy doing the limbo under a flaming stick. "The Strength and Style of our Navy Tradition," by John Fitzgerald Kennedy.

"Oooh, let me see that when you're done," she said.

"Oh, I'm done, alright." He put the magazine on the glass top covering the old lobster pot that served as their coffee table and turned on the TV to CBS to watch The Twilight Zone. Rod Serling's rich voice came on: "Respectfully submitted for your perusal—a Kanamit. Height: a little over nine feet. Weight: in the neighborhood of 350 pounds. Origin: unknown. Motives: Therein hangs the tale, for in just a moment, we're going to ask you to shake hands, figuratively, with a Christopher Columbus from another galaxy and another time. This is the Twilight Zone."

"Goddamn," said Clifford.

"What now?"

"It's a rerun. I know what happens. Christ."

"What happens?"

"Outer space guys eat people. They got a cookbook."

He rose, turned it off, and said he was going to bed early. "Leave it on, Danforth. I want to watch."

"But I just told you what happened."

"I didn't listen. Nighty night."

"Goddamn."

Clifford elbowed Kate several times that night.

"I can't sleep," she said.

He said, "I'm sleeping like a baby. Why can't you sleep?"

"Because you keep hitting me! How can you sleep?" she said.

"Easy peasy. Put head on pillow, close eyes and, walla, I'm sleeping."

"I mean about your job. What if they fire you?"

"For what?"

"For refusing to install those phones up at Bishop's."

"I'll install them right after I walk in that goddamn front door. They got double front doors. I only need the one of them," said Clifford"

"I just think you should swallow your pride, go in where they ask, and keep your job," said Kate.

"I'll go in where they ask, alright, as long as it's in the front door. Or they can get someone else to put in those almighty phones. And you know what, I'm tired, and I'm going back to sleep," said Clifford.

"Well, I can't, so I'm getting up and I can't sleep because of you!"

"Then we have something in common because I can't sleep either. You know why?" said Clifford

"Let me guess. Hmmm. Because of me."

"Bingo. Now good night."

Clifford awoke to the smell of coffee, noticing the alarm clock hadn't rung yet. It read 4:23, and he said, "Goddamn." He got up anyway and grumbled a good morning to Kate, who was at the kitchen table reading Life. She nodded in the direction of an egg sandwich on a plate. "Yours if you want it," she said. Clifford nodded a thanks back, poured coffee into his thermos, and put it down as he grabbed the sandwich and put two cinnamon donuts in a paper bag.

"Where to?" she asked.

"Clear some lines up near Sharp's Cove. Staticky, supposedly. Probably just a branch on 'em."

"Pete Mather know?"

"I'll call him later. He gets up at a reasonable hour."

"Put in for overtime, then."

Danforth was up on a pole thirty minutes later, calling Pete at home and waking him to say he was clearing a branch off the line and fixing some wires. Pete asked if he had to wake him to tell him that. Danforth said he was lonely and if he could get up early so could Pete, so could the entire county as far he was concerned.

Done fixing the line, he went to the truck to get himself a mug of coffee. The donuts were there. The thermos was not. "Goddamn," he said, remembering he'd left it at home. He thought about calling Kate and telling her to bring it up but he was already in the doghouse over the lost night's sleep and decided to pick it up on his way to the phone company. He'd get another few donuts too in case Pete was also in a mood. Everyone was in a mood these days, thought Danforth.

Kate was still at the table when he walked in. Without looking up she pointed to the thermos on the counter. "You left it."

"Don't I know," he said. He poured himself a cup and grabbed another donut. "Want one?" he asked.

"Don't try to charm me, Clifford Danforth. I already ate anyway."

He picked up Life and sat in his chair sipping his coffee when he heard a car, actually several cars, driving past. "Early," he said to himself and then thought no more about it until they slowed and stopped at the bottom of his driveway. He looked out to see three Ford Galaxies and a Lincoln Continental, black, shiny, and brand spanking new.

Four men in suits got out of the Galaxies, looked toward Clifford at the window, nodded, and then looked up and down the empty road. One opened the door to the Lincoln and gave a little bow, or so it looked, and held the door as a handsome man, about his age, emerged. The man straightened, looking like he was in some pain, holding a hand to his back. He was summer stock, clearly, in chinos, tortoiseshell Ray-Bans, blue boating sneakers, and wearing a remarkably snug light-blue sweater with a dark T-shirt hem escaping beneath it. Clifford's first thought was that the sweater must belong to the man's wife. With the Secret Service suits surrounding him, including a sheepish-looking Woodcock, the man walked up to the front door just as Clifford opened it.

"Kate, you'd better come out here, pronto."

The man waved and gave a well-known toothy smile. Kate, at Clifford's shoulder, put her hand over her mouth and said, "My God, you are in trouble now. They're going to arrest you! My God!"

JFK stopped at the bottom of the steps and reached up to

shake Cliff's hand. "Mr. Danforth, I presume. I hope we're not bothering you too early, but it's about my phones."

Clifford just nodded as Kate put her shaking hands on his shoulder.

"As a favor to another Navy man, could you get them in?"

"Yesss, sure, yess, I mean . . ."

"That's wonderful. As soon as you can would be great. Jackie wants to call the kids. They're with my parents in Hyannis. I'll tell the boys to keep the front door open."

Clifford nodded again as Kennedy eyed the Life Magazine in his hand. Pointing at it he said, "Good article."

"Mr. President, would you mind signing it?" asked Kate.

Sure," Kennedy said. It came out as "show-ah" with that Boston accent. "But I've got to be honest. I didn't write a word of it. I've got people that do it for me."

"You don't say," said Clifford Danforth. "Who would've thought?

(Author's note: JFK wrote an article for the August 10, 1962 edition of Life magazine on FDR's Naval Art collection. The main article was titled "The Full Story of the Drug Thalidomide." The front cover featured a photo of a very perky Janet Leigh with the caption "Janet Leigh Breaks Up the Boys at the Lodge.")

18.

Today You Are a Man

Jay Hyman cringed beneath the Ark.

His eyes were lowered in what could have been mistaken for an effort to hide emotion, tears. Indeed, many watching smiled at that; it was a big day for Jay. The cringe, however, was in anticipation of the Rabbi's final words. They would be, of course, harmless, congratulatory, a simple Mazel Tov followed by a chorus of Mazel Tovs from the Jews sitting in the massive and modern sanctuary, plus a few from the handful of Gentiles who'd been invited. After that, there would be some self-conscious Mazel Tovs from the remainder of the unchosen less familiar with the iconic phrase.

The cringe had nothing to do with Mazel. It came from Jay's hours of repetition of the components of his Bar Mitzvah, the big BM as he called it, the various portions he would recite this day leading to his final thank-you speech to one and all. He'd heard many others' speeches and he figured on a simple thanks and generic nod to how much this meant to him. He had gone over it so many times that it was automatic. In his sophomoric mind, those words always concluded with the Rabbi saying, "I now pronounce you man and wife."

The humor helped keep his nerves down.

Lost in the muscle memory of the ritual, he half expected those very words going as far as to raise his foot in preparation for smashing a glass and only stirred with the Rabbi's gentle hand patting his shoulder.

Then Jay heard the Mazel Tovs and looked upon the tears and cheers of the collected faces with the embarrassment only a somewhat plump, short, bespectacled thirteen-year-old boy dressed up as a middle-aged accountant can feel.

It was at that precise moment that he affirmed his faith in the almighty: "Thank God it's over."

But it wasn't quite over.

Sitting in the front row, spotlighted by a rogue ray of sun that bypassed the stained-glass window of Moses with the Ten Commandments, was the shining pride of Jay's mother as manifested by a smile glowing from newly whitened teeth. She took a deep breath, her breasts heaving in the act, forcing Jay to squint as that ray of sun reflected the diamond-encrusted hamsa straining around her neck. She touched a tissue to a tear, taking in the multitude of Mazel Tovs from surrounding guests coming to congratulate her.

One would have thought it was her Bar Mitzvah. Jay said as much to her one day, sarcastically suggesting maybe he could play a role other than the entertainment. His father raised a hand as if to slap him but just shook his head. It was his mother who slapped him with a "stai zitto," Italian for "shut up." She would revert to such phrases periodically which enchanted his father.

Jay didn't want any of it. He had proposed a Bar Mitzvah in Israel as much for a cool trip as any religious longings. He argued it would be more meaningful and when that failed that it would save enough money to cover a semester at a decent private college. His father was almost moved by that, suggesting Jay would make a good lawyer and went off on that tangent.

Then Mama intervened. Mama, born Marissa Gianetti, said she hadn't gone through the "God-you'll-pardon-my French-damn conversion" just for a trip to Israel when her side of the family expected a big Jewish affair. Jay's father gave her a hug because she hadn't said big "Jew" affair.

Besides, she'd say, they didn't have a daughter, so an expensive wedding wasn't in the cards, and didn't she always know what was best? Hadn't she been serving polenta at Passover even before the Committee on Jewish Law and Standards ruled it okay? Jay always thought maybe his mom's "Uncle" Carmine, the one with "connections," had made the Committee an offer they couldn't refuse. He was her godfather, the real deal. They also called him "the butcher" because he had, well, the butcher concession at Key Foods locations throughout Brooklyn. No one shared the joke with Carmine.

His Bar Mitzvah, maybe, but her party, one she arranged in the finest Northern New Jersey Hebraic detail down to the Mercedes of challahs delivered that very morning from Orwasher's on the Upper East Side, chopped liver, smoked salmon and sable from Zabar's, all to be centrally displayed. The band, which played at Jerry Seinfeld's wedding, would offer up chosen klezmer tunes and conclude with a crooning of "New York, New York." Flower centerpieces would go to the person who found a red circle under their chair. Iceboats of caviar and broiling platters of rumaki would be discreetly off to the side.

Jay characterized all this as over-the-top extravaganza more suited to the wedding of the only daughter in a large Italian family than the son of a moderately successful orthodontist. "Che la luna" swam through his head. He imagined a Vito Corleone in the Rabbi's sumptuous office divvying out favors before the dreaded party that was soon to be. It was going to be a circus down to the sideshows.

The sideshows? Jay had balked, but Mama had insisted because hadn't every Bar Mitzvah she attended had sideshows? There is a competitive element to suburban BMs. Jay wanted something subdued, maybe a band for the adults and an ice-cream bar for the kids. But at his shul, the sideshows were de rigueur; the nerdy magician, a slick DJ you wouldn't want your daughter to date with his entourage of super-attractive dancers jumping and grinding inappropriately with a crowd of aroused thirteen-year-old boys. Don't forget about the photo booth that could hold half a dozen adolescents mugging for the camera, pinball machines, lots of them, the bizarre glass closet blowing dollar bills for kids to grab (talk about your cultural stereotype), face painters, colored hair sprays, artificial tattoos, and the ice-cream bar with vanilla, chocolate, and strawberry. And hot fudge. Jay insisted on that.

On the way to the show, Jay's mother hugged him constantly in the back seat, periodically spitting on a tissue to rub into oblivion her lipstick residuals. His father turned from the front seat at least a dozen times to say how proud he was. Jay tried counting but stopped after eight. Even the driver caught on with a Mazel Tov in a distinctly Latin accent.

Jay was biting his tongue, trying to imagine the gifts that were his due. An attempt to loosen his tie met with a mild slap from his mother across the back of his head, causing him to bite harder on his now bleeding tongue. She said he had to look good — "like a mensch" — for the photographer. It came across as "metch," but at least she tried. It wasn't the right word exactly, but Jay's father added "Listen to your mother," sealing the deal.

The photographer started snapping the moment the car stopped in front of the club, trying to position Jay in various spots around his parents, relatives, and complete strangers offering more Mazel Tovs. Oh, and envelopes. Lots of envelopes. One casually dressed man in plaid pants seemed to take offense saying somewhat aggressively he was a member and not part of some damn wedding. Jay imagined a parenthetical 'Jew wedding' was implied. Any discord dissipated when a large man in a small suit whispered something and the member hurried off. The large man returned to open a car door for Carmine, displaying a "whatever" with his left hand and an unlit cigar with his right.

"Hey, Giacobbe," said Carmine, gesturing Jay over. He put a thick envelope in one of Jay's inside pockets and a cigar in the other. "Cuban," he whispered. "For later."

Later couldn't come too soon. There were the usual prayers to start things off led by a musty-scented great uncle spitting when he spoke. Then there was the second event Jay dreaded: the mother-son dance. In dance practice, he begged his mother to forget this part, but she insisted. When she put on her too revealing BM dress, he begged once more, on his knees, for her to wear anything else. His father advised, "When you got 'em flaunt 'em," which pleased Mama to no end. "Don't forget, Jay-bird, you're half Italian and you should be proud of that." How that played with her ample bosoms, he didn't know.

Then there was the grandmother-grandson dance, the silver lining of which was that Bubbi couldn't dance very long. And then the asshole band leader insisted the girls dance with the Bar Mitzvah boy, to oohs and aahs of the collected. Enough adults had crowded the floor to allow Jay and friends a ready escape, only to be trapped by the DJ and his bimbettes, as Jay's friend Eli put it, and the roving magician who interrupted everyone engaged in close conversations with his raccoon puppet and red sponge balls. The little children seemed to like his act until they grew bored. Those kids were surrounded by thirteen-year-old girls babysitting them until the girls got their turn mugging in the photo booth. Jay's cousin Vinnie, his mom's side, who at fourteen almost had a mustache, asked, "Whose idea was all this?" Jay shrugged, allowing several envelopes to fall from his jacket pocket. "Marone! How much? Seriously. Count it. Oh, yeah, Mazel Tov."

Jay liked his cousin, especially liked his attempt to be a tough kid who mimicked any number of characters from The Sopranos. "It's an Italian thing, so va fangul," he'd say. Jay called it an affectation, reminding Vinnie that while he might be from New Jersey his father was an oncologist at Memorial Sloan Kettering and his mother taught English at Barnard, to which Vinnie would make rude noises with his hand under his armpit and offer a "fuggedaboutit."

131

It was Vinnie, holding the cigar Carmine had given him, who said to Jay, "Stogies!"

The pair attempted to edge away unnoticed until the DJ pointed to Jay and said, "And Mazel Tov to the man of the hour" through his mike. Jay thought he'd forgotten his name, which was just as well, until the DJ said, "Come up here, Jay, and show us what you got." Two of the more bimbo-esque of the bimbettes put their arms around him, gave him slobbery kisses, and danced around him while Jay concentrated on "Yankees five, Red Sox three" or iterations thereof. None of his friends joined in, but the slew of the youngest guests danced with the remaining bimbettes yelling, "All fall down!" periodically to hearty squeals.

Jay slunk off the dance floor, flaccidly embarrassed, until pulled aside by Vinnie with a cigar in his mouth waving a $20 bill in front of his face, "Want me to ask if they'll give you a lap-dance?"

Jay cringed yet again; it was entirely possible that Vinnie would do just that.

"C'mon, let's get a drink," said Vinnie.

Jay's tippling heretofore had been limited to a syrupy Pass-over wine and not much of that and a sip of a similarly sweet whiskey sour his father had allowed him at his grandfather's eighty-fifth birthday party. It wasn't the first thing he wanted to do. But it wasn't the last thing either. No, the last thing he wanted to do was stay in the rumpus room, get more Mazel Tovs, kisses from aging aunts, or teases from the bimbettes. At least not for a few more years. Anyway, his friends seemed content with the sideshows. He turned to the screams out of the money booth where Arnie Moskowitz had just grabbed the only $50 bill in the sea of ones.

"You coming?"

Vinnie led the way to the quiet end of the long bar, pulling on Jay's sleeve the whole time. "Watch this," he said. Vinnie gave a "pssst" to a young Hispanic bartender, who first shook his head, looked toward the busy bartenders down the rest of the line, and took the $20 bill Vinnie left on the counter. He nodded with his head to just behind the bar where Vinnie dragged Jay out of sight. Moments later there were two whiskey sours, each with two maraschino cherries and an umbrella, left at the edge of the bar.

"Cousie, it's the only cherry you'll pop today," said Vinnie with a grin and then downed the drink in three gulps. Jay took five.

"Line 'em up, Gustavo!" Vinnie said, leaving a $20 he'd taken from Jay's pocket.

It took them a few more gulps to finish the second batch and when Vinnie went for another $20, Gustavo shook his head, mouthing the words "no mas." Jay allowed that he was feeling no pain anyway, to which Vinnie shrugged his shoulders and dragged Jay outside.

It's possible that had they stopped there, the next thing wouldn't have happened. But no. Vinnie lit his cigar, put it in Jay's mouth, and lit Jay's for himself. "To Carmine," he said. They puffed away. And away.

"Jay-bird, where have you been?"

It was Mama, a little tipsy, Dad in tow.

"They want to cut the cake."

Dad, with his doctor's eye—or dentist's anyway—asked if Jay was feeling all right. Vinnie answered with a shrug. "It's the Bar Mitzvah thing. It's a big day, you know, in a Jewish boy's life." Jay shrugged in sympathy.

It might have been that shrug, enough of a movement to challenge the equilibrium of two young men who'd drunk whiskey sours on empty stomachs followed by puffs on particularly strong Cuban cigars known as Churchills.

If Mama thought something was amiss, she didn't show it but pulled Jay back into the club, climbing the steps like a rocky boat hitting waves, with Dad pushing from behind and Vinnie trailing at an increasingly slow pace. Jay held closely to the arm of his mother, who thought that was an adorable display of affection as they went bouncing up the stairs. "I love you, too," she said.

In the dining room was a massive cake with the words Mazel Tov written in the same blue that adorns the Israeli flags, yellow stars of David on the cake's borders. Jay had the wherewithal to think those were in poor taste, but that thought gave way when his mother pushed him to the cake emitting its rich odor of marzipan — a flavor his mother insisted upon. His father was already there, beaming and mouthing the words "I'm so proud of you" as he handed Jay a bright cake knife that flashed into his unfocused eyes.

The crowd stood for Jay's final thanks, their mouths already forming for yet another Mazel Tov and saliva accumulating in anticipation of the marzipan-laden cake they could smell even at the tables where distant relatives were made to sit. Mama said words he didn't hear, which he thought ended with "I love him so much" when she leaned over, almost spilling out, and hugged him. She wouldn't let go, his face smothered into her, as tears rolled down her chest, reinvigorating the potent scent of La Vie Est Belle Intensément by Lancôme.

Lancôme's description boasted that "Intensément introduces an addictive fusion of red iris and red vanilla, bringing a floral and warm vibration to the iconic perfume." To an inebriated thirteen-year-old reeling from a rich Cuban, Intensément was the final straw on a nauseous camel's back. Upheavals, plural, were the result.

The first was over his mother's dress. With the hands she'd clasped around her son's head she thrust him back, his blue suede yarmulke embroidered inside with the word's "Jay's Bar Mitzvah" flying off. To Jay it felt as if his brain went at a faster pace than the rest of him until he stopped, at which point his brain rebounded forward, his second upheaval following suit over the cake, overpowering the marzipan scent.

Mama ran off to the bathroom streaming tears of another emotion along with some choice words one doesn't hear at a Bar

Mitzvah. His father dunked a napkin in cold water and wiped Jay's head. Jay thought he heard "I'm not proud of this" but couldn't be sure.

Gustavo now played the part of busboy and pushed the table holding the cake away from the crowd. He kept his head down, gagging on the noxious smell but keen to escape.

Having given his son a glass of seltzer and dirty looks, Jay's father took the mike, strained his facial muscles with a forced grin, and apologized, sort of. "It's been a big day for Jay, and I think it all got to him. The caterer has cookies and cannolis in the back, so let's give Jay one more big Mazel Tov. A few unenthused Mazel Tovs followed the retreating crowd. Lagging behind was Uncle Carmine who, with an uncharacteristically Jewish gesture, tossed his hands in the air.

Vinnie put a hand on Jay's shoulder. "Hey man, I'm really sorry about the trouble."

Jay looked around at the emptying hall and took a breath of relief. This day now was over. For the first time that day, he could smile. "Huh?" he asked. "What trouble?"

19.

Trays

It was the witching hour at The Willows, the hour when the lights went down, and voices settled into whispers before stopping entirely. A handful of the devout sat in the library, all looking toward a bookshelf, which was covered by a faded white sheet, a makeshift screen, as they waited for the glow to appear. Those who could leaned forward as the glow became an image, an unfocused scene of space and stars. In one corner stood a man, his demeanor sincere, his eyes intense. He spoke familiar words, words they'd heard for so many years. They still paid close attention as if the words might change, though they were able to recite them with his same cadence, with his same tone. Some nodded their heads silently, mouthing the refrain. Others sat, eyes closed, heads resting on their shoulders, grunting as if lost in a dream.

A thin plume of smoke rose from a cigarette the man was holding at his side. The stance, the cigarette, were part of the ritual, so much so that the watchers paid no heed to the cigarette, dangerous though it was in this time. None of them smoked, not any longer. Even if they wanted to, they wouldn't. They couldn't. "No smoking" was the rule in every nursing home across the country; the Willows was no exception. Octogenarians, nonagenarians, and the occasional centenarian dragging oxygen tanks daren't so much as light a Sabbath candle.

They learned that lesson the hard way on Mrs. Gittleman's one hundredth birthday.

But smoking? Most had given it up by the time their kids were born, and their kids were easily in their fifties and sixties. That monochromatic man before them, the man on the screen, died young from his smoking habit. That wisp of smoke disappearing into space was as fine a Twilight Zone allegory as there ever was. Alas, for the man on the screen, Rod Serling, that particular allegory was as unintentional as it was prophetic.

Thursday night at 9:30 was Twilight Zone night for the handful of diehards who managed to stay up until lights out at 10:15. In the library, the final image would go gray when the aide turned off the DVD player, the lights would come on, and those who'd fallen asleep were tapped awake by hovering aides and quietly wheeled back to their rooms.

The tap on Peter Siegel's head came from the rubber-capped end of a wooden cane wielded by Ed Mulcahy.

"What the heck? I'm watching the show."

Mulcahy leaned into Siegel's face to tell him he was snoring by the time Serling finished the introduction. Siegel insisted he'd watched the entire thing and recited, verbatim, Serling's introduction: "Sunnyvale Rest, a home for the aged, a dying place and a common children's game called kick-the-can, that will shortly become a refuge for a man who knows he will die in this world if he doesn't escape into . . . The Twilight Zone."

"Get that? They seek out the Fountain of Youth, Mulcahy. And find it. All except for one dirty old curmudgeon who I bet was stuck in his room reading old copies of Playboy. Reminds me of someone."

Siegel might very well have been awake; it's true. But then he'd seen episode 21 of season 3, "Kick the Can," no fewer than a dozen times since the show first aired in 1962, plus an additional six times while at The Willows because it was one of the less-scratched DVDs in the facility's sparse collection. Only The

Golden Girls DVDs were more worn. At his age, at all their ages, long-term memories were stronger than their short-term ones.

They were two lonely old men who had become best friends.

Siegel met Mulcahy when he first arrived. He was walking, by himself, a badge of pride for the residents, past Mulcahy in the interior garden, or the "atrium" as they called it. Siegel was wearing a faded sky-blue cap with "Tufts 1955" embroidered in an ugly brown over the brim. Mulcahy stood up, only two inches shy of the six-foot-three frame he had in college, blocking Siegel's progress with that cane of his. "Go Jumbos. Here for the class reunion?"

Friendships are a good thing at any age. But to the residents of The Willows, especially those who retained their marbles, new friendships went all too quickly with the body and mind both on borrowed time. When friendships came, they came with the intensity of a burning fuse. Mulcahy would say the basis for their friendship was that 1) they could hear each other, 2) they could remember each other's name, and 3) they had something to say other than "Huh, what was that?"

Siegel would joke they'd been making hay while the sun set. "It wasn't a match made in Heaven by any means. But it was a match made on the way."

They hadn't known each other at college and neither one had a yearbook to jog memories of what they looked like way back when. It didn't matter. They talked about their lives after Tufts, their careers and families, and played what Siegel called "Jewish Geography" to see if they knew anyone in common. The game went something like, "You're from X, do you know Y?" They came up empty. Mulcahy was from a Boston Irish family and in the Boston Irish frat, a dilapidated brick house with green shamrocks on the shutters and beer bottles on the lawn. Siegel was from the Upper West Side, a dermatologist's son, and in the Jewish frat, the one with full bookshelves and a lights-on-all-night study room.

It was an awkward reminiscence at first, a strained attempt to find common ground until Francesca Vavavavoom oscillated by. Francesca was a curvaceous nurse leaning into a cart laden with pills and catheters for inmates in the memory ward. A stale egg-salad sandwich that had fallen on the walkway jostled the cart, and several boxes of men's incontinence underwear fell off. Siegel and Mulcahy watched carefully as Francesca bent over to pick up the spilled contents. "There is a God," said Mulcahy. Siegel nodded his head slowly in ready agreement as their eyes followed the nurse's sway down the path.

"I forgot what I wanted to say," said Siegel.

"Maybe you should head over to the memory ward."

"You think so?"

"Depends."

"Do you mean that as a contingency or are you incontinent? As for the nurse, amen to that."

Common ground was found. They also found a common room in an unused coffee lounge.

The lounge was always empty except for them. It was the last spot at The Willows that hadn't met ADA rules, meaning there were rugs scattered throughout the room, no wheelchair ramp at the entrance, and no supervision. The exit door had a faulty alarm, and the room's heating system was in competition with massive picture windows that leaked cold like a sieve. If there was a draw-back to the room it was that they had to bundle up in winter clothes to contend with the room's inadequate temperature, the same temperature, though, that kept everyone else away.

But it wasn't yet off limits to the residents, and Siegel and Mulcahy coveted their limited independence. For the mobile duo it had a view, privacy, and a K-cup machine, even if the only coffee available was Green Mountain Light Roast and a vile blueberry decaf with an expiration date so far back in the past that it had faded off the cover from the room's abundant sunlight. Siegel was there one wintry day, dusting a powdered cream substitute into his watered-down coffee. Oh, how he missed his Starbucks ventes. He damned the doctor who warned him off too much caffeine.

Mulcahy came down the steps that should have been a ramp juggling a tray of Old London Melba Toasts and cottage cheese bowls—standard snack fare from the dining hall—and another tray with a paper towel hiding two deliciously greasy glazed chocolate donuts. He'd bought those from Desmond McCauley, the empathetic Jamaican janitor who was raising two children on his own and ran a geriatric black market. He smuggled in those donuts for $4 a pop and an herbal brownie every so often at $10. Donuts, and definitely herbal brownies, were not part of the regimented diet, where dessert was generally limited to lime-green Jell-O cubes and gelatinous butterscotch-flavored pudding cups.

Siegel and Mulcahy picked carefully away at their donuts to draw out the experience. They concluded by wetting their finger-tips to dab the last crumbs from the plate. Siegel pushed the tray away with his foot, spilling the Melba Toasts and cottage cheese onto the floor. "I'll be Goddamned," he said. "At least it wasn't the donuts." He put the tray on the floor while he cleaned up the mess.

"Trays," said Mulcahy. He got up and walked to the coffee machine and picked up a tray and tossed one to Siegel. Then another. Then another.

"What the hell are you doing?" said Siegel, batting them away as they flew at him.

"Trays," repeated Mulcahy. He held one to his chest like it was a life preserver.

Mulcahy pointed with his sharp chin out the bay window. Beyond was a wooded hill, part of the conservation land at the rear of The Willows. It was snowing hard, adding powdery inches to the heavy accumulation of that winter.

In the infinitesimal intersection of their college days a Venn diagram might show, trays would stand out.

Their college was on the high mound of earth rising on the border between Somerville and Medford, Massachusetts and affectionately called The Hill. It was a term coined by graduates who had made careers in advertising and utilized it to headline fundraising efforts ahead of class reunions, as in, "Let's meet back on The Hill!"

No student referred to the school as "The Hill," not when they were there. But all students were keenly aware of the topography, especially after a snowstorm, when vast numbers of cafeteria trays disappeared under winter coats. From the top of the hill students would sled past professors who were angry that students were wasting time when they should've been studying, and envious of their freedom. They sped past townies looking forward to pounding the spoiled kids some night. They zipped past screaming lunch-line ladies demanding the return of the plastic trays that would inevitably crack apart after runs.

And though they didn't realize it, there was one time when Ed Mulcahy and Peter Siegel would have crashed into each if not for Mulcahy swerving at the last minute to grab the edge of a tray beneath a girl he wanted to meet.

"Cans," said Mulcahy. "They're our cans."

"Huh? What are you talking about? Or is this your effort to get a sponge-down from the lovely Ms. Vavavavoom?"

"The trays. They're our cans. Don't you get it?"

Siegel looked out to the snow-covered hill. He couldn't help but smile.

An aide felt the cold breeze as he walked past the lounge. The outside door was wide open. He went to close it, but not before following a pair of footprints in the snow leading up the hill. The prints were jumbled on top of each other like one person was helping another along, or maybe it was a couple of kids pushing each other into the snow. Through the trees and blizzard, the storm had grown harder. He was almost sure he heard two kids screaming "Gangway!" as they sped down the slope.

20.

Here Kitty Kitty

He wished he'd thought more about that black cat when he first saw it earlier that morning. Black cats are bad omens, right? Maybe the omen was the cat itself, a "here kitty kitty" gone very wrong. Now, though, as that morning led into the afternoon, he saw that cat again in front of him, staring and swishing its tail not five yards ahead.

He knelt and held out his fingers, feigning the act of teasing a treat like he would do for a dog; he was not a cat person. The thing screeched at the gesture, then hissed as its back arched, the hair standing on end, its mouth opening to reveal sharp teeth. It positively leaped up several feet, flinging itself backward by an equal amount; sat down again, calm; and, swishing its tail, just glared.

Yeah, in retrospect he should have paid more attention to it, the nasty thing. Early on when he started the hike, he saw it staring at him from back in the woods. It looked healthy, not lost or wild, and had a collar, a wide one, so it must have had a home. The collar warranted attention. It was a fiery thing, blaze orange with black markings on it. He paid more attention to the collar than the cat.

Orange, he thought at the time. Orange. Maybe its owners put it on to signal hunters, now that it was deer season. And then he'd thought that no one could confuse a housecat for a deer, even a large cat, like this one, with or without an orange collar. And the eyes. Those eyes blazed as much as any orange collar.

What were those markings on the collar? From a distance, they had looked like etchings of evil things. Monsters maybe. Some remnant from Halloween. With the cat right in front of him, close, he saw those were witches on the collar. Hideous witches and vicious cats. The cats had arched backs and frightening sets of teeth in gaping maws. It was a Halloween image—it must've been—but certainly over the top. It wasn't something a normal person would put on a housecat to greet trick or treaters. Had he seen that earlier he might have turned around. Should have turned around.

When the cat screeched, he stumbled back over a root and was left sitting on the trail, his rear end screaming from the fall. He felt that familiar twinge in his lower back; a spasm wouldn't be far behind. This far out on the trail, this far into the day, it was the last thing he needed.

The thing ran off when he yelled.

Standing, he had to shuffle his feet in the four directions of a compass to look around the trail; twisting irritated his already tightening back. The indignity and imposition of chronology, he thought. He wasn't too old, not yet, but his all too frequent back spasms reminded him that "old" was a state of body as much as a state of mind.

Shadows were starting to lengthen. It was getting colder, too. Purple-grey clouds were gathering in the north. A bit colder and it could snow. It was pretty, actually, majestic even. It was also, he realized, time to turn back or press on. There was a road somewhere ahead. The map had shown it. He could hit that and walk back to where he'd left his car. Better to take the road than the trail. Things got dark early this time of the year. He knew he should have taken a flashlight. His phone might have sufficed if it had enough juice left.

And Aleve. The spasm that had started in his lower back had spread to his middle back. It was okay with small steps on flat parts of the trail, of which there were very few. On the rough remains, the lower spasm would fire one way and the middle another, causing him to twist for one, exacerbating the other. There were frequent stops with gritted teeth and piercing breaths as he tried to find the equilibrium to go on.

At least the cat was gone or, anyway, out of sight. He didn't like the thing's screeching. He didn't like the thing at all. It being out here alone was weird, even if these woods weren't far from civilization. A reservation, they called it, conservation land. Thirty-five miles of trails that promised solitude. It was a promise kept; he hadn't seen a soul in the last three, no, five hours. That wasn't so odd. It was on the chilly side, even when the sun was out earlier. But with those purplish clouds getting thick, the sun wasn't providing much warmth and it was supposed to get colder per the weather report he'd read on his phone that morning. He just hadn't expected to be out so damn long. *"Where did the time go?"* he asked himself.

Then he asked the damned cat, now sitting on a glacial erratic ten yards from where he stood. "Where did you come from?" He grimaced as he leaned over, saying, "Here kitty kitty," and grabbing a sharp white stone, quartz, wincing as he rose to throw it as hard as he could.

He didn't mean to hit it, didn't expect to. The cat soared up five feet as if launched and then screamed as it did a double axel, landing on its feet. *"An 8.3 from the Soviet judge,"* he said to himself. The cat gave another loud hiss, bared its awful teeth, and tore off down the path that curved over dead leaves and around a rocky hill. He followed. He had no choice. By now he had to be near the end of the trail and the road that he'd follow back to the car. If only the trail was better marked; hell, marked at all. Or if he had a map, like the ones in the wooden box nailed to the little welcoming station in the parking lot that displayed warning signs about

Lyme disease, poison ivy, bears, coyotes, and hunters. There was no sign about black cats. He had to laugh about that.

There was a request that hikers sign a guest book with their start time and sign out when they got back. He'd laughed about that, too. It was just a set of trails in the suburbs, or rather the exurbs per the hiking guide he'd left home. Now he was asking himself what was the difference between suburbs and exurbs. Exurbs would be the worse, he thought, and got a chill with the idea of it being worse.

"Dumb idea," he said aloud. "Dumb, dumb, you big dummy."

He looked back down the way he'd come, seeing only an empty path that didn't look like it has been walked on by anyone, let alone him just moments before. Robert Frost came to his mind, *"And both that morning equally lay in leaves no step had trodden black."* He imagined a blur at the corner of his eye, a black image flying over the surrounding rocky ledge.

He looked to where he imagined was the road and trudged on.

It was there again. It looked bigger now, arrogant as it circled. When he leaned over to get another stone, it jumped back, giving itself distance. He didn't throw the rock this time, just squeezed until it hurt his hand, until he'd get a better shot. He wanted that shot and put a few more stones into his pocket for reserve.

The cat moved parallel to his path. He was looking sideways to the cat that moved from stump to stone to fallen logs, and it angered him that the cat had protection. He was pissed off that the cat didn't look at him, wasn't concerned with him, but just sashayed at an easy pace while he struggled, trying to hold one eye on the cat, one eye on the trail, while tripping on the rocks or slipping on the slick leaves, each small move sending spasms of pain through his torso.

It meowed a loud meow, almost like a call, and then floated ahead not making a sound as it did so. "Damned cat," he said to no one. "Good riddance."

He picked up his pace and started to sweat despite the formerly cool air turning cold. He wanted off that trail, wanted some sign of civilization, and considered turning around. No, that was stupid; he was hours from where he started. Maybe he'd lost the right trail. Anyway, it would be dark before long. Heck, it was kind of dark already.

To his right was that granite ridge rising some seventy-five feet. It would be lighter up there, fewer trees hiding the setting sun. From there, he might see the road, or something, maybe even other hikers. Or, maybe, he shouldn't leave the trail, always a bad idea in the wild, but then he wasn't in the wild at all. That's what he told himself. Hell, there was probably a Starbucks within ten miles. The wild, he thought, what a crazy idea, a stupid idea. He smiled at the very notion and walked toward the base of the cliff.

It wasn't an easy scramble. The rocks were loose, and every other step dislodged bowling ball–sized rocks that bounced down the steep slope dislodging even more rocks. He learned quickly to test what he grabbed, lest they'd pry loose, and he'd end up dropping like a stone. But he got his rhythm and clamored up the last twenty feet, the steepest part by far. It was open at the top and he caught an early glimpse of the moon and, very close now, an easy walk, a road. He couldn't hear the car, its headlights already on, but was gratified at the sight. No, he was more than gratified. He gave a yell of relief and took in a few deep breaths knowing that this day would come to an end. He promised to bring the map next time. And a flashlight! A whole survival kit come to think of it. A big dog, too. A big dog that doesn't like cats.

Going down was harder. It would have been hard to make out the handholds and footholds on the dark granite at any hour of the day, but with the sun already low on the other side of the ridge, he had to descend by feel. He was doubly cautious with his back spasms, which made any movement painful, especially agile moves. Grasping for a hold had become impossible.

That was why he was gripping a crack with the tips of his fingers on a near-vertical slab. His feet managed to find small ledges, allowing him to traverse the slab, but those ledges were mere nubs. Looking down he guessed the drop couldn't have been more than fifteen feet. Maybe he could just fall and be okay. If only there weren't so many boulders waiting at the bottom.

The right side of the slab had more of those little ledges and then gave way to boulders that sloped more gradually. The crack that his fingers were in went all the way over to the boulders. Those would give him more edges to grab and, not without spasms, he could ease down and relish the reward of a short, flat hike to the road. There was a vial of Aleve in his car. He'd take four. He could do it.

What made him look up wasn't so much a sound as a sense. Overhead was a metronome, its hand silently moving forth and back with an easy tempo. Then its eyes opened, two yellow eyes with which he was now familiar, unblinking and just staring. He called out, "Scat!" but the metronome just beat, those eyes simply stared. He screamed it then, or tried to scream it, but his heart was beating too fast and his back spasmed as he breathed in air. He wanted to move his right hand to his pocket, to retrieve a stone, but his grip wasn't that strong, his balance not that good, and he needed both hands to hold on.

That's when the metronome leaped into his face, using it like a gymnast's mount to spring to safety on the very boulders he'd been trying to reach, giving his right eye a sharp swipe with its claws. There was no thought when his hand went to that eye.

He had been wrong. It was a twenty-five-foot fall. And, anyway, he wouldn't have seen the cat turn when it landed and certainly didn't hear it purring as it gazed at the broken skull, smashed on the boulders at the base of the ridge. The cat looked up when it jumped onto the body, toward the sound of a horn on the nearby road.

21

A Brush with History

It was a bitter winter that year, 1954. The coldest that century, they said, and fifteen-year old Ernie Remsen was freezing; the layers of sweaters underneath his blue cotton mechanic's jacket, a "Texaco" patch on the breast, couldn't keep out the chill. Maybe Sal had had better success with it. Sal was the name embroidered over the left pocket. Ernie didn't know Sal but was grateful he'd donated it to the church rummage sale that winter. It was almost better than nothing.

Still, Ernie had stolen a kid's coat, a real winter coat, hanging from a hook outside the gym's locker room. Ernie was either stupid enough or cold enough to wear it around school. The coat didn't even fit him; his arm dangled beyond the sleeves and he couldn't zipper the front. Had its rightful owner, a boy named Sokol, gone up to him and said it was his coat, Ernie would have given it back then and there. He wasn't a bully; he just wanted a warm coat and there it was. Sokol wasn't about to confront Ernie, though. Sokol wasn't the type to confront anyone, and Ernie, well, Ernie Remsen wasn't a kid to be confronted. Avoided was more like it. You don't mess with kids who never smile. You don't mess with kids who mumble to themselves. You don't mess with kids who once came to school with a black eye.

It was Principal O'Brien's call to make: suspension or community service. Ernie was half hoping for suspension because any time out of school was as good as time in school. But his mother would have had a fit and if his father came back this time, Ernie would end up with a black eye and that was only because he'd grown too big for a belt.

He choked up when he offered an apology, saying he didn't mean any harm and just needed a warm coat. He hated himself for that and choked up some more.

The principal told Ernie to stay seated and not touch anything in the office. He went to the storage closet that housed the lost-and-found bin and rummaged through it until he found a suitable coat too large for most kids in his high school. It was a dark plaid thing, wool, that had been turned in after a football game last season.

"Here," said the principal. "No one's claimed it. Probably belonged to someone from a visiting team. A big someone. Anyway, it's yours so you don't need to borrow one from a kid half your size."

Ernie looked up through reddened eyes and said a quiet, "Thanks."

"Now, Mr. Remsen, what to do with you?"

Ernie chewed on the ragged end of a well-chewed thumbnail while staring down at his feet. He hesitated before saying, "I don't know," his stock response to questions in school even when he knew the answer before catching himself. The principal was looking at papers on his desk, not at Ernie. The question, Ernie now knew, was rhetorical.

"Ernie, do you know what 'intimidating' means?

Ernie nodded his head.

"Has anyone ever told you that you look a bit scary?"

Ernie was about to answer no but stopped. He hadn't been told he was scary; no one would dare. No one ever said much to him, unless there was a problem.

"When something goes wrong, everyone kind of thinks I did it. Like when a window gets broken or when the woods caught fire that time. It was like, 'Ernie, did you do it?' I guess I look that way."

The principal looked at Ernie for a long while. Ernie looked out the window, then back, then away again. What else, it would be suspension. Maybe that wouldn't be so bad. Ernie had that term paper on his mind: "A Brush with History." The idea was to write about something in his life that brought him close to the past and so far he'd come up empty except to blame his father's behavior on three years as a POW, though his mother had said he'd been a jerk long before that. Maybe he'd go hang out at the town's library, figure something out, if he could ignore the constant stares from the librarian who would ask him why he wasn't in school. Or if she didn't kick him out.

"It's not fair, is it?"

Ernie nodded in agreement. "You know what they say."

"What's that Ernie?"

"Don't judge a book by its cover. I guess I have a bad cover. I needed a coat. I was going to give it back at some point. I think."

The principal smiled for the first time that morning.

"Well Mr. Remsen, you don't need a coat now. Nor do you need a suspension. I've got community service in mind unless you insist on suspension. Which will it be?"

Ernie didn't expect a choice. He mumbled, "Community service."

The principal smiled again. "Good choice," he said.

Thaddeus Seymour, age 96, lived alone in a house he built in 1897. He'd lost his wife in the Spanish Flu Epidemic. Their daughter, too. The son, a mining engineer, was killed exploring a mine in Colorado. Their spouses had remarried and moved on with the grandchildren to parts unknown. His friends had left him, too. The last one to go was a dog who died when Seymour was 90. Fifteen-years old that dog. Seymour couldn't go through that again. Hell, he could barely take care of himself these days.

Seymour didn't drive, not anymore, even if he wanted to. His license with a rare three-digit number had expired years before. And it was doubtful his Ford Model A would start assuming he had the strength to work the crank. So, he would walk to town to shop, get his haircut, get out of the house, get moving. If he had more than one bag of groceries, he'd make multiple trips that would take up his entire day. He'd amble down the road, waving off people offering a ride and eventually make it to wherever he was going. Mike Abernathy, the local police sergeant, once asked him if he wouldn't rather get there sooner. Seymour groused that then he'd have nothing to do but go for a walk anyway.

"You ever hear the story about the tortoise and the hare?" Seymour groused. "Speed only gets you nowhere sooner." He didn't wait for a response. He looked at the time on his pocket watch, adjusted his tie, swung his cane, and continued on his way.

It would have been a treacherous walk for anyone. That day powdery snow hid slick ice under which roots had lifted the cracked sidewalk into a series of little random ridges, valleys, and glaciers. But it was Wednesday, and every other Wednesday he went for a haircut and a shave. It had been a routine etched into his life for 50 years always at the same barbershop, though the original owner was long gone. His grandson, Joe, no spring chicken, ran it now. Joe offered to come to Seymour's home, especially in rough weather. Seymour would have none of it. "And would you bring the rest of your ugly customers with you? How about those girly magazines? No? Then I'll come to you."

Before and after his haircut, Seymour would sit in the shop—outside if the weather was fine—and talk to anyone who bothered to listen or listen to anyone who bothered to talk. If no one was talking, he'd read magazines like the Police Gazette, Esquire, or Argosy. And if it wasn't one of those every-other-Wednesdays, it didn't matter; it was a place to spend time haircut or not.

The snow had dulled the sheen on his cracked leather brogues. Maybe he'd get a shine if the boy was in the shop that day. Next time he'd wear the brown shoes and get these resoled again; the soles were worn smooth. He could use new laces, too. He was thinking about that when the tip of his cane found a narrow crack in the sidewalk that wouldn't let go. Seymour held onto the cane a moment too long. The cane held fast and Seymour tripped over a thick root that had grown through a crack, his arms splayed out in surprise and his face meeting the snowy pavement shattering his wire-rimmed glasses. He was lucky he hit the snow. The only damage was a badly twisted ankle. He recovered the cane and managed to get on his feet. It took him an hour to dodder home.

The doctor making house calls told Seymour to ice his leg and keep off of it. Seymour smirked. He rose and limped to the kitchen returning with a glass of bourbon on the rocks. "See Doc? It's got ice. I'll deliver it internally."

Members of the Ladies Auxiliary from the Methodist church brought over meals and did some cleaning. It was always the same, chicken pot pie. "Easy to chew, easy to stomach and, damn good," was what he'd say.

Seymour was sitting back in his armchair, bouncing one foot on the floor and alternatively tapping the armrests with his hands. He was staring at the four walls, complaining to infrequent visitors that he'd be climbing them if not for his "damn leg." The church women thought they were doing him a favor by leaving copies of the Saturday Evening Post and worn editions of Reader's Digest. Seymour could have cared less for any of those even if he could read them, which he couldn't without his old glasses. The new ones wouldn't arrive for a couple of weeks.

"He needs a helper, someone to read to him. He likes history," said Joan Wright, Chair of the Women's Auxiliary, to Principal O'Brien. "And, let me be frank, he could use some help with, I don't mean to be rude, the toilet. You understand? It should be a young man. I thought you might have a student, perhaps a scout working on a merit badge. Someone who could use a little money. We're offering $5 a week."

The principal was delighted.

"I have just the fellow."

Ernie made his way up the walk to the porch and knocked on the door. A voice called out, "It's open. Wipe your feet"

He did as instructed and closed the door behind him.

"Umm, hi. I'm, uhm, Ernie Remsen and —"

"I know who you are and don't mumble. Come over so I can get a look at you."

Ernie wiped his feet again and stood before Thaddeus Seymour. "My eyesight, you know. They're working on new glasses. Take a seat. Now tell me, do you know what day it is?"

Ernie shrugged his shoulders, "Wednesday." It came out more as a question than an answer.

"Wednesday is right. That's why I look handsome. Got a haircut. And a shave. Joe came over from the shop. Did me the honors. I don't want to look like some ragamuffin for those church ladies, do I? "

Seymour pointed to a stack of magazines on the chair next to him. "He left those."

"Magazines," said Ernie.

"You might as well start your job. Choose one. I don't care which."

For the next two hours Ernie read to Thaddeus Seymour with two breaks to help the old man onto the toilet, discretely standing outside the room until called, and another break for a trip to the kitchen where a plate of cookies had been left by the ladies of the Methodist Auxiliary.

"Take one for yourself. Hell, take two. I can't eat 'em all," said Seymour.

Ernie had hoped Mr. Seymour would have fallen asleep so he could get to that term paper; he was struggling with his particular brush with history. Seymour wouldn't cooperate. As Ernie read, Seymour would interrupt constantly. On an article about Teddy Roosevelt's Sagamore Hill being turned over to the family trust as a museum, Seymour said, "Voted for the man. Twice. But that Rough Rider stuff? Waste of time. That Hearst fellow just wanted a war to sell his papers."

Ernie read a Life Magazine piece on the Supreme Court's ruling on school segregation. Seymour piped in. "'Bout time, too. Colored kids just the same as you, only darker." He giggled at that. "Get it?"

Then Seymour started to nod his head.

"I saw a lynching once."

He closed his eyes, still nodding, and stopped speaking for a moment

"Really?" said Ernie. "Was it awful?"

"Well, I didn't see the murder, just the boy hanging from a tree the next morning. Fifteen he was. His mother – I guess it was his mother – was trying to get his body down. A crowd stood around doing nothing. Happened right here in Maryland if you can believe it."

Seymour leaned over to get another magazine. "What's this one?"

Ernie picked up a magazine whose cover had been torn off. He opened to an article and read the title, "The Flight of John Wilkes Booth."

Seymour nodded, "Go on."

The article described Booth sneaking into Lincoln's box, stabbing the Major who was with the president, breaking his leg when he leaped onto the stage yelling "Sic semper tyrannis," and then limping off to make his escape. Ernie stopped reading periodically when he got caught up in the drama. He was fascinated.

"Good story if you speak up," said Seymour. "Truth is better than fiction if you ask me." The story went on how Booth was killed in a tobacco barn after a 12-day manhunt. Seymour kept asking Ernie to reread parts, offering comments like, "Yup", "Nope," and the occasional, "Ha."

155

When he'd finished, Ernie looked up to see Seymour, eyes closed, sitting back in his chair. He got up to go shovel snow off the porch; part of his job was to find things to do. "I'll just go clear outside. Can I get you anything?" he asked. He whispered, thinking Seymour might had fallen asleep. He hadn't.

"They always get that part wrong," he said.

"What's that Mr. Seymour?"

His eyes remained closed. "That 'sic semper' nonsense. They always get that wrong. It means 'Thus always to tyrants.' Virginia's state motto. Bet you didn't know that. Booth didn't say it. Bet you didn't know that either." Ernie sat back down. "No, I didn't."

Seymour's eyes opened and looked at Ernie. Maybe his eyesight was poor without his glasses but his focus suggested he could see perfectly well. He nodded his head holding his stare.

"Well, he didn't. I can tell you that much."

"No?"

"No! First, he screamed. He wasn't as loud as Mrs. Lincoln, who was screaming too, but Booth was plenty loud. He tried to say sic something, but what came out was 'The south is avenged.' Then he dragged himself away. He still had that big knife waving everywhere. They said he was trying to scare off the actors, but I think he was just trying to keep his balance. Then everyone started screaming when they figured he wasn't part of the play."

Ernie shook his head, at first, thinking Seymour was telling a story he once heard. When Seymour returned with slow and deep nods, Ernie had to ask, "How do you know all that?"

"It was my birthday," he said. "April 14. Still is by the way." He laughed to himself. "Still is."

"Paps wanted to go," Seymour continued. "We lived in Maryland, just over the border. You could spit into Washington we were that close. I was seven, sitting in front with my parents. I didn't pay much attention to that play, but my parents laughed and laughed so it must have been funny.

"Me? I was looking at all the uniforms. That's what a little boy cares about. I was dressed up like a soldier, too: blue jacket and brass buttons. Paps was a doctor in one of those military hospitals. A Union man, make no mistake. He kept elbowing me, pointing to the stage, but I didn't care. I was looking up to the box, you know, where the President was. He was laughing, too. Having a grand old time.

"And I'm telling you, he caught sight of me, he did. I waved a little. Know what he did? He waved back, just a little wave. Gave me a smile. And winked. Imagine that. President Lincoln winking at me. Then all hell broke loose. I wasn't 15 feet from Booth when he dropped. I saw him spit when he yelled. That's how close I was. The things you remember. And that is the truth and I'll swear it on a stack of bibles."

Seymour leaned forward, his eyes never leaving Ernie, and said, "I must be the last person alive who was there. When I go, they'll be no one to fix that sic semper nonsense. A shame, too."

Ernie probed him for details—Was he scared? What did his parents say? Where did he go after that? Did they ride in a wagon? Ernie wanted it all. Seymour's eyes were wide open when he recalled holding his father's belt when they carried Lincoln's body across the street. His mother pulled him back. "I remember looking down at the cobblestones. There was blood on them. Lincoln's."

He directed Ernie to a roll-top desk. In a slot meant for letters was a small folder. "Take a look," said Seymour. Inside was a yellowed paper rectangle, the ink faded brown with age. "Ford's Theater" was printed at the top and below, in handwritten script, the words "Washington D.C. April 14, 1865. Maj. T. C. Seymour has secured seats 29, 30 and 31 in Orchestra."

Then Seymour stopped, dropped his head, and started to snore. Ernie went to shovel off the porch and spread sand on the walkway. He only left when a stout lady wearing a thick wool coat arrived with a dinner of chicken pot pie. "If I knew you'd be here I would've brought two," she said. "What about tomorrow?"

Ernie loved chicken pot pie. He came back every day for the next few weeks, even after the county decided a live-in nurse was needed. He'd read to Seymour who didn't mention he'd received his new pair of glasses. If Seymour was tired of Ernie's questions, he never mentioned that, either. When the county nurse eventually showed, she took charge, cleared up the magazines, and shooed Ernie away. "You're exhausting the old man," she said.

Not long after that, Seymour was sitting in his chair, staring outside while the nurse made herself a cup of coffee. He brushed his fingers through his hair and frowned. It was a Wednesday. He managed to get himself up, cane in hand, and walked out the front door. He probably didn't see the sheet of ice that formed a small skating rink on his porch. His obituary said nothing about the night of April 14, 1865.

Ernie got a C on his paper, "The Last Witness." His teacher thought he made most of it up. He resubmitted it as a short story to Argosy Magazine, which published it and paid him $100. The story became the basis for a Twilight Zone episode some years later.

Ernie Remsen wrote the screenplay.

22.

Heaven is Restricted?

His GI dog tag had P on it. P for Protestant. Hardly unique given that ten million dog tags had P's on them. Problem was that Ish Kabibble was Jewish. He hadn't touched a slice of bacon until he was drafted and then couldn't get enough, a change he didn't mention in letters home.

The P was a white lie. If captured, his thinking went, P would better than H, at least to a German. H meant Hebrew. And, if there was ever a chance for a promotion, a P might do him better service than an H. Ish noticed there weren't a lot of Cohens or Goldmans getting saluted.

His name wasn't Ish Kabibble. Kabibble was a semi-popular cornet player, who was lanky and goofy, with a bowl haircut like Moe of the Three Stooges. They could have been twins. His name was actually Leo Lavin. The story is that at the immigration line, his grandfather's speech impediment turned Levine into Lavin. The inspector, who had just spent the morning tallying up a boatload of Irish immigrants, took the mispronounced Levine in stride.

It was just as well. A Levine would have caught the attention of any semi-astute anti-Semite, P or no P, but that was never an issue because he wasn't captured or promoted. The issue was he was dead.

How he died isn't relevant to subsequent events other than to say they needed his tags to identify him, hurrying his corpse off to a temporary morgue in the basement of a Hotel de Ville somewhere, spooning what was left into a coffin, and then interring him in a US military cemetery. There, over his poignantly simple grave, at attention, stood a brilliant piece of Lasa marble in the shape of a cross.

The authorities couldn't be blamed; his dog tag did have a P on it and who was the American Battle Monuments Commission to raise a challenge? All his mourning mother knew was that he was buried somewhere in Normandy, and, as upset as his step-father was, he was comforted that he wouldn't have to pay for a funeral. And there Leo lies to this day in the midst of 10,000 similar white crosses, despite Leo's protests.

Protests?

Lavin passed Heaven's initial muster outside the Pearly Gates, where an extraordinary crowd had gathered to wait and wait and wait for clearance to enter. Millions were milling about: soldiers and sailors, throngs of civilians of all ages, from all walks of life, now victims of war. Suicides, too. The idea that suicides are barred from Heaven is utter nonsense.

It was not an unpleasant wait. In fact, it was entirely enjoyable, and no one was in a hurry to leave even if entering eternity on the other side promised, well, Heaven. Flapping about, leaving feathers falling like snow, were overwhelmed angels directing people to designated points of collection, trying to encourage some order to the pleasant chaos. They also wanted people to feel welcome. It was their job; they were, after all, angels.

Leo was taken under the wing of one and encouraged with a gentle maternal push toward a plaza. In place of cobblestones, was a layer of cottony cloud like a shag carpet. Leo noticed that many had taken off shoes and were wiggling their toes as they perused their options. Around the plaza were cafes, bistros, cafeterias, restaurants to fit any taste. The aromas were enticing, the offerings abundant, the bills paid for including a 20 percent tip for the immaculate service. Cloud carpet streets led off this plaza to an abundance of parks where archangels gave uplifting talks. Apart from the parks, there were gazebos with music from every corner of the world. And street performers whose talents must have grown with passing. They passed their hats, which the audience filled with joy. Literally. The performers would sprinkle it on themselves, then toss it to their audience like a magician tossing confetti instead of a hatful of water.

Saints and prophets gave away books, toys, autographs, anything to tide people over for the duration of the wait. Saint Christopher was especially popular with his endless supply of medallions for safe travel. "Trinkets," he would say. "Just trinkets. I was thinner in those days." Everything was free because, well, it was Heaven. Leo got one for himself. He also picked up a silken yarmulke that was spun out from under the leg of an ancient rabbi. "Wear it with pride, boychik!" he said. The rabbi was wearing a Saint Christopher medal. Everyone was wearing a Saint Christopher medal and then some.

Leo couldn't believe the variety of uniforms. Many he didn't recognize. Many were mere rags. He noted there weren't many swastikas about. He asked an angel, who merely shrugged her wings, tapped the side of her nose, and looked down.

"May I?" The angel, a not unattractive blonde, lifted Leo's dog tag and pointed past a gazebo holding a Salvation Army band that stood next to a crowded beer hall. "Protestants. They'll narrow it down from there. Presbyterian, Methodist, that sort of thing." The angel said Baptists could be sticklers about mixing but they get over that. "Not much of a sense of humor, either. You're not Baptist, are you?"

He was disappointed. "Figures," he mumbled. "Even heaven is restricted."

The angel looked at him with beatific sympathy. She teased him with a flirtatious if angelic wink before turning to help another angel struggling to explain things to a group of Soviet

Commissars who, heretofore, didn't believe in Heaven. Leo gave her wing a soft tug. "But, you see, I'm Jewish. They don't want to bunk with me." The angel started to weep so Leo added, "You know, goyim can be funny that way."

She wiped a tear from her cheek and sneezed into her wing. "Damn allergies. Look, cock-ups happen. "

Leo swept his arms wide at the throngs of humanity. "But all this? It'll take forever."

"Patience. This is an eternal paradise." The angel's wings fluttered when she was jostled by a group of torpedoed sailors heading toward the beer hall. She sighed, acknowledging they hadn't been prepared for so many. "God looks at the big picture. Details? Not so much. Hence only ten commandments."

A gang of emaciated children in filthy striped pajamas ran around, kicking up clouds, laughing as they banged into people. They held rainbows of ice cream cones that a litter of squealing yellow pups was jumping to grab. The angel spread her wings and lifted a few feet off the ground. The children stopped in their tracks. It was "oohs" and "aahs," and "when can I get wings?" The puppies jumped at the feathers that drifted about.

"Now go find your parents," she said.

Paying no attention, they ran off to a clown tying balloon animals.

"The clown, was he in a camp?" Leo asked.

"No," the angel replied. "Heart attack. In a Stockholm circus. The naturals get lost in the crowd."

She pointed Leo down a road. "We're trying to organize by groups, you see, to sort out the paperwork. Religion, country, town, street, that sort of thing. Until we get organized."

"A bureaucratic nightmare, huh?'

"We don't use that word here. It's just a delay. Go enjoy yourself—try the brick oven pizza. Take in a show. Glenn Miller is performing later if you like that sort of thing."

Leo was fine with Glenn Miller. He wasn't fine with how he

was sorted, arguing he'd rather be with a Jewish group: sense of humor, irony, angst, and all that. The angel gave him a "you people" roll of her eyes. The tag said "Protestant" and there was nothing she could do at the moment. Then her halo brightened. "You should meet up with Unitarians. Lovely people, though a bit bored here. Nothing to complain about, I suppose. A number of them were Jewish, I think."

Leo had no choice but to follow the road, noting that it always seemed to go downhill and there was an encouraging breeze on his back.

He went back to the plaza and had a delightful croque monsieur in a bistro to shame any in France albeit with friendly waiters and menus in English. There even was a soup kitchen, very good soup mind you, manned by smiling Unitarians. It wasn't clear if the soup kitchen was to keep the Unitarians busy or if people actually chose to eat there.

He followed signs pointing to "US Military Personnel Protestant Zone" but veered when he saw another zone, with a sign reading "Fresh Bagels & Bialys" in front of it. That sign read "US Military Personnel Hebrew." A stocky Marine leaning against a palm tree grumbled out, "Hey, pal. Where do you think you're going?"

Leo tried to explain, but the Marine was having none of it. "Yeah, yeah, I've heard that one before. Being Jewish is so 'in' these days. It's Jesus, you know."

Leo was confused. "Jesus?"

"Yeah, Jesus. Son of God? You may have heard of him. Well, don't you know he was Jewish and hangs out with, yeah, Jews. His seder was huge. Italian guy, Bacchus, catered. Now all these Christians are like, 'I want to party with THAT guy.'" The Marine started chanting, "Toga, toga, toga."

Leo looked around for a guy in a robe and sandals. He turned back to the Marine. "So, can I get in?"

The Marine barked, "The tag says 'P,' you're a P. You can

always file for a transfer. Meantime," he pointed away, "try the pulled pork."

His stroll was continuously interrupted by wonderful distractions. There was a foot reflexology spa, for example, though the line was long. People gathered in animated conversation at cafes, in parks, and at designated family gathering points. There, families reunited, reunited families argued, arguing families reconciled. There are no bad endings in Heaven. Soldiers played craps where no one seemed to lose, and harp players entertained, though the crowds around them were decidedly thin. Sidewalk preachers laughed with delight, "There's nothing to repent for! Get a massage!"

A miles-long line of soldiers queued up before a sign that read "Entering US Protestant Zone. Non-personnel to Registration." Leo was getting a coffee and hot cinnamon donut from a smiling USO matron when a voice called out, "Kabibble?"

His company sergeant, Ed Morgan, pulled him out of line.

"Sarge! What a surprise."

"Yeah, yeah, big surprise. Maybe you didn't hear there's a war on." Morgan had a nasty snarl that masked a nastier snarl. "Say, Kabibble, aren't you Jewish?"

Morgan's snarl twisted as Leo explained. "That's Heaven for you. Hurry up and wait. Follow me." He cut to the front with a series of "scuse us." Leo heard one guy say, "Hey, that's Ish Kabibble." Several GIs in the line leaned out for a look. He had to sign two autographs.

Leo registered. In a space left for comments, he wrote that he belonged in the Jewish group. The registrar was a red-faced master sergeant with zero tolerance for anything, especially anything out of order. His stint in heaven hadn't softened that feature. The sergeant looked at the line going off into the distance and thumbed Leo into the "P" zone. "Barrack's the same, entertainment's the same, waiting's the same. Food is different; they're Kosher and get more holidays off. Don't think pleading the Jew case gets you off duty.

Leo looked at Morgan. Morgan looked at the sergeant. Both asked, "Duty?"

"Old habit," said the sergeant. "Bunk with the Unitarians. Next in line."

Leo was about to follow the arrows pointing to the Unitarian section when Morgan punched him in the shoulder. "Kabibble, what are you doing?" Before Leo could explain, Morgan punched him harder, reminding him he wasn't in the Army and didn't have to follow anyone's orders.

"But," Leo said. "The angel, they all said . . ."

"Hello. Anyone home? You're one of the Chosen. That carries some weight around here."

Leo nodded in dubious agreement. Being Jewish had some advantages? It was hard for him to fathom, but there was the Jesus thing. Made sense when he thought about it. After all, even Leo was looking for fellowship. For the first time in his life, he prayed for Jesus.

And there before him, in a coarse robe, rough sandals, hooked nose covering much of his face, dark curly hair falling over an olive complexion, and tired eyes bearing the weight of the world, was someone who didn't look like any Jesus Leo had seen in the movies.

"You Levine?"

"Lavin. Leo Lavin."

"Same difference. What's with the P?"

Leo repeated his plight, said he thought he should be in the Jewish group—his ganze mishpocha as it were, though his curiosity got the best of him. "Why are you, Jesus Christ of all people, interested in me?" he said. "How do you even know about my dog tag?"

Jesus picked at a space between his teeth with the edge of his pinky nail. "People talk."

A large crowd gathered around them, some on knees, some crying, some with arms spread wide because it didn't make sense to raise them to Heaven, did it? Jesus turned, offering his sad smile of love, held his palms out, and spoke words of kindness

and joy concluding with, "Now scram. I'm talking to this guy."
The crowd parted like waves on the Red Sea. "Walk with me,
Leo Levine."

"Lavin."

Along the way, Jesus was forced to touch innumerable heads
as the masses bowed before him instinctively crossing themselves. "Please don't do that," said Jesus, looking at his palms. To
disappointed faces, he added soothing words. "You're fine." "All's
well." "No problem." "Lovely day." "Shalom to you as well."

"So, Levine, what's the problem? You're here. You'll be there.
Everyone's talking about this rogue Jew whining. Relax."

Leo was relaxed. Everyone was relaxed. It was hard not to be
when you were walking on clouds. Still, he said, something wasn't
Kosher. He had a weight over him and it didn't feel quite right.

"You got a P?" Jesus asked.

"I'm fine. I went earlier. I never used a bidet before."

"Oy, pischer. P like the letter."

Jesus swept aside the clouds below to reveal the white cross
with Leo's name. "You know the expression 'bearing a cross'?
Well, that's yours. Trust me, I know. Come."

They went to a jeweler's workbench behind which sat a Jew,
gray bearded, with payes touching his drooping shoulders. He
looked up from his hammering. "So, what can I do for you?"
He gestured to a display case filled with elegant if understated
jewelry. A cigar box that served as a cash register was brimming.
Business was good in Heaven. He gave Jesus a long-suffering
look. "The Second Coming? Need another cross?"

"Clever," said Jesus. He lifted up Leo's dog tag, which the
jeweler scrutinized through his loupe.

"Nu?"

"My friend Levine here is Jewish."

"Not according to the US Army."

"A mistake. He is one of us. Can you help?"

The old jeweler sat back down. He gave a smug sigh; "You

sing, I dance." Leo handed over the dog tag. The jeweler hammered away, polished the tag, and smiled at his handiwork. "Today you are a mensch. No charge."

Jesus said his work was done "In heaven as it is on earth." And Leo Lavin felt a weight drop. He went to the Jewish barracks, where they were lining up for Glenn Miller's show. A few whispers of "Isn't that Ish Kabibble?" went unnoticed.

Visitors to the US Military Cemetery in Normandy walk amongst graves. They focus on the names, the ages etched on the stones. Scant details of people who died for them. As the years go by, few have any direct connection to the dead; families, friends, comrades have mostly passed on, too. The pilgrims have to imagine who these soldiers were, and who they could have become, based on the inadequate information etched on crosses and stars.

Jews in particular are drawn to one that stands at attention. It's an especially brilliant piece of white Lasa marble in the shape of a star bearing the name Leo Lavin.

(This story is based on a little reality. About 550,000 Jewish Americans fought in World War II, making up 3.4 percent of the 16 million Americans who served. The cemetery at Normandy only had 149 Stars, but statistics say there should have been about 330 Jewish grave markers there, and there are many seemingly Jewish names on graves there marked with crosses. In recent years, some of those markers have been changed to stars. The same is true with American cemeteries elsewhere. Sometimes it was simply a mistake. The military simply put crosses on the graves of some Jews who died on the Bataan Death March. In other cases, like with Leo, Jews scratched out the 'H' on their dog-tags or got new ones to avoid the inevitable difficulties if captured by the Germans. Indeed, several Jewish POWs were sent to a concentration camp and suffered other indignities, though the legacy for the most part of Jewish POWs was one of equal treatment to their non-Jewish comrades.)

23.

The Old Clock Stopped

The old clock stopped. Facing it was its chronological counterpart: a mirror suffering age spots that distorted the clock's image stuck at 6:32. It stopped there like the final date on a gravestone. Its brass pendulum dangled dormant below the face.

It was new on their wedding day. The groom's father had proudly called it a "Regulator," an accurate wall clock in an oak cabinet that would ring out the hour twenty-four times a day.

"There," his father said, starting the pendulum on its swing. "It will be a friend forever, beating its heart to mark where you've been, where you are, and . . ."

"Where I'm going." The groom, his son, finished for him.

"Hah. And where all of us are going. It will mark time as we all step ahead. Would that it beats long after I'm gone."

It was a clock you'd find in a train station or classroom, accurate and utilitarian, efficient and practical, the way his father expected his son to lead his life.

The Regulator had to be key-wound each morning. And the son did just that, wound it while his wife, and later the cook, made breakfast. Then children would do it, fighting for turns until the day arrived when they'd argue that it was someone else's chore. He was happy to take back the job.

It had ticked and tocked across from the mirror since the first Roosevelt had been in the White House. The Gustav Stickley

169

mirror came from her widowed mother. She never knew her father. He died just before she was born from — so it was said — a mini ball that entered his spine at Gettysburg. On that wedding day, when they got the clock from his father, her mother stood in front of the mirror and said, "It's so you can look at yourselves as the years pass and remember all that is reflected." She looked around to make sure no one was listening and then whispered to her daughter, "I believe that mirrors hold those images forever."

The bride rolled her eyes. Her mother was, after all, a spiritualist, forever holding séances and playing with a Ouija board to her daughter's eternal amusement. Decades later, when Ike was in charge, that same daughter sat back into the comfy armchair under the clock lullabied by its soft ticking and her memories. She smiled into the mirror believing at that moment that her mother has been right all along. She never woke up.

Her children teased each other over elements of the will, minor things they could laugh about, but agreed that the clock and the mirror should stay together facing each other as they always had. The daughter got them because she still had young children. They would sit in front of the clock counting as it chimed out the hours. She would tell them the mirror held the memories and, if they were patient, they might see themselves growing up, as she could, at one time, see herself and her mother and her grandmother.

"It's like beating the speed of light and looking back!" exclaimed her eleven-year old son.

Or maybe the mirror holds memories in its heart," said the mother. "And how on earth do you know about the speed of light?"

"Star Trek!"

Five-year-old James climbed the chair to put his ear to the mirror. "I can hear, too. And I hear the clock when it was little!"

There was a practical element to her getting the clock. Her husband was a mechanical engineer who liked to tinker. If the need arose, he could fix it. Other than polishing the wood and oil-ing the mechanism, he never had to do anything beyond the daily wind. That came to an end when the children would play "Inka-dink, a bottle of ink" to determine who would wind it. Then they moved out to college, careers, life, and another will.

James was given the task of emptying out the house. His brother didn't care.

"Give that stuff to Goodwill," he'd written in an email to the estate attorney.

That directive generated a phone call.

"But what about getting ahead of the speed of light! Remem-ber that?" James asked.

The older brother said he didn't know what he was talking about.

The sister asked for some photo albums and that "Dear Na-vaho rug Gramps got when he worked on the reservation."

James reminded her that it had been appraised on the An-tique Road Show for $28,000, and she retorted that they always "hyped" the values. After some back and forth and one angry hang-up, she agreed to reduce her share of the inheritance by $10,000 to cover the rug. He could have everything else in the house.

"But you pay for the hauling. It's only fair." His sister was adamant about that.

As it turned out, Goodwill happily sent a truck for the con-tents. He took the clock and mirror. And the tax break. It was only fair. The drivers admired the furniture, commenting that they knew how to make things back in the sixties. They didn't see much demand for shaggy carpets or the avocado-colored re-frigerator, but "who knew," they said, and took it all away. Ev-erything, except for an old clock and a cracked cherry frame that held a blotchy mirror. The driver told James, now in his sixties, that the mirror could be replaced at Home Depot. "The frame might be worth something," he added.

They were the last things to leave the empty home.

James placed them facing one another in his home office and wound the clock for the first time since his mother had died months before. He tapped the pendulum with his fingertip to get it beating, adjusting the hands to 4:17. He had to smile at the Roman numeral IIII. His grandfather once explained that this is what was done for symmetry; "See, Jamie, there are four numbers with Xs and four with Vs and four with only Is. You're right, it should be an IV for the number four, but then you'd have too many Vs."

"And balance, too!" Jamie said. "Eight would be the only number with four letters: V, I, I, and another I. Only the four could be done that way, I, I, I, and I."

His grandfather looked at the clock, figuring out that James was right; no other number could have four Roman numbers. "Well done, Jamie. Well done." His grandfather looked at James differently after that.

That evening, the clock rang out at five, six, and seven. James lifted his head at the familiar sound, then gave his full attention to an episode of *Mystery* on PBS. It was only when the show ended that James realized he'd stopped hearing the chimes. A flick on the pendulum resulted in a lifeless swing slowing into a flaccid dangle. He tried winding it. The clock offered a few hopeful tick-tocks, the pendulum moving in a feeble arch, the chimes ringing the eight bells they'd lost two hours earlier. And as if exhausted by such effort, the clock came to a rest.

His father would know what to do, but Dad was gone these thirty years, and James had to watch a YouTube tutorial before changing a light bulb. He searched the site for antique clock repairs and found dozens of videos narrated by strange men with odd tools or odd men with strange tools hovering over the autopsied remains of once upon a time.

The instructions offered were strikingly similar; open the clock face to reveal the works. But when it came to the levers —

172

half a dozen whose names didn't match to their purpose, to say nothing of an escapement, gear train, and more wheels than a Good Year dealer — James suddenly felt lost.

And so it stayed. Sometimes, James would wake to imagine he heard the chimes. What woke him weren't the rings, but the loneliness of their absence.

He wasn't the only one to feel that way. "Gramps," a visiting granddaughter reminded him, "can I wind it, please?"

"Oh, that thing stopped. Busted."

"Forever?"

"I don't know. Maybe. It's an old thing like your Grampa." That didn't get the laugh he'd hoped for.

"Will they throw it away then?"

Throw it away? James hadn't thought about it, didn't want to think about it. If it was up to his brother and sister, that timepiece would have ended up in the trash heap. Goodwill wouldn't sell it, couldn't sell it. But he kept it. He kept it on the wall, wound it, polished the thing. It wasn't just some busted eyesore. He told his granddaughter no, they wouldn't throw it away. All she said was, "Good." It was all she needed to say. Calls to clock repair shops came after that. Futile calls. The problem was antique clocks were no longer in vogue and the clock repair trade had followed. When James googled for repair shops, the few websites he went to advertised that the URL was available. Others teased with phone numbers no longer in service. And when a connection was made, the voice on the other end of the line was usually gruff. "Not that old," they'd tell him. James did find a place that called itself The Clockery. The Clockery was now fixing phones. He got his cracked screen replaced for a reasonable price.

"Phonery didn't sound very good, so I kept the name. My dad does, or did, the clock thing," said the owner. "A labor of love. Not a labor of a living, if you catch my drift."

"Do you think he'd do a special job for me? I'd pay for it."

"If you ask, he'd say yes a thousand times."

"That's great!"

"Hold your horses. He'd say yes a thousand times because he'd forget he'd just said yes. He's in a memory facility. Somewhere. Can't exactly remember where."

"You don't know?"

"Joke. I know. But I'm sorry to tell you he couldn't fix a light bulb anymore."

He considered a replacement. It wasn't the cost; the lack of demand that squelched the repairmen's lot also dampened the price of antiques in perfect repair. Old they were, but new to him and that made all the difference. He almost bought one, an Ansonia. The clock, though it was from a town that had rusted out years before, still ticked nicely. The gong was crisp. But it hadn't ticked for his family. It was a foster clock.

Family couldn't help him. Nor friends. Nor could a query on Craigslist. The latter generated curious responses, including one teasing a better time than any clock's hands could provide. He was impressed with the creativity, even if they didn't promise to ring his specific chimes. It was back to YouTube and a regret that his mechanical insights stopped at righty-tighty.

"Jim, it's me. You'll never guess what I found."

It was a call from a friend who had come across a shop somewhere in Vermont that claimed it could fix old clocks. The name of the shop, displaying evident Yankee frugality, was The Clock Man. James asked about a website. His friend cautioned that he'd be lucky if they had a phone. "It's not exactly a state-of-the-art facility. Maybe it was in '98; 1898. But I'll tell you, Jim, they got all these clocks that ring out at the same time. That's got to be a good sign."

James googled the shop and found an address, a name, and a URL from a *Yankee Magazine* piece on back roads of New England from 1983. A photo of the shop looked like a set for a Norman Rockwell painting.

James called and called and called again. There was no answering machine and he very much doubted it was a cell phone that would notify him of each missed call. Luck finally struck one morning.

"Hello? Is this 'The Clock Man'?"

A voice said, simply, "Clock Man." James was able to get in a few words, but after the word "Regulator," he was interrupted by a loud gulp of some liquid and a brusque admonition that he couldn't tell a thing without looking at the clock "in the flesh."

James thought he had to provide more information, or anyway get some, so he tried to ask if Clock Man had worked on a Regulator. Before he could finish, Clock Man confirmed that he'd worked on some.

"Not a lot, mind you, a few dozen. I hate those Regulators."

That comment worried James. How could a clock man hate a clock?

"Mr. James, was it? They made them to put a clock repair shop like mine, which was my father's, by the way, after the war, the Great War that is, out of business. You follow?" James explained it was just James, no need for Mister, and that he only sort of followed.

"Best damn clocks to tick themselves into oblivion. If they hadn't gone under in the Depression, we might have gone under. German springs, you see. Tariffs did 'em in. US of A springs didn't hold up, and don't ask about the junk from Japan. Then it was electric clocks. I hated those, too. Real crap but kept the business up. Do you know the Kit-Cat Klock?"

James confessed he didn't.

"Sure you do. Cat's eyes move one way, tail goes the other, belly is the clock face. Sold thousands. Had a running ad in *Yankee Magazine*. Thirty years it was. At least. I think that's why they did the piece on me. Pulled it next year. Know why?"

James confessed he didn't.

"Started making them in China. Not red China, but China still. Think I'd sell something made in China? Think again."

James let Clock Man go on though he didn't think he could have stopped him except by hanging up the phone, and he still had the issue of his broken clock. Clock Man went off a while about being retired, but not really, worrying who'd take over when his "spring got sprung." He sounded teary about the fine clocks no one bothered to pick up and how he thought that was cruel.

"I see it in their faces, you know. I mean real clocks, not those electric gee gahs, and I don't touch ones that glow. You don't have one that glows, do you?"

James reminded him that his was a Regulator, but Clock Man stopped him. "Oh, yeah, I hate those, but if anyone alive can fix it, it's probably me. Bring it in tomorrow."

"Tomorrow? Bring it in? I could FedEx it if that is any easier."

The phone went silent for the only dead air of the call.

"You care about this clock? You told me it's been in your family over one hundred years. Would you be okay if FedEx broke it? Lost it? I don't have a lot of time on my hands. Don't have a lot of time, period. I fix clocks that people care about. You care? You bring it wrapped in a thick blanket."

James replied, "You're right, of course," embarrassed that he'd be so cavalier as to think he could post it in the mail as if it was some Amazon thing made in China. "And I'll put it in bubble wrap for protection."

A burst came through the phone. "No bubble wrap! A blanket, wool if you have it. You want to keep it warm. Keeps the oil from gunking up. Worst thing you can do to a Regulator. And keeps the veneer from cracking. You know it's got a veneer. Walnut. They really knew how to make those Regulators, why, I could . . ."

Clock Man went on again. James listened at first, then offered a series of "a huhs," managing to finish the *New York Times* crossword for that Thursday when Clock Man suddenly asked, "You still there?"

James coughed out a thanks for the fascinating history, intrigued by the man's knowledge, trying to recall some details from Clock Man's oration to prove he'd listened the whole time before finishing off with, "And no bubble wrap."

That Vermont is a rural state will come as no surprise. But just how rural the part of Vermont where Clock Man took root surprised James. He drove on a dirt road that edged beside a meandering river with ice forming along its edges. He passed sorry-looking dairy farms with sagging barns and broken silos supplemented with rusting "Genuine Vermont Maple Syrup" signs. The handful of Holsteins still in some of the fields made him wonder if there'd be more once they'd uttered their final moo.

He almost missed a faded wooden sign in desperate need of paint that stood in front of a home demanding a painter in equal measure. And carpenter. And roofer. The sign read "Clock Man" and, with the meticulous clarity of the man himself, "Clocks and Repairs" below that.

James jingled the bells that hung from the door marking the workshop. A gruff voice said, "It's open." He opened the door but wasn't sure he could make it any farther. Confronting him was a wall of clocks, all registering the exact time of 8:52, and boxes and tables covered with more boxes, along with the internal organs of innumerable clocks. A voice at the far end of the room commanded, "Go left." James was just able to squeeze through a narrow gap into a canyon of clocks that ended at a counter. An elfin old man in overalls sat behind it. He squinted behind thick glasses, his head tilted to one side, assessing James on his approach.

"Buying or selling?" asked the old man.

"Repairs, actually. I called."

"Good, because I'm not buying, and if you said you were buying, I'd drop dead of another heart attack. A repair maybe I can do. Where's the patient?"

James retrieved the blanket-wrapped clock, again having to edge sideways down the aisle toward Clock Man. He moved at a cautious pace, taking in the mixed aroma of sawdust, shellac, oil, and age. The old clock faces looked down on him, stoic and proud.

Had it been any other time, seconds earlier, seconds later, things would have been different. But it was 9:00 on the button, and right as he put his arms forward to lay his clock on the counter, the chimes of thirty-three clocks rang at once. As a startled James jumped back, the clock leaped forward, and the two feet separating them from the counter was enough to allow the clock to fall mightily to the floor.

Clock Man leaned over the counter, watching James as he collected the remains of an 1897 Regulator Clock. "You'll want to watch that glass," he said, handing over a brush and a dustbin. He went on with a set of aggressive — no argument — instructions: "Bring the works up here," "Mind that spring," "Don't bend the hands." Each order was connected with a "dammit." James did as he was told. He felt like he was a five-year-old who'd let the puppy wander out the front door. When he'd put the debris in front of Clock Man, he had to wipe his tears with his sleeve.

James looked at the pile of broken wood, shattered glass, and unknown components of steel and brass. The only thing more or less intact was the face. He thought about a burial. He thought maybe he'd collect it all and just keep it in a box, pieces of a past.

Clock Man rummaged through the heap, dividing the remains into random piles, "ahems" and "ah hahs" accompanying the effort.

"No problem."

"What?"

"Well, not a major problem."

He looked past James and let out a cheery, "Hello." James turned to follow his gaze. There was no one. Perhaps Clock Man's springs had sprung after all. Clock Man maneuvered himself around the counter, holding its edge for support, his eyes searching down a narrower aisle than the one James had taken.

It was a slow amble marked by the ticking of the surrounding clocks. James started to count with the ticks but lost track after twenty.

Clock Man stopped halfway down the aisle, looking up. "Hey, give me a hand here." James joined him to stare at an Ansonia Regulator, same model, same year, same face as his own. Identical almost. Had he not just shattered it he would have sworn that this was his. But, the more he studied the Regulator, the more he could see the differences. The veneer wasn't quite so crinkled. The luster was brighter. The pendulum lacked dings. And it was working. The ticking, the tocking, the movement were jittery; not quite what he was used to. Clock Man reached up and moved the hour hand ahead. The chimes were sharp and loud. James had expected softer bongs. James felt the pang he'd had when his mother passed away at 106.

"Can you take that down for me?"

"Thanks, but you know it's just not my clock. It's a beauty. But, I don't know, it sounds . . . odd.'"

"Good ears, huh? They come in handy. Now, if you don't mind." Clock Man swept his hand in front of the clock.

Clock Man led the way back down to the counter. He used his arm to move the piles aside and helped James lay the new clock down. He gave James a wink and opened the clock face to reveal the mysterious works behind. His eyes went back and forth, from the new clock to the piles of innards of the old one. He took his time. If he heard the array of chimes sound yet another hour, he paid no attention. Nor did James, wondering what he was up to, too anxious to ask.

"Yep, I can do it. Gimme, say, three weeks. Maybe less."

James apologized for not believing what he was hearing.

"It's smashed to smithereens. How?"

He didn't explain so much as instruct. He reminded James of an earlier talk about the Regulators being well made, exceptionally so. The works, as he put it, are what's important. The works

179

were what kept the time, made sure the thing chimed when it was meant to. And the works could be put back together. The face, too.

"But it won't be the same."

Clock Man smiled. "The heart of it, the brains, the voice, they'll be the same. The face, the face you've been watching, that'll be the same. The box? The box is just the wardrobe. You change your clothes?"

James nodded.

"Ever buy two of the same shirt because you like 'em?"

James nodded again.

"Same clock, different shirt, simple as that. Its heart, really all that matters, will be yours."

James's nodding this time was slower.

He came back three weeks later. When he entered the shop, the only ticking came from the clock hanging behind the counter. "Turned the others off for you," said Clock Man. "How's it sound?" James smiled into the familiar face before him. He didn't even try to hide the tears when the clock struck nine.

He paid cash as Clock Man had insisted. He paid for the restoration and for the other clock that was, as Clock Man put it, the donor. James asked about its innards. Clock Man smiled. "Gotta guy who has a Regulator some jackass made electric. Time to give it back a heart."

24.

Admissions Process

It was not as if the boy's pleas were falling on deaf ears, not at all. Henry Munroe heard him loud and clear, his impatience growing each time the child asked. Was he oblivious? If a teacher meant no, did he physically have to say no? Perhaps subtlety had been removed from the standard curriculum along with Tom Sawyer, The Odyssey, and decent handwriting. Or was this guy, this teenager, just another one of a litany of spoiled, entitled kids, in this rich island of a town in the midst of a sea of rich towns, who had never been told no?

Honestly, Amherst. Did he expect to get into Amherst?

Munroe cleared his throat with a studied ahem that came out as a cough. "Look, Robert. I've had you for less than one semester. I hardly know anything about you. I wouldn't do you justice."

Munroe didn't mean justice. He meant that he didn't want to be bothered by Rob; no one called him Robert. Munroe didn't want to be bothered by anyone, certainly not some half-wit student seeking to get into his alma mater.

"But you wrote one for Janet Markovitz. And Fleming, I think. He said he was going to ask."

Munroe looked away for a second, tightening the ends of his bowtie as he thought about Janet Markovitz. She was a different kettle of fish. Smart, to be sure, and engaged. She positively raved over Munroe's fiction work he rarely shared and was more rarely published. The girl had an eye for talent, a rare quality amongst the grade grabbers that dominated his classes and the school in general. She gave him his desired respect. And she was very unpopular for it.

It was no wonder she was nervous when she approached him.

Munroe always made a show of his disdain in writing recommendations. When he saw a request coming, he'd roll his eyes up, close his lids slowly, lean his head to one side and inflate his sunken cheeks just before offering the deep exhale of discouragement.

These were the contrived clues he wanted to provide, to make the students know they were the ones in need of a favor and needed it from him. In return, he wanted to make them sweat. Happily, he got few requests. But in recent days, he'd give in a little if the student was smart enough, if the student was deferential enough, if the student was lonely, nerdy, an outsider. If the student was like Henry Munroe had been. Janet hit all the high points.

In these recent days, it was less a pain to write a tight handful of chosen recommendations than to confront, once again, with the administration on the issue of his attitude. In these recent days, they had measurable objectives, metrics they called them. Metrics to prove you were a good teacher by the number of students who wanted your class, by their SATs, by where they went to college. And by how many college recommendations you wrote. Even the union insisted he try to get more involved with the students on that one.

Munroe was never criticized for his teaching; there were no metrics for students actually learning.

Fleming, Ian Fleming of all things, was Munroe's type: offbeat, slight, and slightly effeminate, probably gay, but didn't know it and bullied like most sensitive kids and probably couldn't stand Sunday nights. He found Fleming once trying to hide in his locker in tears. Munroe considered putting his hand on the boy's shoulder but thought better of it. He told Fleming to take a deep breath and that he'd be happy to hear what was upsetting the boy.

Fleming dismissed him with a "It was nothing" and brightened up. "Hey, Mr. Munroe, I reread 'Paul's Case.' I liked it, though I think you're right, Holden Caulfield is the more tragic figure. That was a good class."

Munroe lifted his chin in acknowledgment, thinking, Screw that Ratemyteacher app.

For those types, those kids, Munroe could write decent recommendations, even great ones. For the few he wrote as a sop to the Union, his recommendations would merely be okay. For all the others who would dare ask him, it was a finger-pointing down the hall, to some else, someone who'd give the child in question the praise they "undoubtedly deserved" but weren't about to get from Henry Munroe. Those kids got the point.

"Mr. Munroe?"

Munroe looked back to Rob. "Well, as I suggested, I think there is a teacher who could do you a solid. (Munroe was pleased that he could come up with such a colloquialism.) I've seen you positively animated with Mr. Glascock." The image gave Munroe a moment of satisfaction.

"He's a gym teacher! I need someone from humanities. And English is an humanities."

Munroe tilted his head and said, "An humanities? I see. Is that your intended major?"

If Rob got the slight, he didn't show it.

Munroe wanted to say no. He wanted to be strong, definitive, to tell Rob he'd write a lousy recommendation because that's what he deserved. He wanted to say that the only reason he never reported his frequent absences and tardiness—he couldn't bring himself to say latenesses—was because he didn't notice and didn't care one whit about him or his jock friends or the fact he drove to school in a car Munroe couldn't afford.

"I'll give it some thought, but don't think I'll change my mind. You do the same. Come up with an alternative and we'll compare notes."

"You're great, Mr. Munroe. Simply the best. Thanks so much. This is a real relief."

Munroe's left arm rose in wonder. His right arm would have risen as well but then the armful of books would have fallen to the floor and those included not only Moby Dick but the Moby Dick SparkNotes he would need to reread. He tried to say to Rob, in no uncertain terms, there was nothing to thank him for, not at all. He hadn't said yes; he had merely not said no.

In the teacher's lounge, Rick Goldman, AP calc and stats, sipped his coffee and shook his head with a grin that spelled trouble. "Munroe, is it true? You're writing a recommendation for Robby Montgomery? Talk about opposites attracting."

"Whatever gave you that idea?" said Munroe.

"His dad," replied Goldman.

"HIS DAD?" said Munroe.

"Yeah, I ran into him with some lacrosse recruiter. Bowdoin I think, maybe Colby. Someplace in Maine."

Munroe stammered that he hadn't said yes. All he'd said was that Robert — Robby — would do better with someone else, someone who knew him; he left out that he didn't like him, not one bit. He pushed Goldman, asking whom he thought would be better.

"Search me. He's an obnoxious prick. He asked me, and I said no. Fact is, I asked him to drop stats, but he rallied. Doing quite well, to be honest. And I can use extra bodies in class."

Extra bodies. The administration was constantly looking at the less popular courses and cutting them for classes that made the school look good on paper, in papers, and in the college acceptance statistics. Munroe was momentarily grateful he taught a core curriculum course.

He was not, however, grateful for his inability to get one student to grasp his meaning, his nuance, to say nothing of his genius. He envied Goldman's direct if somewhat coarse demeanor. His was too gentle, too cerebral, too fey, and now, not for the first time, he hated himself. How could he extricate Henry Munroe from being Henry Munroe?

"Well done, Munroe!"

He turned to face the smoker's rasp of the department chair, "Oh, hi, Allison. I didn't see you there."

"Lost in thought? Thinking about Robby Montgomery's letter, no doubt."

"Yes. I mean, no. Ah, a bit maybe. How do you know about that?"

She explained, "Good news travels fast. Surprised, I must say. Goldman mentioned it."

GOLDMAN.

"I didn't offer, Alison. He just pleaded, really, and . . ."

"And your heart melted. Happens. No matter. It's a good thing. Takes the edge of your elitism. Wears the leather patches off your elbows, so to speak! "

Munroe asked about trying to find a substitute, his subtlety giving way to desperation. He got no takers but did get responses:

"Can't stand the kid."

"Smart with emphasis on alecky."

"Cuts corners, cuts classes. Did well on the boards, I'll give him that."

And finally, "Me? I've got enough of them. Couldn't do him justice anyway. Say, did you try Glascock?"

Munroe tried not to think about Rob, but the more he tried, the more he thought about him. He kept his distance from most students, all students, deliberately. The privileged few he'd written recommendations for were easy enough. After all, he was an English teacher and writing recommendation letters came easy, easier than his fiction. But he resented being asked and resented not being able to say no. With Rob — Robby — Montgomery, he was cornered.

185

The hard-copy form Rob brought to him said explicitly it was to be submitted electronically. "These are some ideas, notes, you know, about me. Highlights," said Robby. Attached was a sheet of handwritten scribble. At least it wasn't written in crayon.

Munroe looked down his nose, or tried to, but Rob had four inches on him. Instead, he looked as if he was preparing to put in eye drops.

"Are you having a nosebleed, Mr. Munroe? I can get some tissues."

Munroe lowered his chin. "I'm fine, but these notes. You understand this is my appraisal, not yours."

"Sure, of course, I just wanted to give you some pointers. Mr. Goldman suggested it."

Goldman, again!

That night he sat with a glass of Armagnac and set to it. "Team player" didn't easily roll off Munroe's keyboard. He tried to come up with words as generic and noncommittal as possible but felt they didn't do justice to him—to Munroe, that is—in the literary sense. This was for Amherst, after all, his alma mater. With a self-loathing that forced his hands to shake he typed in the word "bonhomie" under the section "Positive Attributes." It took him fifteen minutes to come up with any others.

He wasn't ready to give up on his creativity but did give Rob's notes the once over. He got no inspiration. After a while, and another Armagnac, he was rewarded with a load of immature conceit hidden behind naïveté.

It must have been the Armagnac, because Munroe started to write what was in his heart. He wrote he knew Rob, hardly. Perhaps he was an adequate student. He could be polite—an odd thing to write, and Munroe smiled at doing so—which stood in contrast to the brazen bravado the three-time captain of the lacrosse team more consistently demonstrated. He'd answer if questioned, would contribute if pushed. Beyond that? "I can safely say he can both read and write but whether that's to Amherst's standards I offer no further comment."

Munroe was pleased. He'd written nothing untrue. He'd given Rob ample opportunity to choose another teacher. If Amherst thought of it as a half-hearted recommendation, they'd be generous. And besides, what he wrote would stay between him and the admissions officer who'd read it, assuming, which he assumed would not be the case, Rob's grades were sufficient to get his application past the initial scan.

Months later, word came in.

Janet Markovitz decided she was a lesbian and chose Smith. Ian Fleming decided on a large state college in the Midwest, for mechanical engineering, on an ROTC scholarship of all things. X got into Y. A was rejected at B but got into safety C.

Rob said nothing. That raised Munroe's curiosity each time he glanced over at the boy. Not a word to relay his disappointment? He'd become a more engaged student, remarkably so, since asking for the recommendation. Munroe wondered if he didn't deserve some solace for inspiring the boy. He thought maybe he'd been too hard on him. He thought maybe Robby didn't get into any school.

Which was why he was caught by utter surprise when Rob lifted him off the ground in an enormous hug, his tears staining Munroe's bowtie. "I made it. Off the waitlist. Thank you, thank you, thank you, Mr. Munroe. A thousand times and then some."

"Huh?" came back Munroe.

"I'm in! Amherst. First choice. Thank you, thank you, and thank you again."

Rob danced away, leaving Munroe shocked and confused. How had this happened? What had happened? Had he once more found himself too subtle for his own good?

A single call gave him the answer.

Before he could finish saying he wanted to offer the school his gratitude for accepting his student, the receptionist in Admissions interrupted. "Oh yes, we've been expecting you. Just a sec." She immediately put him through to the Director of Admissions.

"Munroe!!!" boomed a voice at the other end of the line. "How the hell are you, you dweebish pansy. It's been, what, twenty-five years?"

"I'm sorry, who is this?"

"Gordy Goddamn Adams!"

"Adams? What on earth?"

"Director, Admissions, you douche. So, you're teaching English now? The great American novel still on hold?"

Munroe stumbled, trying to convey he'd had some things published, mostly regional journals, but found his passion in teaching.

"Hah, and getting kids into college, too?" said Adams.

"Well, I wanted to express my gratitude, appreciation, for Rob—Robby. I must admit I wasn't fully confident he'd get in," offered Munroe.

"No thanks to your recommendation. Lucky for him it fell onto my lap."

"Yours?" said Munroe.

"Yeah, mine. I couldn't believe anyone could write such a thing, and then I saw your name and, like, duh, of course, you would. I called his dad, a big donor by the way, and asked for one more recommendation to get him over the edge. Math guy named Goldman. Yours I rolled up and put in the smallest room in my house. None the wiser. Get it? Anyway, the lacrosse coach wanted him. He was a shoo-in."

"A shoo-in?"

"Shoo-in. And Munroe, you don't want to pull that shit again. Okay?"

Over the next year, Munroe wrote a series of recommendations for Amherst and managed to get one more student jock in. She played lacrosse.

25.

Return of the Blob

The film had only just started when the blob filled the screen, blackening the panoramic shot of the upper Amazon, the foothills of the Andes in the distance, cinematography that demonstrated why it won the film an Oscar. The mass started on the left working its way painfully across "oompfs," "ouches," "watch-outs," and "what the hells," until it enveloped the area around one viewer and collapsed into his lap. A pained screamed that sounded like, "Oh God, my knees! I heard a crack," was followed by a perfunctory "'Scuse me," in a voice reverberating across the theater that echoed into a series of "quiets," "shut ups," and a "Christ almighty."

The mass rose, edged further down the row. He stood tall as the film rolled, taking his time to remove his coat and put down his goodies: a thirty-two-ounce keg of soda and a bucket of artificially buttered popcorn, its chemically rich odor wafting to the balcony while murmurs of "down up front," "sit," and "please, we're trying to watch the movie" wafted back. At last, Stanley Polodski sat down.

The film rolled, the rainforest sounds of birds and monkeys giving way to wind in the canopy and a fierce storm. Those explained the Academy Awards for sound editing and mixing. Offscreen, those in the theater heard munching and slurping, sounds emanating from Stanley as he bulldozed popcorn into his

189

chomping maw with one hand and sucked up the melting residual of ice through the straw in the super-sized cup grasped in the other.

A voice came from the seat behind him. "Can you eat any louder? Jesus." Stanley's arm shot up, and with a backward throw, a handful of greasy popcorn spread in a wide array toward the voice.

The now popcorn-covered patrons in the rows behind Stanley started to make their feelings known: "What the hell?!" "Animal." "Jerk!!" "Can't you shut up?" "We're trying to watch the movie."

One man, Greg Janner, sat quietly on the aisle seat of Stanley's row, annoyed but patient. He tapped the arm of his wife and whispered, "What a flaming asshole." She nodded and gave a "shh" that he barely heard. He took a few kernels of popcorn from the small box at his lap and relaxed in his seat while an immense anaconda slithered across the screen toward its prey. A tremendous eruption made him jump, made a lot of people jump, as Stanley belched most of the CO_2 that had once been in his container of Dr. Pepper. A loud "Pardon my French" followed.

"Disgusting," "Pig," and "Oh, my God" were now heard from the far corners of the theater. Most of the man's small box of popcorn flew up when he jumped, and much of that found its way onto the theatergoers surrounding him, including Stanley Polodski, who took not one but two handfuls of popcorn and threw them in Janner's general direction. Most landed on the people sitting between, but a particularly gooey clump landed on his wife, who yelled, "Gross!" as she used her fingers to pick through the well-distributed particles in her hair. '

"Right!" An athletic-looking man, late middle-aged, whose five-foot-seven frame belied his physical capabilities, stood up. He edged through the now standing audience to confront Stanley, whose bulk remained in his seat and whose elbows hogged the armrests on either side that he had obtained by steadily forcing off the arms that had been there originally. "Out!"

"Make me," said Stanley over the angry voices of pretty much everyone in the audience.

"You are ruining this for everyone. You're disgusting."

Stan took one handful of popcorn to his mouth and while chewing managed to say, "I mow you tar ut hot mam oy."

"What?"

A visible lump traveled down Stan's throat, not unlike the capybara the anaconda had just swallowed whole up on the screen.

"I know you are but what am I?"

A crowd gathered round, yelling at Stanley. An usher with Coke-bottle glasses and a hearing aid came forth, flashlight beaming into a full-moon face. "Stan. You better get going or I'll call the cops. I really will this time."

"Chill."

"No, Stanley. Anyway, how many movies can you watch in a day? I can't believe you're eating again. Honestly."

"Four."

"Four? We're only showing three."

"I liked Deadpool. Saw it twice."

The film stopped, and the lights came on. A tall, thin, young man sporting a hipster beard and an ill-fitting burgundy blazer with the theater's logo on the right breast pocket stormed down the aisle. He shook a five-D-cell flashlight, looked grim, lips pursed, eyes glaring. The gauges dangling from his mutilated earlobes made his ears flap back and forth like a charging elephant. He shoved the usher aside and raged over Stanley.

"Dude, out, now . . . got it?" He pointed over his shoulder with the flashlight, temporarily blinding the usher who cringed behind him.

"You almost blinded Algernon," said Stan.

"It's okay, Stanley," said the usher.

"Algernon?" came from several people, including the manager with the gauges who turned to look at him.

"It's a stupid nickname. My name's Herbert."

"Algernon's better."

"Keep out of it, Stanley!"

When the movie started up again, the manager yelled to the film booth, "Elmo! Stop the goddamn movie, you moron." Then he said to the audience, "We'll start from the top when Moby here leaves.

"And no previews!" yelled someone upfront.

"Can't help those," said the manager. "They're in the loop."

"I like previews," said Stanley.

"You are out of here unless you'd like a preview of this," said the manager, waving his flashlight over his head.

"I'm not sure I follow," said Stan. "I see a flashlight. You're threatening me with it. Where's the preview?"

"You're outta here."

Stanley stayed in his seat and much of the seats of those on either side of him. He retrieved the bucket of popcorn he somehow managed to squeeze between his thighs and threw it over the manager, who was joined by a very large and solidly built black man in a rent-a-cop uniform. The people surrounding him applauded.

In one stride, the guard stepped over the row in front of Stanley. In a very loud and very deep voice, he said, "Alright, pal. Done and done. Out!" Applause rose from throughout the theater.

"I haven't finished the movie or, for that matter, these . . ." he waved large boxes of Sno-Caps and Milk Duds and shook them like maracas. "Cha cha cha, amigo."

"Eat 'em elsewhere!"

"Alliteration. Not bad," Stanley said, opening the Sno-Caps and pouring out a large handful. Then he started tossing them, one by one, at the guard, who caught one in his mouth and immediately spat it out, hitting Stan square in the eye. He then attempted to lift Stan out of his seat.

"I can't budge him," he groaned, whereupon the manager joined and managed to pull his arms up, leaving the rest on solid ground. A muffled but distinct explosion, a rift of liquid rips, came from somewhere down in the seat. "Body-burp. Must have been the Indian food," said Stanley, settling back down.

A collective groan emitted from the dispersing crowd. One young woman, short, a tad heavyset, in a dusty blue business suit, stood on her tiptoes at the back of the throng. "What's going on?" she asked a man standing next to her.

"They're trying to throw that fat guy out."

"Why?"

"He's a pig and won't move."

"Ah," she said, swinging her briefcase to make room and moving to stand by the exit.

"Right!" The manager then pushed three buttons on his cell phone, tapped the speaker, and held it up for all to hear.

"9-1-1. What's the address of your emergency?"

"Bijoux Cineplex Three. We have a man disturbing the peace . . . He won't leave . . . He's throwing popcorn and stuff . . . Yeah, all over . . . Huh? No, won't leave . . . No, this isn't a crank call.. . . . What? Yeah, I'd say he attacked, with popcorn. And Sno-Caps . . . I am serious . . . Do I feel threatened? Yeah, I'm threatened . . . Okay."

Moments later two burly policemen parted the people in the aisle and approached the manager, guard, usher, and Stanley.

"He won't leave. He's throwing things."

The one with stripes on his sleeve glared at Stanley. "Why are you throwing things?"

"I'm not."

"HE IS!!!" shouted the crowd.

"Settle down, settle down. I'll handle this. What's all the popcorn doing on the floor then?"

"I spilled it."

Again, the crowed chimed in: "He's lying!" "We saw him." "He won't shut up!"

"Relax! Buddy, they say you made this mess and won't leave. Why don't you just make it easy? You don't want us to pull you in for disturbing the peace, now do you?"

"Is that really a crime, disturbing the peace?"

The two cops looked at each other, eyebrows squeezed. The one with the stripes took a deep breath and shook his head. "One of those nights," he said.

Algernon stammered out, "Stan, you don't even have a ticket. You're just going from movie to movie, and that's not allowed."

"Tattletale," said Stanley, tossing a Milk Dud at him.

"Trespassing it is! You're coming with us," said the one with the stripes. Stanley threw a Milk Dud at him as well.

It was only when he pulled out his Taser that Stanley put his hands into the air and stood, with effort, saying, "Top of the world, Ma. Top of the world." The audience cheered as he was led out in cuffs. On the way, the short woman edged toward Stanley and thrust a card into his pocket. Holding a pinky to her mouth and thumb to her ear, she mouthed, "Call me." The usher snuck the remaining box of Milk Duds into the pocket of his burgundy polyester vest.

Stanley was taken to night court, where the judge warned him he could get charged with a variety of offenses, not the least of which was contempt of court. Stanley belched, loudly, after the judge asked how he pled. Then he said, "Not guilty."

"You're kidding?"

"No, your honor. Not guilty."

"Look, Mr. Polodski, this is a misdemeanor. A $100 fine and you're out, done, go home. Stop wasting your time . . . and mine."

"It's the principle."

"What principle?"

"Innocent until proven guilty."

"I think an audience full of pissed-off moviegoers is pretty convincing evidence that you should just pay the fine and maybe start eating better."

"My lawyer says otherwise."

"Your lawyer?"

"I plead the fifth."

"I drank a fifth!" said a swaying man who was yet to be brought before the judge on public intoxication charges.

The judge rolled his eyes, as did the policemen behind Stanley, the clerk, and the two kids who'd been arrested for stealing a radio from a BMW. Then the judge set the date for a hearing. Stanley agreed—under duress, he said—to pay a $100 fine for littering.

He fingered his pocket, hoping for a lost Milk Dud, but only found a business card of one Amy Resnick, Center City Defense, with a crude drawing of a well-built man in a dark suit holding a briefcase. Stanley wasn't sure if it was meant to be a lawyer or criminal. He called the number, 462-2424, because the letters preceding it read, "IMA-BICH." He liked that.

"Center City Defense. Resnick speaking. How can we protect you?"

"Uhh, I found your card in my pocket. I was at the movies and . . ."

"Stanley Polodski, right?"

"Yeah. I paid a fine but they . . ."

"Want you back for a hearing, pending trial on a series of petty issues that in aggregate could get you a hefty fine and a record and you need a defense."

"I'm not sure . . ."

"Don't interrupt me. You need a defense. That's not a question. That's a fact."

"Okay, but I don't want to pay . . ."

"Much. No one does. We're a public service. Non-profit. We defend the innocent against the guilty. The little man against The Man, the . . ."

"I'm not little, I'm pretty . . ."

"Physically challenged. And discriminated against. There's more prejudice against people who are overweight than any other group . . . race, religion, even gender. Did you know that?"

"No, I . . ."

"It's not a question, it's a fact."

"Well, if it's free."

"You pay what you can afford. $500 should do it and, Stanley, trust me, the fines they'll put on you will be far more than that. And a record? Hah. That'll cost and in other ways."

"I already spent $100 on the littering fine."

"What? $100? Why'd you pay that?"

"The judge said so. I could leave if I paid, and I did throw stuff."

"You spilled it. I heard you. It's coercion and they won't get away with it. We'll get the money back and then some."

"You're hired!"

"You're represented!"

Two weeks later, the court clerk asked Stanley Polodski to come forward. A sweaty, nervous, and tired district attorney read details of the events in question. The judge occasionally looked over his half-glasses and either smirked or frowned as he read, "Trespassing, disturbing the peace, malicious intent, resisting arrest, indecent conduct, threatening behavior, attempted assault, littering . . ."

"Objection!"

"Who are you?" asked the judge.

"Amy Resnick, attorney at law. I represent Mr. Polodski."

"Counselor, this isn't a trial. It's a hearing. On misdemeanors, if I heard this fiction right."

"Then I want these outrageous charges dismissed."

"They are not charges yet, Ms. Resnick. This is a hearing to see if he should be charged. At your client's insistence."

"Oh. Well, throw out the littering."

"That's funny," said Stanley. "Throw out the littering. Get it?"

The judge banged the gavel. "Please keep it quiet. Now, why would we throw out anything yet, Ms. Resnick?"

"Double jeopardy! He paid a fine. Which we intend to recover."

"Again, counselor, he's not on trial and he paid a fine. It's done."

"Then why bring it up again?"

The DA intervened. "Hmm. Popcorn, Milk Duds, Sno-Caps, and the popcorn container. There are several instances."

"It's one instance, not several."'

"Ms. Resnick, how many hearings have you been involved with?"

"Your honor, that's not relevant and would prejudice the jury."

"Ms. Resnick, I'm asking out of curiosity. Let me point out there is no jury in a civil hearing. It's just me."

"And me," said the DA.'

"Whatever," said the judge.

"This is my first."

The judge looked hard at Amy Resnick. "Why am I not surprised? If this were a trial I'd sustain your objection, by the way. Listen, he paid the fine. However, if you say the charge was wrong, I would have to let the evidence go forth. Love the law, Ms. Resnick . . . by studying it. Please continue."

The DA raised his hand, signaling he had nothing further to add. The judge pushed up his glasses with his middle finger while eyeing Stanley. "You paid $100 for littering. I'll fine you $100 for each of the other offenses and dismiss assault and resisting arrest with or without the offending Milk Duds . . ."

"It was a Sno-Cap, your honor," came from the DA.

" . . . the offending candy and let you go your own way. That's $400. No record and, depending on what I hear next, I will or will not add a restraining order on your attendance at the movie theater in question for a period to be determined. Are you okay with that? Fine."

The DA pushed aside the papers in front of him and reached for a new folder for his next hearing.

"OBJECTION!"

"There's nothing to object to, Ms. Resnick. I saw your client nod his head. And anyway, it's a hearing. There's no evidence to object to!"

Stanley piped in, "I believe there's no evidence to which to object, your honor."

"Stanley, keep quiet and be done with it before I put a restraining order on you on behalf of this court," said the judge.

"Your honor, my client will behave. As he always has."

"I hope not, Ms. Resnick," said the judge.

"These accusations are simply unfair. Mr. Polodski has a metabolic issue that is behind his physical state. He is tormented by it. He's been teased, abused, harassed, and his emotions were taut that night, that very night, as he attempted to move to his seat. And he was attacked."

"Attacked, Ms. Resnick?"

"He was hit by the guard with a Sno-Cap! The manager threatened him with his flashlight!'"

"Where is this going, Ms. Resnick?"

"Bear with me, sir. He was already in an agitated state and to calm himself, he found comfort in food, in this case, Sno-Caps, Milk Duds, and well-buttered popcorn, after, again, sensing the prejudice against him as an obese person. The sound of him eating, well, he was only seeking a safe place."

"Ms. Resnick, he snuck into that theater without a ticket."

"Your honor, we can only imagine the contempt and derision Mr. Polodski received in each of the other theaters. He couldn't enjoy those films under the stares and sneers. But did he object, complain, yell, and make noises in those theaters? No, sir, he did not. Rather he left those theaters to seek the entertainment he'd paid for but was unable to enjoy. It should be Stanley Polodski complaining. Clearly, something happened in that second theater . . ."

"Third. He was at the third."

"Third then. Even worse. The poor man. Something happened that provoked him, and I put forth he was the victim of a societal view of what makes an attractive physique."

"And the throwing of food?"

"Defense, your honor. Self-defense. Beneath their cruel words and admonitions, he had no way to defend himself, and it would hardly be fair for him to have left the theater because of, because of a characteristic that others didn't like. Have we not moved beyond such a system? Do we apply Jim Crow to waistlines? A gentlemen's agreement to double chins?"

"He made obscene noises."

"When is flatulating—yes, let's call it what it is—a crime? What it is, is a digestive disorder. Would a sneeze expelling pathogens have been more acceptable?"

"The officers who escorted him out of the theater said he refused to cooperate until they had threatened him."

"Scared, your honor. My client is a lonely, scared man. He was only trying to show the officers that he was, ahh, umm.. . . ."

"What, counselor?"

"That he was worthy of their friendship, hence offering them Sno-Caps."

"By throwing them?"

"By giving them in the only way he could. It's hard for him to lean over. Due to his disability."

At this Stanley leaned over an inch and groaned at the effort. "So true, sir. So true."

The judge rolled his eyes again and looked at the DA.

"Do you want to add anything to this?"

"Sir?"

"You're the DA. Do you have anything to say?"

"Well, no. I mean, it's about a few fines, really. I was looking at the next case."

The judge's eyes rolled. Down went the gavel. "Done. Counselor, please advise your client that if I see him in here again with any of this nonsense, I won't be so generous. I'd advise you to advise him to keep away from that theater. Tell him to try Netflix."

"I watch Netflix," said Stanley.

"Good. Try The Crown. $400 to be paid to the clerk. And restitution to the Cineplex: three movies broken into. That's $40."

"I paid for one ticket."

"$30 then. And quiet in my court."

Amy Resnick cleared her throat and waved her hand. The judge looked up, a frown on his face.

"Yes?"

"About the first $100 fine, your honor. Under the circumstances, I think it's only fair . . ."

The judge pointed his gavel menacingly toward the back of the courtroom, his eyes wide, and nodded his head at the doors. Amy Resnick smiled; elbowed Stanley, whose eyes had closed; and exited the room.

"My first case!! I won it."

"Yeah, but I'm out $500."

"Chump change. No record."

She attempted to give Stanley a hug, her arms fitting only partially around his torso, and Stanley reciprocated with a wet kiss on her lips, which she immediately wiped away with her arm.

"Stanley, that's not appropriate."

"What about attorney-client privilege?" he asked with an oddly flirtatious smile and a leer in his eye. She grimaced, backing away, and said he could expect copies of the relevant court papers as well as her bill.

Some weeks later, well after her second overdue bill was sent to Stanley, Amy decided to go to the last theater in the city playing Lady Bird. She went alone, as usual, but it wasn't all bad.

She could buy a large bucket of buttered popcorn and not feel self-conscious.

The only seats available were in the middle of the rows, single seats. She bent forward, apologizing as she squeezed through the narrow gap between the rows. Amy sat just as the lights dimmed and the coming attractions started to roll. It was during the trailer for the next Deadpool that she became aware of grunts, complaints, and a general disturbance in front of her. A mass was working its way up the row, stepping on toes, stumbling into people, and taking an inordinately long time to get to the one empty seat. It sat there, causing the metal frame to squeal under its weight as its limbs pushed aside the arms that had been on the armrests. It sat forward several times, loudly unwrapping boxes, before putting on a ski hat that stood up like a fez, largely blocking Amy's limited view.

"Excuse me, sir. Do you mind taking off your hat? It makes it hard for me to see the movie. Thank you."

Amy was immediately coated with most of the contents of a super-jumbo bucket of popcorn that Stanley Polodski tossed over his head.

26.

Sliding Home

Charlie O'Brien thought he heard the bell ring, although these days he could never be 100 percent sure. His hearing, which hadn't been great to start with, had grown lousy with the years. If indeed it was the bell, it would mean it was 3 p.m. Not that it mattered. He had an internal clock that ticked away in very accurate time, a talent he had gained over the last several decades. His ears may have missed the bell, but that internal clock told him school was out.

He went to his janitor's closet, his inner sanctum, and extracted the waxing machine from its spot. The thing had been in that closet of his almost since the day he'd started this job and it still worked like a charm. It was a heavy old aluminum buffer, and the old gal could still polish up a mirror finish. He'd replaced the pads on it at least thirty times. They were made of wool in the old days, lasting longer and buffing better than the new ones, which were probably made from some hifalutin stuff and came in colors that made his eyes water. Those colors turned to a shiny grey once the wax went on and buffing got started; it showed they were doing their job.

He loved the way the machine would slide across the linoleum floor and bring a glow to the dull sheen after the kids had scrambled over it. The routine was to buff them all once a week, but one hallway got it every day. He liked routines. Over the years, people from various school committees had passed through the halls of his school. If someone saw him tinkering with the waxing machine, they'd ask if he needed a new one. Charlie would look up from his reflection on the floor. No, he would say, this old one worked fine; always had, always would.

It was the grips he grew to love. When the machine hummed, those grips vibrated enough to give his hands a massage and, he was sure, tingle away the pain of his arthritis. If they ever forced a new on one him, he was determined to take this one home. Maybe he'd just let it vibrate in his hands. He'd had his hands massaged that winter in Belgium. It was in some basement that passed for an Army hospital, from an angel who passed as an Army nurse. She didn't speak much English, and Charlie didn't speak more than a few words of French, and he never did get her name. But he'd fallen in love with her, especially her smile.

He was reminded of that smile every morning. In his wallet was a crinkled photo of her, in her nurse's outfit, probably when she got out of school, she was so young. That smile was there with some French words on the back that Charlie never did understand and didn't dare to. He wanted to think she'd given it to him because she liked him and that the words said something like "to my love." He did recognize "mon chéri," and he hoped the smudge that followed was his name. Tears caused the smudge, he imagined. She'd gotten two packs of cigarettes from him the day she gave him that photo. Every morning when he looked at her face he worried if it was nothing more than a trade. And if it was, he thought, he'd got the better deal: a lifetime of "maybe."

Charlie kept all that a secret. And anyway, whom would he tell?

A few kids, not many, always stayed late after school because their parents wouldn't be home. A couple of them only had the one parent. A teacher would get paid a bit extra to watch over them in a classroom. It was usually the same group of kids. They got along, behaved nicely, and got a jump on their homework.

These were young kids, elementary school, meaning lots of energy, and it bothered Charlie that they were cooped up when they should've been out playing. Heck, thought Charlie, they could see kids playing kickball just outside. He felt bad for those kids left behind.

Which was why, first thing, after three every day, he waxed the floor outside that particular classroom, even when it didn't need any waxing. His kids would stand inside the doorway, watching as he talked to himself and moved the humming machine back and forth down the hall. Right as he turned the corner at the end of the hallways, he'd signal the children with a thumbs-up. They'd already have their shoes off, boys and girls both. They'd run halfway down the hallway to locker number 122 before sliding as far as they could. The furthest anyone ever slid was to locker number 156, a record set in 1958. Once, every few years, Charlie would paint those lockers in a dull institutional green, every one except for 122. That one he painted orange to mark the starting line. He then put a star sticker on 156 to mark the record held by Ross "Gasser" Gassior. Hundreds of kids over the years had tried and failed at beating Gassior's achievement. None made it past 148.

Charlie played the role of the official for this after-school challenge. He'd stand at the end of the hallway, making sure the kids started at locker 122 and determining where they stopped; someone was always trying to eke out a few more inches to get to the next locker. That was, at least, what the kids thought Charlie was doing. In reality, Charlie was there to make sure no one got hurt if they slipped. The teacher, who was, in theory, supposed to oversee the after-school program, might get in trouble for letting them out of her sight.

He remembered back to when it started. A Miss Faucett was the teacher. He'd forgotten her first name, if he ever knew it, a first-year teacher of the third grade. She was nice to him, not condescending, always asking about his day. She called him

Mister, formal, but respectful. She reminded him of that Belgian nurse. Charlie took a liking to her. He would smile, his eyes looking down, but he had little more to offer. That little more was brushing the snow off her car when the weather demanded it and throwing some sand under the tires so she could get out. Later, he did that for all the teachers, but it started with Miss Faucett.

Those smiles stayed with him even after he watched one afternoon as a man, younger than him and without a limp, picked her up in a green sports car, a Triumph TR2. The man had a grey tweed jacket, an Ivy League crew cut, and pearly white teeth behind an assessing smile, which he somehow managed while biting on an unlit briar pipe. Charlie's eyes fixed on the thick silver ring on the pipe's stem. The man jumped out of the car to give her a big hug and kiss — inappropriate around the school, Charlie thought.

She wouldn't be interested in a guy like him, who walked funny, didn't have much of a job, rarely had much to say anyway. Also, he had that hearing issue, a result of the explosion that hit his leg. Earned him a Purple Heart and got him on a ship back home. This is the sob story Charlie told himself whenever he took a fancy to a new teacher or most other women on the rare occasion he met someone new. He was just Charlie, the school janitor.

"Charlie, do you have a moment?"

It was the principal, Mister Barrone, the new guy, who'd only been at the school a few months. He took the helm from Waldo Weatherbee, the man who'd hired Charlie way back when. Charlie liked Weatherbee. He almost got as much of a kick out of his name, a name he shared with the principal in the Archie comics, as the kids did.

Weatherbee was also fond of Charlie. He'd taken off a couple of years to serve, like Charlie, and also got hurt in his leg. "Well, Mister Charlie, I'll hire you and you know why?" That's what he asked when Charlie applied for the job. "I'll tell you why, young man. Because if I have to chase you down for something, you won't outrun me!" Weatherbee's belly, which had already started to expand, jiggled with his deep laugh.

His esteem for Weatherbee grew from then on but surged one day when an old prune of a teacher, Florence Bragdon, had sent an eight-year-old boy crying to the principal's office with the rolled-up copy of an Archie she had whacked across his face when the boy started giggling over the name Waldo Weatherbee.

Weatherbee was walking down the hall just as the boy was walking to him. "Now, son," said Weatherbee. "What can all these tears be about? What can possibly be so bad? I can't imagine anything."

The little one stammered about the comic and how he'd laughed over the name Waldo Weatherbee. "Hmm," said Weatherbee to the boy. "That doesn't seem like a federal crime to me. Did you really read the comic?"

The boy nodded his teary face in a guilty yes.

"Well, that's good. It's good you're reading. Between you and me, I thought they stole that name from me. I probably should try and get them to pay for using it. What do you think?"

The little boy smiled and said that seemed about fair.

Weatherbee walked the boy back into the classroom and dragged Mrs. Florence Bragdon out. "Flo, honestly, it's just a comic and an amazing coincidence to boot. Let it be. In fact I'll just go and tell the kids I'm not THAT Waldo Weatherbee, even if we do look somewhat alike."

Bragdon's lips stiffened as Weatherbee entered the classroom, and you could almost hear her jaw cracking from the way she gritted her teeth when the class started laughing. Bragdon forced a smile, adjusted her hair, and feigned a laugh when she went back in.

Charlie watched the whole episode. Bragdon retired after that year.

The new principal, Barrone, smiled a lot. He would walk around the school, smiling at the kids, usually saying, "HI, kiddo!" or some variation. He said it to the teachers, too. "Hi, Miss," or "Hi, buddy," or "Hi, pal." If a member of the school board or a parent came around, Barrone knew their actual name readily enough. He'd take their hand in both of his and shake as if he was trying to take their arm off. Then he'd whisper, the smile replaced by an intense look of interest, and walk them to whatever destination he had in mind. If Charlie ever heard him call a teacher by their name, he didn't know about it, but then Charlie's hearing wasn't so very good. Maybe he'd just missed that, but he doubted it.

"How's it going, Charlie?" That was the first time Barrone had ever addressed him by any name. It was always like "Hey, buddy, do this" or "Pal, there's a leak in the girl's bathroom. Did you see it?" Charlie was pretty sure Barrone didn't know his name. He certainly didn't know Charlie. If he had, he wouldn't have asked if Charlie knew about a leak in any bathroom.

"No complaints. Everything's working, you know."

"Ah, that's a good thing at your age, I bet!"

"I mean the school. Equipment and such. Everything's good. I might have to change some of the tiles in 132. The art room. But I got those. This weekend I'll get to it."

"That's what I want to talk to you about."

Barrone leaned back in his chair, a new one he'd ordered, and that Charlie had put together. It was what they called Danish Modern, chrome and black leather and able to adjust so you could do what Barrone was doing just then, leaning way back. The older chair that Weatherbee had used for years worked just fine, thought Charlie. He didn't like the way Barrone could lean all that way, nearly touching the radiator under the window, and looking down his long Roman nose, his foot tapping the edge of the desk. The desk, a birch-colored wooden thing that felt flimsy when Charlie helped carry it in, was also new. It only had a couple of drawers. Weatherbee's old one had plenty of drawers. A principal needed that space. Charlie wondered where Barrone kept all of his work, all the notes on the kids.

"Charlie, you've been here . . . what . . . thirty years if it's been a day. I just received a note that you've hit retirement age. Past due in fact. Shit, Charlie, you could have retired years ago!"

"I like what I do."

"Yes, you do," said Barrone. "And you are damned good at it." Charlie didn't like Barrone swearing—twice so far. A principal shouldn't speak that way, even if it was a compliment. If that's what it was.

"But it's time. You've got a nice pension coming. Very nice. And I gather there's the disability from your time in the service?"

"Yeah, the war."

"Yes, the war. Why, between the two, you'll almost make more than me, and I've got a Ph.D.!" Barrone's mouth opened with another smile, and he tapped a finger to the side of his nose. Charlie didn't think it was any of his business.

Charlie wasn't listening very much after that and he'd stopped looking at Barrone. He fixed his gaze out the window at the kids on the playground, thinking he saw the slide shimmying as they went down. He'd have to cement it at the base, maybe Friday, so it would set over the weekend. Barrone went on looking at the ceiling, at some papers on his desk, that unchanging smile sticking to his face. He's got good teeth, Charlie thought, I'll give him that.

"So we're all set?"

Barrone was now looking at Charlie, his smile replaced with arching eyebrows and lifted cheeks in what could pass for a smile or a look like he had just caught the scent of a dead animal. Charlie smirked at the image. He recalled such a smell from years back when a rat had died behind a panel in the school's library. He once saw a similar look on Mr. Weatherbee's face.

"Charlie, something smells to high heaven in there," Weatherbee had said. "Would you mind taking a look? Durned stink of the thing makes the kids want to barf, pardon my French." After that Charlie put out traps, well out of any child's reach, and soon the rats were gone. Ike was President then, Charlie remembered.

"Charlie?

"Sorry, Mister Barrone. My mind was elsewhere."

"It's a lot to take in. We'll throw you a party, of course. Next week, just before spring break. I'll have my gal arrange it. There's a teacher's day Wednesday. That work?"

"Wait just a second. You want me out next week? What if I want to stay? That would be okay, right?"

"Charlie, Charlie, it's time. At your age, you're past the mandatory. The union is, well, we've spoken to the union. They won't fight it. We checked."

"I haven't been to a union meeting, ever, I don't think. What if I want to stay on?

"Sorry, Charlie. No can do. They, the union, have some guys they want to bring up. Hell, Charlie. Christ, most people would be thrilled to be in your spot."

"My spot? I'm getting fired for wanting to do my job."

"Charlie, you are not getting fired, not in the least. You're getting retired from the rat race. You beat the rats!"

He'd beaten the rats twenty years ago, maybe thirty years. "We got a rat problem, ya think?"

"No, Charlie. It's an expression."

"I was being funny."

"Oh," said Barrone, who sat back in the chair and laughed too loudly. "Very good, very good." He got up from the chair, leaned on the desk, which Charlie worried might break it was so flimsy, and offered his hand. "Good luck, Charlie."

Charlie got up and brushed his hands down his green shirt and pants. "My hands are kind of dirty. Next time maybe."

"Sure, Charlie. Next time, next time."

The word was out about Charlie's retirement. He got some hugs, a handshake or two, and a theatrical kiss on his lips by the school nurse, a voluptuously late-middle-aged Miss Fuller who squeezed her phone number into his hand. "Stay in touch. Let's have dinner. At my place. Soon." He pocketed the note. A few tears were shed and there were a lot of pats on the back.

"I'm right behind you, my man," said Tom Collins, the gym teacher. "I've got a few Carlings on ice. Come by later." Charlie passed. He didn't think it was good to drink in the school.

It wasn't much of a party. Barrone came in, put his arm around Charlie's shoulder, thanked him for his thirty years—it was closer to fifty—and said he had to leave early to go to a board of ed meeting. "We'll miss you, pal," he said and left in a rush still grinning.

One by one, the partygoers left, as well, careful to put paper plates in the garbage bin. Some offered to help clean up, but that was Charlie's job, as he made it clear. After he shut the lights off, he went to his closet and put fresh wax on the buffer for a final shining. He wished he'd put in for a new one so he could take the old bird home. He went over all the floors, proud of this sheen, and then did it again. He was going to write a note for the new guy telling him to wax the floors first thing so the kids could skim on it but figured it wasn't his place. The union would tell the guy what to do.

He put the buffer away, wrote out labels for the bundle of keys, and left them on his chair for the new guy. He wrote down his phone number, too, with a note, "Call me if you have any questions. Charlie."

Charlie wanted to be sadder than he was. He looked up and down the halls, thinking about kids come and gone, teachers he'd known, not sure what he was feeling but sure it wasn't just sadness. It was the hall, the tiles, and the wax smell of the buffing job he'd just done and done again. The school would miss him. This very hall would miss him. And he'd miss it, too. He stared down the main hall, admiring the double waxing job and the especially bright shine it gave off, the shine he'd given it, for the final time. The new guy wouldn't do it twice. Union rules. That idea made him sad, sadder than he'd been feeling. He felt bad for the floors: his shiny floors.

A desk stood outside the after-school room with an old chair by it, one that was supposed to be used by the teacher who was on monitoring duty, though, these days, it sat empty. Maybe it was loose. Some of these old wooden seats could splinter, too. He didn't want to leave it that way.

He jiggled the chair about. It was solid enough. The seat was worn, but hardly threatening to puncture a teacher's rear end. The desk was clean, too. He'd dusted it just a week before. He sat down trying to figure out if there was a problem, why no one ever sat there. Then he remembered: the chair was there for the kids, the after-school crowd. The only ones to use the desk these days were those kids. He smiled seeing that and at his increasing forgetfulness.

He looked down the hall again, at his work, and with his left toe took the right shoe off and then took the left shoe off, revealing white socks that were almost blinding against the gleaming brown linoleum floor. He rubbed one foot against a smudge he hadn't noticed until the spot glowed again. He walked around, seeking more smudges but finding none. It had been a good job and a long day.

Charlie put a hand against one of the lockers, admiring his work, and felt his finger on a slightly protruding edge of the little metal label. With his fingernail he pushed the edge back down; a kid might cut himself. The number on the label was 122. Charlie shook his head with a smile. Locker 122. Then he did something he'd never done in all his years. He walked back to the start of the hall and tore off fast as he could, almost hearing high-pitched squeals behind. When he reached the orange locker, 122, he slid and slid and slid. The momentum carried him to locker 162 for a new school record and a fitting end for Charlie O'Brien.

27.

A Winter's Walk

It was just the two of them, trudging along for what felt like an eternity. They walked that first night and hid the next day. At some point they'd given up on trying to hide; there was no one to hide from. The weather had been kind enough at the beginning: cold, not too cold, and kind of dry. Until today. A thick fog had come in, heavy and wet, and there was a rumble off in the distance. And flashes. Lightning maybe. Or guns. Probably guns. It was getting really cold, that damp cold that crept under their skin and made them shiver if they didn't keep moving. It felt like rain, maybe snow, and they weren't prepared for it. They had the one blanket between them, a thin old rag borrowed from what was left of a farmhouse, and they split that in half. It barely wrapped around the helmets. The short one said, "You look like that grandma, in that town, the one that had her hand out." It wasn't meant to be funny. The tall one was limping from the shrapnel that had passed through his calf. A flesh wound, the medic had said, not worth one of the few morphine vials he had left. Had it only been a couple of days back? "You'll live," he'd said. "Just don't think about it too much." The tall one just nodded. He never did say much. There wasn't much to say.

The tall one had to stop. The short one stopped too. "Bad?"

"Kind of burning. Let's go easy, I'll be okay." The short one thought they had been going easy but didn't mention it.

They'd only been together for a few weeks before the battle, both of them replacements called up. They stuck with each other because the older guys in the unit didn't want to know them. Replacements, after all. Replacements didn't last. They hadn't been treated poorly—just pretty much ignored. "Go there, dig this, hold that . . ." Nobody asked their names, where they were from. Not mean, just not interested. That's probably why they were put on the far right of the line.

The medic had been okay, gave them a flask of something, calvados maybe, and told them to keep quiet or everyone would ask for it. He then ran off to another hole where someone had started yelling out, "Medic, medic." "Why now?" the short one asked; they hadn't been shelled in half an hour. Maybe he was knocked out and just woke up, the tall one suggested. Maybe, said the short one. He took a swig from the flask and handed it to the tall one. "It's for you, really."

It got colder as some fog rolled in, but they didn't notice much because the explosions got going on their left. When they stopped, the two of them heard someone, probably an officer, shout, "They're coming." As soon as he said that, the attack started. The two inched up over the edge of their foxhole to get a better look. The flashes were nearby. They could hear the guns, yelling. But they had nothing to shoot at, no one to see, so they just stayed low, scared and waiting. Even the bad guys were ignoring them now, joked the short one. "I hope they keep it that way."

After a while, the firing came closer, much closer, then settled down and moved away, behind them. They heard some more yelling, distant screams, and voices, not English, not their side, so they slunk deeper into their hole. The heavy snow muffled even those sounds. When it was quiet enough, when quiet could mean safe, the short one poked his head up and saw nothing, not a soul. The battle was well behind the two now. It had passed right by them.

"Maybe we should move," said the short one. "Can you walk?"

"Where you wanna go?"

"I don't know, but this can't be good. We're alone out here. Head back to our lines, maybe."

"I can walk."

The short one helped the tall one out of the hole, took his rifle, and bent low, lower than the tall one, as they stumbled along, stopped, listened, and moved on. He was going to tell the tall one to get lower but didn't. Why bother? With his leg wound, it was enough that he was moving. Besides, he didn't want to admit it to himself but the tall one made a bigger target.

But they encountered no one, no soldiers at least, their side or the other. In the distance, they heard fighting, but it could have been miles away—dull explosions, not small arms.

That first day they came upon what was left of a farmhouse, partially bombed but quiet. Muddy boot prints, broken bottles, and opened tins told a story of soldiers having come and gone. The pair looked for something to eat but found nothing and shared the last of the rations they had on them. They finished what was in the flask. It had a sweet almost vanilla taste that burned its way down their throats. It was a good burn, too, it almost felt like warmth. Whatever it was, they toasted each other on the last sips.

They moved along a muddy road, crunching the ice that had formed on the edges of potholes. It sounded incredibly loud. Every house they came to was either destroyed, looted, or both. In a stone barn, the short one ran after a few scrawny chickens that flew up into the rafters. The tall one was about to shoot but the short one said no, it might draw attention. They threw rocks at them but didn't hit any and moved on. The tall one said he didn't know chickens could fly. The short one shrugged his shoulders and said, "Tell them that."

The tall one's limp got worse. He was using his rifle as a crutch. He was slower now, even slower than before, but didn't complain. The short one said they should surrender if they could.

215

He had a white cloth ripped from a curtain tied to his rifle. He thought about throwing the thing away but worried what an officer would say if he showed up unarmed. They'd call him a deserter for sure, so he kept the rifle and held it at the ready. Just in case. He'd claim the white rag was camouflage.

Sleet started to come down, making the mud icy and slick. The tall one slipped twice. The short one helped him back up. They didn't speak much. They weren't just tired, but hungry and lost. As prisoners, they'd get help. If they found their unit, any unit, they'd get help. They couldn't imagine why they met no one.

Up ahead was another farmhouse, with a thatched roof and a dead cow in a small field, its stomach bloated and legs sticking straight up almost comically. Large black birds were pecking at its head, which was turned away from them. The tall one stopped for a second as if contemplating butchering the thing but caught the putrid scent and hobbled on.

The short one was well ahead by now. He turned and waved that he was going in. The tall one stopped, leaned against a tree, and gestured that he would take a rest.

The door opened to a small room, which smelled of burnt wood. It was beaten up, like the others, having seen soldiers come and go, their cigarette butts, empty cans strewn about, drawers and cabinets left open, not caring if this was someone's home. There was a bed, muddy but standing, and some down comforters leaking feathers, dirty but dry. They'd rest this night. The short one walked over and kicked a can he hadn't noticed. Peaches, in heavy syrup. Rations. They'd eat tonight then. He looked out a window, preparing to shout over to the tall one, who was still leaning against that tree, eyes closed, not quite asleep.

Then he opened the can, drank the sweet liquid, and ate the peaches as fast as he could. He poured some water from his canteen and swirled it around, drinking that too, and tossed the can onto the floor with others that had been left behind, opened, empty.

He let the tall one take the bed that night.

28.

The Fish Went One Way

The trout went one way. Foster went another.

He leapt out of the water, arching over its surface, and then diving into the depths of the cold pool. For a trout, such a move is a graceful display of instinctive acrobatics whether to catch a fly that's risen off the surface or to argue with the bite of a hook in its mouth.

For Foster, the move was simply his attempt to get out of the water he'd fallen into when the fish, a large one, indeed a very large one, took him and his fly and his light rod by utter surprise. The rod had slipped out of his hand, already numb from the cold of the water, and he followed after it, slipping off a slimy rock he hadn't noticed beneath the surface and into the river.

In the millisecond before his face went under, he noted the dozens of stoneflies on the surface and was pleased for a brief moment to think that at least he had the right fly on. Then he went below the film and realized that of course he had the right fly on; the fish had taken it, didn't it?

Foster half swam, half crawled along the bottom, spitting out the cold water, worrying he might get giardia and not wanting to swallow the rising stoneflies, though he never heard of those causing any problems. He had managed to hold onto the rod, a spanking new $850 contraption with an equally obscene reel, which along with the fly line would have cost nearly $2000 to replace. He would have kicked himself had the water-filled waders not been holding down his legs like the lead attachments to Navy frogmen. The reel alone had cost him $900. It was an Abel, the Mercedes of fly reels, with the Dancing Bears of the Grateful Dead engraved on its surface, a limited edition he justified as an investment.

Those costs were actually only his third concern. His second was that the fly at the end of that line had worked and it was the only one of its kind that he had with him. The fish, fortunately, had kept the fly without breaking the line.

Foster's first concern was that he was soaking wet. He felt a damn fool for chasing the rod, the reel, the fly, and the bloody fish that got away, and falling into such a pool, a deep one, on a day like this in a spot that had to be a good three hours from his car. What would that be in miles? Walking at two miles an hour would make six miles, but then how fast could he walk in his soaking waders, and what if he saw fish rising along the way?

His waders. He'd dragged himself to the bank, thinking how lucky he was that he held onto that rod. Then he'd calculated how much it would have cost if he'd had to replace it. Only now did he realize how cold he was. The water had gushed over the top and into his waders, filling them. If they hadn't already leaked so badly, he would have noticed the additional cold water sooner.

On the bank, he turned onto his back and lifted his legs into the air, kicking like a little baby to allow the water to gush out. That water fell out all right, splashing over his belly and flowing down onto his already chilled head. So much water, gallons it seemed. That was way too much to get in. Where was his wading belt? He remembered cinching it tight at the car, having let out just a bit more of it to accommodate his slightly expanded gut, and thinking again that maybe he should try to lose some weight, but that might mean exercising more and fishing less. And like on previous occasions when his wife or his doctor had made the suggestion, he concluded that it wasn't an option.

Foster looked into the river, trying to see if he'd lost it in his fall, but through the glare of the sun on the water, he couldn't see more than a blur. He felt for his glasses, the expensive polarized ones with the magnifier clipped over them. The glasses were missing but the clip-ons had fallen into his waders. "I'll be goddamned," he said to no one but himself before tossing the magnifiers into the brush.

A cold day to start with was made colder by his now soaking wet pants and socks. Foster sat on the bank pondering his options. One, stay in the waders and very wet clothes, get colder but fish anyway because once he started fishing again he might forget about his discomfort. Two, take off the waders—a difficult task—wring out his clothes, put the waders and boots back on—a more difficult job—and fish in still damp clothing, and hope he'd forget all that. Three, call it a day, walk back to the car, and keep warm by moving. Or four, make a fire, dry off, and resume fishing.

When taking off his boots, Foster managed to pull a muscle in his lower back trying to get his feet out of the Neoprene socks attached to the waders. It took several minutes to get the actual waders off, and then strip off his wet socks and pants, although he left his underwear on for modesty's sake, even though there was no one around. He took off his fleece sweater and wool turtleneck, wrung them out, and immediately put them back on. Part of that was the cold; goosebumps rose off his skin when a breeze combed the exposed parts of his body.

The other reason was that the soaked sweater and turtleneck hid his girth. He looked about as he tugged the fabric away from his belly. He really had put on some pounds, he thought.

He pushed some rocks into a circle and filled the space with twigs and dried leaves. He added some bark he ripped from a birch tree, remembering from his scouting days that birch bark made a brilliant fire starter. Problem was he didn't have a match.

Foster thought back to the images of pipe smoking anglers he'd seen in any number of ads and covers of old magazines when he first took up fly fishing. Even one of the major rod maker's logos was of a guy with a bent rod and pipe in his mouth. Foster bought himself a pipe and tobacco aptly called Forest and Stream. He smoked it once or twice but keeping it lit and in his mouth when he was traversing a river proved impossible, even if he admired himself in the reflection. He had a lighter then, a Zippo, which at the time seemed nostalgically appropriate. He gave up the pipe to a garage sale and lost the Zippo who knows when.

The breeze picked up enough to give him a chill, and he started to shake. He laughed at the idea of the pipe-smoking killing him sooner than the cold.

Foster had wrung as much water out of his clothes as he could — now merely drops squeezed out — and he waved them to the breeze to dry them further.

He looked down the trail he'd followed to this pool, wondering if anyone else would show up. Robert Frost came into his head, "And both that morning equally lay in leaves no step had trodden black." No, this wasn't a path many would follow no matter how good the fishing might promise.

Foster gave his clothes one good final squeeze, barely getting a drop out of them. That was good, he felt, he'd done what he could, and he put on his socks and waders but left his pants off. At least the waders would block the breeze and maybe retain some warmth for the trek back to the car. If he hurried, if he pushed it, he could make it in maybe two hours. But he'd have to hoof it. He went into his vest to set the stopwatch app on his cell phone. It dripped as he took it out, and he could see beads of water that had accumulated behind the screen. "Not my day," he said, then yelling to the trees, "NOT MY GOD DAMN BLOODY DAY!" He thought he heard the trees giggle back. A pickup in the wind sent shivers down into the still damp interior of those waders.

He was tempted to throw the phone against a rock, not so

much in anger, but because it seemed the right thing to do. Until he suddenly remembered a YouTube video on using a cell phone for survival. Fire! He could use it to make a fire.

How did they do it? They busted open the case, took out the battery—yeah, that was it—and touched the battery to steel wool, which set it off. Steel wool. Who had steel wool? He scrounged through his fly box and wondered if he could use the thin hooks or unwrap the metallic floss on the nymphs. He started to do just that, unraveling the flies he'd painstakingly tied over the desk in his home office. Feathers and fur got caught in the breeze flying into the stream. He saw one feather floating high on the surface and a trout, a huge one, take it in his mouth, which still had the fly it had taken from Foster minutes before. "Damn fish," he muttered as he went back to work.

He put the handful of thin metal findings on a leaf, took his phone, and smashed it against a rock again and again until the case cracked and he could pry it open. There, inside, was treasure. The video he had watched said you could use the mirror-like plastic sheet under the screen for a signal mirror. The speaker contained a magnet, which could be rubbed along a piece of metal, like a straightened hook, turning it into a compass—if you floated it on a leaf in water. The circuit board could be sharpened to make a knife. And there was that battery.

He stripped off the plastic coating to reveal the positive and negative ends. That's what the video showed. He also found thin copper wire in the works and remembered that's what the video used. Attached to the positive and negative ends, the wire would get red hot and could spark tinder. The recollection was good because as he swung around to his collected twigs, he kicked the hooks and floss over, under, and into the leaves that surrounded him. This warranted another "Goddamn!"

Foster didn't want to take any chances. He shredded the birch bark into the thinnest possible fibers and rubbed dried grass and leaves into a fluff that would hold a spark. The resulting ball he put next to the twigs. He then held the battery in one hand and touched the copper wire to the ends. At once, the center glowed a bright red, which he touched to his pile, spreading a spark into an ember. He blew on the ember until it burst into a small flame that caught the twigs, which, in turn, lit the sticks he'd put over those in teepee fashion, a trick he also got off the Internet.

Or so he had hoped.

The wire never got red. Of course not. Had the battery worked, the phone would have turned on and timed his antici-pated walk back to the car. He kicked the debris from the phone into the stream, half hoping the trout would eat some and choke on it. He was tired now, depressed, and he laid back onto the ground trying to take in some of the bright sun overhead. It must be just past noon, he thought. The sunshine forced him to squint as he looked up. The sun.

He jumped up, pulling another muscle in his lower back that had cramped up from his cold plunge or the uneven ground or all the above combined with the age on his bones and the weight of his belly. If he had hoped to walk quickly to his car, his potential pace had just slowed markedly.

But the walk wasn't on Foster's mind just then. It was on the sun, the sun and his glasses. He could get a spark going. He'd done it before when he was a kid burning leaves and ants. That was, could it be, fifty years ago? Sixty? Yes, he thought, but he could do it. Those YouTube survival videos showed it could be done. And, maybe, he thought, maybe global warming made it easier. He laughed at that, conscious he was laughing alone.

Foster got his pile of tinder back together, took off his glasses, and held them at an angle to the sun to focus the small, bright dot that would start a spark that would spread into an ember that he would blow into a flame. The fire, he determined, would warm him up immediately and dry out his clothes in an hour, maybe less. It would be perfect and a story he could tell his wife, who teased him about wasting all that time on YouTube. It might

222

even be a story, a lecture, at his Trout Unlimited meeting: "What to take with you if you're trekking up a river." Maybe the spill wasn't such a bad thing after all.

He moved his glasses up and down, trying to focus the bright beam that would create the pinpoint of heat. That is, if there had been a beam. Foster moved his glasses up and down, back and forth, squinting to make sure they were hovering over his little pile, which, though just a couple of feet from his face, was a vague blur through his nearsighted eyes.

"Oh Christ," he thought. "Oh, damn damn." He was nearsighted, very. His glasses spread the light out to correct for distance, the opposite of what magnifying glasses would do. But he'd had magnifiers. He'd had them, and he'd thrown them away minutes before. He tried to remember where and didn't want to think about why. Why he'd been so stupid.

Foster looked around, careful now lest he step on the magnifiers. He saw nothing but made a careful, slow circle of the area. He kept his eyes down. He had tossed them, not thrown them. And not into the water, oh, please, not into the water. He was sure he just tossed them nearby. They had to be close.

What caught his attention was not the magnifiers but smoke. Just a thin wisp, far less than a cigarette in an ashtray, but there it was. The magnifiers were dangling from a low branch and the lens had caught the sun enough to narrow a pinprick of hot light onto a leaf. A tiny hole was there, blackened on the edges with a teeny bit of glow from the pinprick of focused light. Foster leaned forward to take the magnifiers. He half didn't believe he'd found them and was back on his knees holding them tightly in his shaking hands.

He recollected the debris into a tinder bundle, fluffing it again, and eyed the still high sun to get an angle. He held the magnifiers between it and the tinder, focusing a bead of light as best he could as his hands vibrated with the cold or excitement, or maybe both.

The bright bead swayed back and forth, but close enough to heat a spot that started to smoke, then show a glow, which spread as Foster gently blew on it. More smoke rose as the glow turned into a bigger ember, which spread into the bundle. He blew harder still, sparks now flying about as he held the precious nest in his hands, ignoring the sparks burning his hands as the ember turned into a coal and then into a flame. He put the fire gently on the ground and covered it with twigs, which caught ,and added larger sticks, more and more until he had a decent fire. "Goddamn," he said with a smile.

He built up the fire, kicking away dry duff so that it wouldn't spread, and walked around the flames, finally warming himself up and drying his increasingly less damp clothes. He took off his waders, pulled them inside out, and held his socks and underwear on a stick closer to the fire. The heat felt good against his bare skin.

"Hey! What the hell do you think you're doing?"

Foster turned around to see a man in a green uniform, a Smokey the Bear hat on his head, and a silver badge catching the brilliant sunlight just so. The man was large, which made the scowl on his face all the more intimidating. Why, wondered Foster, why did he have a hand on that holster?

"Hi! It's great to see you. God, I fell in and, well, it's kind of cold in there." The ranger didn't share his laughter.

"It's not that cold. You're naked. Why are you naked? What about kids seeing you like that?"

Foster started to put his clothes back on, struggling with the damp pants that just didn't seem to want to go on. "Kids? There's no one here. I was worried about the hike back so I built the fire. To get warm, dry off."

"Fires are illegal here. So is prancing about in your birthday suit. I got the call about that."

"The call?"

"Those people," said the ranger, nodding across the river to a group of smiling Girl Scouts pointing down from the top of a hill.

Foster knew they were Girl Scouts from the sashes across their adolescent chests. One waved at him. He waved back.

Turning, he saw the ranger writing in a booklet. "I'm going to fine you for the fire, at least. You have a fishing license?"

Foster held up his fly vest, dripping still, with the license.

"You're okay there. Now, indecent exposure . . ."

"What! I had to dry my clothes. I could have died out here!"

"Died? Mister, you're five minutes from the parking lot."

Foster looked confused. "What are you talking about 'five minutes'? It took me hours to get here."

The ranger looked over Foster's shoulder. "Which way did you come from?" Foster pointed south.

The ranger followed Foster's finger. "Hah! You took the long route, buddy! That trail circles back. The parking lot's this away." He pointed his thumb over his shoulder. Foster felt a warmth, an uncomfortable warmth, rising in his face.

"You're kidding."

"Nope. I'll let the indecent exposure go but put out that fire and don't piss on it." He nodded again to the group of Girl Scouts in the not too distance.

"Goddamn," said Foster shaking his head.

"Mind the language 'round the kids," said the ranger as he handed out the fine. "Nice rod, by the way."

29.

Die-a-Domaceous Death

Tommy Fitzgerald sat stiffly in his truck, toying with a stale Marlboro he kept in reserve in the clean ashtray, a deliberate temptation to prove he didn't have to smoke anymore. It was the last one, and so long to all that. Tommy reached to remember when he had started, what, twenty-five, thirty years ago, after he joined the Marines.

He took care of pools for rich people. His accountant never stopped trying to get Tommy to call them "clients." "In case the IRS overhears you," he'd say with a grin. But Tommy thought that was pretentious and stuck to referring to them as "owners" to the accountant and "Mister or Missus" to their faces if he ever saw them, which he rarely did. For the most part, Tommy cleaned the pools, fixed the pumps, billed them, and never the twain would meet. Except for this one Missus that was always home.

He twirled the cigarette between his fingers, a few dried shards of tobacco slipping out of the business end, and sucked in as hard as he could, almost tasting smoke. When done, he placed the cigarette back down in an ashtray that hadn't seen an ash in a year. It was a ritual once every two weeks when he parked the truck in front of this house and only this house. Tommy once went so far as pushing the truck's lighter in until it glowed and held it in front of the tobacco. When a thin wisp of blue smoke lifted from the end, he put the lighter back and pinched the tiny coal out with a wet fingertip.

Maybe today he'd get lucky. Maybe today she'd be away. Get in, get out, and just leave the bill in the mailbox. It would be a first.

He wasn't lucky.

Pam Gilbert took one long sip, using her tongue to ensnare the two olives left behind. Through a mouthful of dry martini and olive slurry she managed to growl, "Aren't you finished yet?" A deep swallow followed with a slight choke to get the less chewed olive down. "Eh, pool boy? You hear me?"

Tommy looked up from behind the pump. Sweat left trails in the diatomaceous earth powdering his face, matching the color of his grizzled crew cut. He looked up at three late-middle-aged women, who were holding mostly empty martini glasses, wearing shades large enough to could cover most of the bosoms their tops struggled to contain. The two behind Pam were ogling Tommy.

"The filter needed backwashing again, Missus Gilbert. You get a lot of algae with the heat on and all and not enough chlorine."

She tossed her long, bleached hair into the air like a horse swishing its tail at annoying flies. "You said you'd be done by noon. It's almost one. That's an hour longer, in case you don't know."

He wouldn't argue with the math and wouldn't bother reminding her that he never said he'd be done by noon, or that he was always there for more than two hours. "I'm done, but it needs more care, you know. Once, twice a week, at least. It's not difficult. I can show you something."

"I'll bet you can," said Pam. She shushed the women behind her. "Just do it ASAP." She smiled to still more giggles.

"That's why the suction went on you," he said, clearing his throat. "A bathing suit top, I think, got caught in the pump. Chewed to bits. It's clear now, but you really can't throw things like that, towels and such. They clog the system, you know."

"Oh, so the suction went on me? Maybe I just won't wear anything. Hmm, gals?"

One of the ladies spat out a stream of martini, crying she'd "norked" it and wanted a refill.

"Tommy," said the other one, "don't let the suction let go of me!" Tommy waved, picked up his gear, and headed out the side gate, saying he'd leave the bill in the box.

"I'd like to meet this Bill he keeps talking about," said Pam to her friends, one of whom pretty much fell out of her top leaning over to wink at Tommy.

"I like your tattoo," she said.

Tommy looked to the bulldog inked in his forearm, a "Semper Fi" banner above it. "What the hell was I thinking?" he said, barely hearing the catcalls and splashing from the pool. A wet bathing top hit him in the back of his head.

❀   ❀   ❀

Two weeks later, Tommy was back staring into pool water tinged green with algae and skimmers clogged with debris. He had to flush the pump and clean out the filter three times. He also had to extract the remains of another top, or maybe a bottom, that was clogging the drain at the pool's bottom, putting tremendous pressure on the system.

"Really, Missus Gilbert, you've got to be more careful. The pump is going to burn out on you, and they're not cheap. "

"Well, Tommy, exactly what do you expect me to do? I dove in to get my suit, but the suction just held it in. Don't accuse me of creating a problem. You're the pool boy, not me." Without a martini in hand or her entourage behind, Pam Gilbert could be quite the bitch. Or with the martini and the entourage for that matter.

It wasn't the first time Tommy had to explain simplicity or the first time he had to swallow bile. He began with the net, telling her to clean out leaves, grass, and debris every day, and es-

229

pecially after she had the landscapers in. "There's the net right there," he said, pointing up at the retaining wall. "And I could come more often. And," he was looking away now, "and anyway, I can come more."

"That would get costly, no?"

"Cheaper than a new pump and filter system. But you can skim and take crap out of the skimmer drains. You don't need me for that."

"Skimmer drains, eh? Those are . . . ?"

Tommy explained again that they were the boxes at the top of the pool where one puts in the chlorine blocks. He lifted the lid to one drain; emptied it of nature's debris and the remains of butts, a half-smoked joint, and an olive; and added the chlorine.

"You really need to keep chlorine in this. Honestly," he said.

"Don't 'honestly' me, hon. I pay you, as I recall, and it's quite a nice amount for you to sit around and get a suntan."

"I don't mean to be . . ." Tommy was looking at his feet, then into the pool and squinting even though the clouds were hiding the sun.

"Yes? You don't mean to be what?"

"It's just that, and I don't mean offense or anything, it's just that, well, those bathing suits really clog the drain. I mean, the pump gets going when they get hold of them. It's best if, you know, the suits, or towels, were left outside of the pool."

Pam Gilbert moved closer to the pool, sitting down on the stone steps that led to the pebbled walkway. "You are suggesting I swim in the nude, is that it? Is that what's on your mind?" She let down her long hair to cover her breasts as she played with the straps to her bathing top.

Tommy stepped backward, stumbling over a hose, stammering "no" a few times before Pam Gilbert looked up at the sky and laughed for several seconds.

"You are a prude, my working-class hero. Finish off, or I'll take my swim right in front of you." She looked into the sky, flung her head back, and howled a laugh.

That laugh that wasn't a laugh. It was a cackle. He remembered hearing on the Discovery Channel that a cackle was the term for a group of hyenas. "Perfect," he thought.

He also thought Mister Gilbert must have been very lucky because there was no Mister Gilbert. "Dropped dead, the sonofabitch," he heard her say more than a few times to the cackle that hung out at the patio. "Asshole ad man. Had cigarette accounts. Coffin nails, he called them. Best line he came up with and not that original," she'd say. "What can I say? It wasn't cancer research!" They'd laugh as if they hadn't already heard it a thousand times. "Smoked himself to death. Poetic justice."

Tommy thought he'd have something in common with that Mister Gilbert.

He made the final adjustment to the pump, taking down the suction power a notch to reduce the pressure when something would inevitably clog the system. It wouldn't work for long, he knew it, but the lessened strain might give him time to get back and clear the unit before it burned out the motor.

Two had passed, and he was again sitting in his truck twirling a Marlboro. A fresh one from the pack he'd bought that morning. He inhaled for what seemed like minutes, the tobacco tempting him to no good. He flicked his new lighter on and off before putting it in the ashtray with the cigarette while taking a deep breath. "Let's get it over with," he said to no one.

The pool was green, algae creep around the sides. The water was a weak tea color, appropriate given the lemon slices floating around the idle strainers.

"Dead," she said, letting the porch door slam behind her. "Dead as a bloody doornail."

"How long has it been out? You shoulda called me, honestly."

"Do your unplugging thing, Mister Roto-Rooter. The gals and I are having a drink.'"

Tommy did try to get it going. With his bare hands, he extracted bathing suit remains, leaves, grass, and globs of metal-colored plastic. He was already sweating when he realized the pump motor would have to be replaced. That itself wasn't a big deal. Telling Pam Gilbert was another matter.

"Planning a party?" Pam asked, glaring at Tommy and his armful of debris.

"I did warn you, Missus Gilbert. I warned you a lot. I mean, just look at this stuff." He held up the shreds of metallic plastic. "This melted in the pump."

"They're balloons. From my birthday. The girls gave me a shit-ton of them."

"Umm, well, Happy Birthday, I guess. Consider a new pump a birthday gift."

"You can't fix that one?"

Tommy explained it was gone, done, dead. She needed a new one. She looked at him, stared, for a long while, and if she blinked once he didn't notice when he periodically looked back up to her.

"Well?" she asked.

"Well, um. Well, what?"

"When can you get it in?"

"Don't you want to know how much, like an estimate?"

"Tommy boy, I don't have a choice, now do I? It's a new pump or septic tank of a pool, and I'm not filling in the pool. Just get a powerful pump, right, so this doesn't happen again."

He explained through gritted teeth that it wasn't the size of the pump that was the issue, it was the maintenance that someone had to clean the thing out more and keep "crap"—his choice of word surprised him—out of it.

"Fine, whatever. Just get a decent pump, a more powerful one, and get it in today. It's hot out here."

"You don't need a more powerful . . ."

"Get one! I like power. And maybe you should clean the thing out more often."

She didn't wait for an answer, and he didn't try to argue. If she wanted a more powerful pump, she'd get a more powerful pump, and he just happened to have one in the shop from the Seligsohns that was barely used. They'd filled in their pool and replaced it with a hot tub. Screw it, he thought, she can have that one.

Powerful it was. It recycled the water in half the time and pulled like a team of oxen. He adjusted the intake to take it down a notch, but it was still a strong pull. A very strong pull.

"Well, is it working?"

"Yup. It's on. I put those blocks in the skimmers. You gotta check on those. I'll come back in . . . a week?"

"Two weeks."

"But I need to check on the system. You need to keep junk out of the pool, especially cloth stuff. You know, suits and all."

"Two weeks. I just paid a ton for that pump or filter or whatever it is. I'm not made of money."

He tried to tell her again, but she just took a slurp of rosé from a very large glass and waved her hand. He went back to the new pump and turned up the power to keep the flow going. The water in the pool was clearly agitating through the drains, which would help keep the algae from building. He added chlorine and was about to leave when he had a thought. He went back to the pump and turned it up some more.

The day was hot, a real scorcher. Pam had drained her midday martini before the girls had arrived. She was in a wading mood and took the steps down, discarding her top and letting it sink to the bottom, where the suction from the drain lured it in.

"Goddamn," she said to herself, thinking through a fog induced by the heat, martini, and a moment of pool-owner pride over not wanting to shell out another few thousand bucks on a new pump. She dove to the bottom where the drain was sucking in her top, barely noticing the pull as she went deeper. She grabbed the top and played tug of war with the pump. She pulled herself right to the drain, her breasts and hair scraping the pool's bottom in the effort, working to yank out the top, or what was left of it. When the top came free, the pump exchanged its pull for the next best thing. It sucked until the system burned out then let go of its victim.

✽   ✽   ✽

"Freak accident," the police said. They were asking her friends how much she'd drunk, and they pointed to the martini glass and the half-empty bottle of vodka on the patio's table. They weren't there, the friends explained. Found her floating that way. She had a drinking problem, they insisted. Depressed since her husband—a lovely man, they told the police—had died.

One cop walked around the pool while the EMTs lifted Pam's body out of the water. "Big pump," he thought. But then he asked himself, what did he know?

Tommy showed up as soon as he heard the news. He didn't wait in his truck very long. Lifting the yellow tape, he went through the side gate to clean the pool like any other day. He went to the pump, which had stopped when it got too clogged—a good feature on the newer ones—and adjusted the pressure. He really had turned it on too high.

He tossed a pack of nineteen Marlboros out the window on his way home.

30.

You Are So Very Welcome

Ellen Berliner offered the caller a ready excuse that her system was incredibly slow that morning. What with the holiday coming up and Covid going around there were simply an awful lot of calls coming in. It rolled off her tongue like the lines from a well-rehearsed play. Ellen also rolled her bored eyes. "We're experiencing unusually high call volume," a quote taken directly from the Post-it permanently taped to her monitor. She apologized, per another Post-it, and moved to the topic at hand. "Now what date was the claim again?"

An aggravated gasp came through Ellen's headset.

"I've been on hold for like 20 minutes!" said the caller.

Ellen's systems were not slower than usual that morning or any other morning. None of the associates' systems were slower. Ever. It was the standard excuse generated by representatives of the GoToHellth Insurance Company. The real name was United National Healthcare Corporation, a blandly sinister integration of United, National, Health, and, in last place, Care. The employees thought GoToHellth captured the culture better.

What had kept the claimant on hold was Ellen's trip to the bathroom, a stop at the coffee room where she got herself two Keurig cups of hazelnut coffee, a brief exchange with a colleague about lunch plans, and a walk back to her cubicle.

"Is the policy in your name?" she asked.

"My God, I told you already. Yes, it's my policy, for me and my family. I'm on Cobra. That's $1836 per month, and you'd think I wouldn't have to call three times to deal with this…"

"Just a moment," said Ellen. She put the caller on hold to cacophonous sound of a saxophone interrupted every few seconds with a voice that repeated, "Your call is important to us." Ellen did not need to search for the claim details; she had them on the screen all along. What she was struggling with was a three-letter word for meadow. After a minute she wrote LEA in the puzzle then reconnected.

"Yes, the claim was denied," said Ellen.

Ellen and her colleagues had been trained to use the passive voice when discussing the downside of policies.

"I know that already. My question is why?" fumed the caller.

Ellen explained with coached patience that United National required more documentation from the provider to determine the appropriate level of reimbursement. She shared sympathy that the claim was for a procedure that had been submitted multiple times before. "I don't know how this one ended up in that department." Still, she explained, that the cost of the procedure would be allowed; she'd see to that. Then, in a confidential aside, she cautioned the cost of the treatment, in this case physical therapy, would only apply to her out-of-network deductible, which hadn't been reached for the current year. It was, Ellen reminded her, only April.

"There's a list of in-network providers on our website. The deductible is lower if you stay in-network," she added.

The claimant had choice words about deductibles, in-network providers, and co-insurance, fulminating on the BS cost of the plan, and how they denied more than they accepted. She slammed the phone down before Ellen had a chance to ask if she would like to participate in a survey.

It was the third slammed phone that week and it was only Tuesday. She hit 'completed' on the customer's file, putting a conclusion to this claim.

Her phone was ringing again.

"Hello, United National Healthcare where our clients are our most important asset. How can I help you today?"

Ellen didn't need to reference the employee guidebook for that line; she knew it by heart and instinct. The line was part of the collection of studied responses designed by a well-paid neuro-linguistic programming firm to keep interactions unemotional yet empathetic in a noncommittal way. The intent was to avoid tears, screams, pathetic pleas and calls to the state's insurance overseer. There was the unspoken goal of exhausting people into just giving up on a claim or stretch out the process where a successful outcome could be as simple as "Well, you've hit your deductible." It was frankly amazing how often the caller at the other end would say, "Thanks for your help." And Ellen would respond appropriately with a "You are so very welcome."

She left out what was always on her mind at those moments: "what an idiot."

Before failing her physical therapist licensing boards...the first time, not the second time...Ellen would never have said "idiot" out loud about her professors, fellow students, or patients. She did say it about herself when she saw her scores and said it about everyone else when her advisor, Helen Adler, advised a repeat of her senior year. Ellen had said, "What an idiot." Adler returned a smile and with a former smoker's smug rasp said, "You are so very welcome."

Helen Adler's cold response ended that conversation. Ellen made a note.

The recruiter for United National found Ellen's resume on LinkedIn via an algorithm that cross-referenced PTs who had taken their licensing boards and were still looking for work 90 days after the test results were released. The recruiter's database flagged those who'd taken the exam more than once; they'd prove ideal candidates.

"Are you looking for a career in your profession? One where you don't need a license?" These were magical words to the depressed and disenfranchised fretting their limited options, wondering if they'd thrown away years of education.

The recruiter explained the health-insurance industry needed professionals who might be more suited to an office than a clinic, who had the knowledge to understand medical evaluations, and could, "like a detective," she'd said, help determine if a given treatment was genuinely warranted, or, and she left this part out, whether the patient could hobble along in agony for the rest of his or her life and save the insurance company some money.

Never, not once, had the recruiter been called out by someone saying, "So what you need is an unlicensed PT, OT, MSW, fill in the blank, to say "no" to paying for treatment."

Ellen's colleagues accepted their fate or saw it as a temporary step as they studied for another shot at their license. In the meantime, they justified their work with excuses ranging from "well someone has to" to calling it "a crusade to stamp out corruption."

At least it was employment in the once-chosen field for which they failed to qualify and a chance to challenge the expertise of people who did. That made the bitter aftertaste a little sweeter. Ellen was particularly bitter making her particularly good at the job.

"Hello, United National Healthcare where our clients are our most important asset. How can I help you today?"

The caller didn't respond immediately forcing Ellen to repeat the canned phrase. "Yes," came back in a strained sotto voce. Ellen screwed up her eyes as the caller attempted to get to the point. Ellen insisted without initial success to get the caller's ID and group number until, against protocol, she said, "Stop it. I'm about to hang up if I don't get your ID and group number."

"All you had to do was ask," huffed the caller. Or was it more a rasp than a huff? Ellen typed in the numbers. She had a grin like the Jack Nicholson character in The Shining when she saw the name that appeared on her monitor.

"Well now. How can I help you, Helen Adler?" Help was the last thing on Ellen's mind.

Helen Adler's long-winded explanation followed the trunk of a very large decision tree following up and down each branch as the tree grew in length. There was no need. In front of Ellen was the electronic paper trail of a claim filed, sent to the wrong department, refiled, sent back to Adler for more information stating some data couldn't be read even though the scan on the screen was quite legible, and documentation of her multiple calls.

I do understand your frustration," said Ellen. "You don't want to..." Ellen was about to say "go back to school" but caught herself. "You don't want to go through this again. Let me give you a case number if you have to reference this call." The case number hadn't changed in the three prior episodes when, according to the file, it had been provided to Adler.

"Please, I just gave it to that woman, Sheila something, before she transferred me. I was on hold for over 10 minutes."

Ellen took note of that; the usual wait time was slated for at least 20 minutes.

"Give me a moment to review the file. I'm going to put you on hold for just a moment."

Ellen heard an aggravated "But wait" just as she muted Adler's call.

It was clear what was going on. Adler had a simple case of tendinopathy after a week of skiing in Aspen. "She can afford that?" thought Ellen. She bit hard on her sucked-in cheeks at the image of her former advisor skiing in Aspen. And she had dared to see an out-of-network physical therapist, out of state, for an expensive series of treatments. The claims were initially denied due to improper paperwork – older employees of United National called that the 'hanging chad' excuse – but the intent was clear to anyone who knew all 26 letters in the alphabet; postpone. Any fault could be cited,: black ink instead of blue ink, printing a name instead of a signature. Or triple checking the license number for an out-of-network provider.

It was a philosophy United National embraced.

PT claims were habitually refiled, lost, refiled, sent to the wrong department, and finally landed on Ellen's lap. As a trained if unlicensed PT, she was either the light at the end of the tunnel or barbed-wire topping the chain-linked fence at the end of a dark alley.

Ellen was the eternal clerk behind the counter of the DMV; she could either point right, in which case the claim was approved, or left to the "get-back-on-that-line" heap.

The screen in front of Ellen showed that even by United National's standards, Helen Adler's case was a doozy. Several of the procedures had been signed off pending approval. Ellen was in the position to authorize, a.k.a. reimburse, them if she so chose, or send Helen Adler's stone of Sisyphus rolling back down the mountain.

There was a sob followed by sniffles and then a rallying cough. "I've provided 'further details' so many times," Adler said and listed each date, each action taken, and the identity of the United Health employee she'd spoken with. "And, for my records, what's your name?"

"Um," said Ellen.

Ellen looked at the surrounding cubicles. What she needed was a name other than her own. Page 21 of the manual started the ethics section and the ethics section made one thing abundantly clear: you could cajole a claimant to your heart's desire, but you could not handle a claim of someone you knew. That was a conflict of interest that would bring the insurance regulators down on United National like a year's worth of unreimbursed claims. The example cited was of a client who sued United National after his invasive procedure was denied by a still-angry former girlfriend. The state's regulators did their own invasive procedure on United National. United National changed the manual.

"The individual's role was terminated."

The passive voice was consistent with how the firm communicated uncomfortable information. The active tone came in the next sentence. "The former employee cannot legally work in a regulated industry again." That was problematic for Ellen because said former employee had trained as a Physical Therapist. Ellen's duo of inadequate board scores came back in a flash.

"Just a moment," said Ellen.

Her colleagues looked busy. Janet, an obese PT, was talking into her headset. Janet had worked in a clinic, fully licensed, until the weight got in the way, got in everyone's way. Bill – a former chiropractor who had to give up that job due to a bad back – had his eyes closed. He was twirling a pen around his thumb in a distracted way. He must have had someone on hold.

Up and down the cubicles Ellen looked for a name, someone who'd cover for her. Yeah, right. She considered making up a name, but Helen Adler had a case number and she'd entered it in her screen; her name was already registered. She considered hanging up, but Helen Adler would just call back with that damn case number.

Ellen stared at the blinking red light on the phone console that had an angry Helen Adler at the other end. A queasy warmth expanded into her throat causing a slight gag as her whole body started a reflexive heave. Ellen grabbed for the trash bin under her desk, relieved to see the white plastic liner. The heave was about to manifest itself into the bucket when Ellen heard words of inspiration.

"I do apologize. I'm not really sure how this happened, but it all looks good to me. You have more than met your deductible. I'll see you get the allowed reimbursement for this."

Ellen's oozing warmth retreated.

"Please, there's no need to thank me."

It was Janet, now rewarding herself with the first of two Subway Chicken & Bacon Ranch Sandwiches that were her Wednesday's meal-du-jour. She'd gotten thanks for, in essence, applying a claim to a deductible at a petite cost to United National. And when another claim followed? The rigmarole would start over.

Ellen took Helen Adler off hold.

"I'm so sorry for the delay. I had to pull some strings."

Ellen cut to the chase after another ten minutes reviewing the long paper trail Helen Adler had been following. Being deliberate and detailed was also in the manual, though not specifically mentioned as a technique to numb the customer. Helen, too, had met her deductible and so further claims would be paid out at 80% for in-network providers, after co-pays, and 60% for out-of-network. Ellen gave her the website where she could find those coverage tidbits.

"And I've authorized the allowable, the maximum allowable, reimbursement for this claim. That's fifty-six dollars and twenty-nine cents. You'll get that within two weeks."

Nothing came out of the other end of the line. Ellen looked to make sure they were still connected. "Hello? Ms. Adler?"

"I'm here. I'm just, you know, exhausted from it all. But, anyway, thank you. You know, I don't think I caught your…"

"Name? Let Sheila take the credit," said Ellen. "Oh, and Ms. Adler? You are so very welcome."

31.

Ed's Ego

Ed Jesperson combed back his steel-grey hair, turning this way and that in the mirror, patting down rogue strays that refused to behave, and smiled. In the closet, he looked over his vast collection of ties, rubbing their silk fabric to recall the distant days. He could tell by their width where he had worked and when he had last worn them, like counting the rings on a tree.

There were the two bright-yellow ones — "power ties" in their day — he'd wear with suspenders embroidered with garish images of Rubenesque women. The suspenders had lost their stretch around the time B. Altman's had gone under. He'd worn those with French blue shirts, the ones sporting — sporting was an appropriate pretension — garish white collars and cuffs. The blue had faded, the white cuffs had yellowed, the collars had frayed. A line from his father came to mind: "I wouldn't wear those to a dog show." He agreed.

The search narrowed to a tie that was almost in fashion. It was subtle, periwinkle blue, elegant; a good match for the spring weather. He made a knot, thought the narrow part too short, and retied it. He put on his pearl-gray gleneagle plaid jacket, patted out invisible wrinkles, and flattened a brown bag lunch into his briefcase along with the two well overdue novels, yesterday's copy of the New York Times, and a manila envelope stuffed with resumes.

His home was an easy walk to the commuter train, a fact that gave him immense pleasure. It was one smart choice thirty years earlier and a good selling feature today if it came to that. On the platform, he nodded to fellow commuters he knew only by sight and was content to keep it that way.

Ed aped the behavior of others, looking down the track, glancing at his watch, looking back down the tracks, and contriving an impatient sigh. He pulled out his cell phone for a commuter conversation, louder than necessary, rude or oblivious. Or maybe just pretentious. "I'll be in by 9:15. This can wait until I'm there, but it has to be resolved by noon. If I have to fly out to the coast, again, I'll need you to get the driver arranged."

His phone wasn't on. Ed looked around at his fellow travelers to see if they noticed, to see if anyone overheard him, and was disappointed to find people engaged in their own affairs.

He made a similar call on the train, looking apologetically at the people sitting near him. "Sorry," he said, mouthing the word "important," reaching for a sympathetic response. There was none. Others in the car were reading, napping, doing the daily crossword, or working away on laptops, scribbling notes. What do they do? Ed wondered. How did they get their jobs? Keep them? How much do they earn? These questions were the same ones he wondered about the day, week, and month before. His real question was, "What do they think of me?"

At Grand Central, Ed made a beeline to the Yale Club. Upon entering, he said to the doorman, "Good to see you again." After allowing two women to pass, he snapped his fingers and added, "I'll be back in a moment."

The doorman smiled politely and held the door for him. Ed walked around the corner to the Roosevelt Hotel, which teemed with loud foreign tourists. He cleared his throat and looked about with a studied air of contempt, bounded through the lobby with purpose, went up to the mezzanine, and took a seat in one of the comfortable chairs outside the little-used conference rooms. Today, inside one, was a meeting of the "Thirty-Five-year Club of NY Corporate Life Underwriters."

Leaving his coat and briefcase on a chair, he went to the reception table, looked at the nametags, and picked at the free pens and notepads. "Can I help?" said a pretty young thing standing behind the table. "Just looking for my name, but I suspect my colleague picked it up." She offered to make up a new one. "I'll find him," smiled Ed. "He's probably inside saving me a seat . . ." Then, leaning forward, he whispered, "He's up for a promotion and is doing his best to impress me."

She giggled and handed him a canvas bag with goodies inside. "If you can't find him, come back."

"I most certainly will," said Ed, looking around. "Looks like a better crowd than last year."

"Did they have one last year? I didn't think they did," said the young lady.

"Of course, of course. It was the event in San Francisco I'm thinking of. At my age I'm lucky to recall what"—Ed's mind flashed with recollections he wished he could have— "what the housekeeper made for breakfast. Ah, I think I see my colleague."

He hustled off to his chair after picking up a coffee and two muffins at the breakfast buffet. Looking about to see if anyone witnessed his white-collar crime, Ed sat back in his chair, looked over the rail to the lobby below, and closed his eyes to the murmur of the middle-aged insurance agents behind him and the crowd of foreign voices below.

There was a gentle tap on his shoulder. "Is everything alright, sir?" It was a member of the hotel staff he recognized from prior forays.

"Fine, fine . . ." he said. "Taking a bit of a break from . . . the conference. These meetings can be bloody boring, though don't say you heard that from me." The man gave a hospitable laugh and asked if he could get him anything. "I'm fine, fine," he said, and then, "I'm not speaking until after lunch. Closing comments." As he was taking his leave, the young man turned back with a look of déjà vu before continuing.

Ed put his hand over his chest, feeling his rapid heartbeat. Perspiration collected on his forehead. Perhaps he'd used the Roosevelt as a base too much, too long. There had been other hotels, but his welcome in those had eventually worn out. A manager at the Helmsley once pulled him aside from a luncheon, asking if he was an invited guest, and then suggesting he should leave on his own accord. Ed smiled, held his head up, and slowly walked out though closely trailed by the manager, who didn't even offer the decency of a "thank you."

He left the Roosevelt, turning right to head north on Madison Ave. He would miss the Roosevelt Hotel—so quiet, so discrete, so anonymous. And so close to Grand Central.

Across Madison was Tourneau Jewelers. Ed went right to the Rolex counter, the left side, the good stuff. In a New York minute, a salesman showed up. "Hello, lovely day. Can I answer any questions?"

Ed gave a taut smile, a deliberate gleam in his eye. "Yes, you can. I just gave my old one to my nephew. We had breakfast at the Yale Club. He's a freshman, and I'm in the market."

"You are generous. May I ask which model?"

Ed knew exactly which model it would be. It would be the one he always saw in National Geographic ads. The Rolex Edmund Hillary wore when he conquered Everest, not some pretentious jewelry to flash in people's faces to make an impression. No, his would be the adventurer's watch. The real deal. The genuine article. It would be worn by the Ed he always wanted to be.

"Oh, I had it for years. The Explorer. But I'm thinking of the President, in white gold. I must admit, the yellow ones are a tad obvious. Bought it here I don't know when."

"I can look that up, sir! We keep records as far back at the pyramids. And you do know your Rolexes."

"Oh, don't bother!" squealed Ed. "I'm still deciding. Black face or white. Though the deep-blue face, with the diamonds, is rather nice."

"Very nice, sir. Let me look it up for you." He leaned forward. "We offer 15 percent discounts to repeat customers. Watch sales are slow these days with smartphones and Fitbits and what have you. The computer is in the back and that 15 percent might take some of the sting away on a white gold President."

"Um, well, yes, fine, sure, then. Name's Roosevelt. James P. I bought it around, must've been 1972. Yes, 1972."

"I'll be right back, Mr. Roosevelt. You'll appreciate that discount"

When the salesman was out of sight, Ed scurried out of Tourneau, heading uptown. He went to the park, heart beating quickly with his pace, and walked northwest toward the Museum of Natural History. Near 66th Street, he sat on a bench to catch his breath. Nearby, two women, about his age, were jabbering away. He took out his newspaper and a pen and went to the crossword puzzle, in which he would jot something before gazing off as if thinking. Periodically, he would slap his thigh, laugh, and say, "Ah hah" or "Oh, brother" and return to the puzzle.

He looked at the ladies, engaged in their conversation, until he caught the eye of one, smiled apologetically, and went back to his work. The woman said, "Pardon me for interrupting, but you seem to be having an extra fine day!"

Ed turned to the women and said it was indeed a fine day. "I indulge myself when the weather is like this. Do the crossword puzzle, dine al fresco. It's a break from the office." He lifted the brown sandwich bag to show the ladies. "My secretary was kind enough to offer me her lunch. I sent her and one of the other gals off to the 21 Club in exchange." Leaning in conspiratorially, he said, "And I think I got the better end of the deal."

"That is so wonderful. What a treat. May I ask what do you do?"

Ed folded over the paper, hiding the random scribbles he'd inked into the crossword, with a deliberate calmness as he thought of an appropriate answer. "I'm the senior partner at a law firm."

"Oh, which one? My husband is with Skadden Arps. M and A."

"Ah, yes. Skadden Arps. Mine is one you wouldn't know, or I hope you don't. We're a very private firm. Our clients are international, some individuals, families, but mainly governments that need things done quietly. We are very much not in the public eye."

"Oooh, that sounds mysterious. Almost like espionage? You're not James Bond, are you?" she asked with a half-serious laugh.

"There's more tedium to it than mystique. But we do get involved in, ah, negotiations with entities you wouldn't want at a dinner party. We've had a number of kidnappings. Hostage exchanges. That sort of thing. And there's the artwork. We've found looted artwork, stolen by Nazis, and get it back to the rightful estates."

"REALLY? Oh, my," said the other woman. "Anything we would have heard about?"

"Ideally, no. Emphatically, no. Discretion and secrecy. Both parties prefer it that way. But I've said too much, and, in any event, I must hurry along."

Ed insisted that the ladies "enjoy this wonderful day" as if it was his to grant and the women nodded their heads in happy acceptance. He rose and headed west, but not before glancing back to see the two women watching him. He waved, they waved back. He imagined they would talk about him, his hurried exit, speculating on who he was. When out of sight, he tossed the day-old newspaper in a garbage can and ate the tuna sandwich he had made that morning.

Looking up to the statue of Theodore Roosevelt outside the museum, he brushed crumbs from his mustache and stood a bit taller. He deserved it. Roosevelt. What a grand name. Too obvious? No, understated, too historical to be pretentious. Old money. Subtle. He wondered if there were any Roosevelts left to enjoy all that, the mere mention of the name, creating a pedigree. He ran the name Jesperson through his circuits for the umpteenth time in his life and never came up with any Jesperson of note.

Ed wanted to work at the museum, to work with the dioramas. Twice he tried. When he was a child, he'd seen a man in a gray smock with a huge moustache brushing the teeth of the orca. That, he decided, was what he wanted to do. How wonderful it would be to enter the dioramas, dust off the stuffed animals, have children watching, thinking he had the greatest job on earth.

He sauntered around the museum, recalling his father taking him once, though he couldn't remember much else about his father. "Look at those guys," he had said, pointing at a diorama. "Just look at those guys." Little Eddie waved. The man cleaning the orca's teeth waved back. "Best job in the world, working here. I bust my hump and these guys dress up like a dentist with a tie and all, doing what? Let's get out of here."

Ed trailed his father, not wanting to leave, waving back at the man in the diorama. "C'mon, Eddie. Gotta wet my whistle. Get you a burger or something. Let's go."

Ed didn't get the diorama job, but he did apply for others, even in the gift shop, and didn't get those either. He satisfied himself with frequent visits, sitting on the benches before the dioramas, seeing himself there, exploring, wondering what went on in the parts of the museum he couldn't see. Wondering what went on everywhere, offices, hospitals, anyplace people worked.

He took out his notebook and started sketching and jotting down random thoughts, and then he started to draw the muskox in the display nearest him. A boy on a class trip watched. "Are you drawing that thing?" asked the boy. Ed looked up to see him and some classmates staring at his crude drawing.

A young teacher was eavesdropping. "Boys, now leave that man to his work."

"Is that your work, Mister?" asked one of the children.

Ed closed the notebook on his lap, crossed his legs, and put a professorial finger on his chin. "Well, drawing is not my work." He looked to the teacher with an avuncular grin. "No, I'm thinking about a new diorama and was trying to draw up some ideas."

"Wow, a new one!" said a boy.

"Will it be a Bigfoot? Or Yeti?" asked another.

"I like panda bears," said a little girl.

"Well, I can't tell you right now. We're not ready. But personally, I like the idea of sasquatch, but don't tell anybody, okay?"

"I swear," said the boy. "I swear it a million times."

A chorus of "me too, me too" followed.

"Of course we'd have to put it here, in the Hall of North American Mammals. Or maybe the Hall of Primates. What do you think?"

The kids gathered around Ed, their teacher standing behind, smiling as they yelled out their thoughts about where the Bigfoot exhibit would go, advising Ed of their thinking.

"It would have to be a really tall one, like ten feet!"

"They're not ten feet. They're only eight feet."

"Will you have more than one, like a family?"

"Where did you get it?"

"I think they're the same speecee as the abdominal snowman, don't you?

"You need to have plants because they're vegetarians!"

Ed said he'd been given things to think about and thanked them for such great ideas. He stood up and shook each of their little hands. The teacher nuzzled up close and whispered that he'd made their day. Ed smiled and said he looked forward to seeing her again, when the Sasquatch exhibit opened. She squeezed his arm, gathered the children, and moved on.

Ed continued through the museum, standing up straighter, walking more deliberately, and found himself at the massive bookstore. A young man with a student volunteer tag asked if he could help find anything. Ed noticed the tag, which read "Columbia."

"Columbia!" he said to the young man. "What are you studying?"

"Haven't decided," said the young man eagerly. "I'm doing this for an internship. Maybe English. I'm only a freshman."

"Ah," said Ed. "Explore and enjoy. I'm sure the school's changed since my years there, but exploration is the key. Take courses that interest you, not just to get a career. Careers can wait. English is a fine major."

"When did you graduate?"

Ed hesitated, "Undergrad or graduate? Both were long before you were born. Anyway, do you have any books on Sasquatch?"

"I don't think we have anything on mythical beings," returned the boy, looking around. "There's enough real stuff that's interesting, don't you think?"

"Yes, of course. For my grandson, you know. Good luck at Columbia. Headed up there myself, trustee meeting. Perhaps I'll see you there sometime."

He rushed out of the store, a bit stooped, down the front steps toward the statue of Theodore Roosevelt, whose horse's rear-end was staring him in the face. Deservedly so, thought Ed. Deservedly so.

He was watching crowds of people going to places they needed to go, to work, to the museum, to walk their dogs, jobs, to wherever. "Back to the park," he decided. Perhaps the two ladies he'd entertained earlier would still be on that bench. He looked back at Teddy Roosevelt.

Ed thought about the roles he'd been playing. He didn't usually think about that. They just came to him. Today, though, with the kids, it bothered him. They were games. When they were over, he was Ed Jesperson again. Ed Jesperson looking to be someone other than Ed Jesperson. "Resolved," he determined.

He'd volunteer at the museum. Why not? A docent. A guide. He'd tell stories to the kids. It was a role that suited him.

He stood taller when he turned to cross back over Central Park West, thinking about his future. He was not thinking about the traffic light that had turned green or the cab that was going too fast with a passenger urging the driver to hurry for a meeting at ABC. When it hit him, he was flung to the curb, a crowd gathering around. He was bleeding, had broken a hip, he was sure—a bad thing at his age.

A man put his coat under Ed's head. Camel hair, Ed noted. "We called 911. An ambulance will be here in a second." Ed looked up, whispering. The man moved in close to hear what Ed was struggling to say.

What he intended to say at that moment, that moment when he felt his life fading, a life so very different than his dreams, was something to the effect that the man should call the FBI. That he should tell them what happened. That he should relay, and this Ed would emphasize was most important, that he had been right all along, and that they would know what to do.

He opened his right eye, the sclera crimson from internal bleeding. His left eye was swollen shut. If the man leaning over Ed hadn't been looking for the flashing lights of an ambulance, he might have seen a glimmer in that right eye.

"Tell them, tell the museum."

"What? Tell them what?" asked them man.

"Bigfoot, the . . ." Ed was spitting out blood.

"Bigfoot? You said bigfoot?"

Ed managed a pained smile. "The abdominal snowman," he said.

The man nodded, assuming the man on ground was delirious. Ed's eyes closed and never opened.

32.

Last Remains

Deano bent over the camping gear in the attic, brushing away the cobwebs and dried-out flies, careful not to lift his head to the sloped roof with nails sticking down through any number of the shingles that had been put on over the years. Behind the sleeping pads, almost hidden in the depths of fiberglass insulation, lay the utilitarian urn that contained half his father's ashes. He smiled when he saw it. He remembered where it was, after all.

He hefted up the urn, surprised at its weight, and put it upright on the floor, wondering for a moment about the heavy gold bridge—the sanitary pontic—his father got thanks to a US Army dentist during the war. It was a story his father never tired of telling all the way to the day he died. Literally. That very day he opened his mouth for the nurse administering his morphine drip and told how his jeep had hit a mine, emphasizing it was a "kraut" mine, rolled into a ditch, and he'd broken several teeth. A "million-dollar wound," he called it. "Better than a Purple Heart!"

Always to Deano he'd say, "It'll be yours someday if you can pry it out! Worth its weight in gold. Get it?"

Oh, Deano got it, all right. If not the first time, then the hundredth time. He never did get the pontic though, his father disproving the rule that "you can't take it with you." He did, however, leave pretty much everything else to Deano's sister Marion. To be fair, Deano didn't need the money and had acquiesced when his father discussed the will and, for the umpteenth time, opened his mouth to display the gold mine inside. "Must weigh an ounce if it weighs anything," he'd laugh.

He thought for a moment about sifting through those last remains. An ounce would be close to $2000. His father would have wanted him to sell it. In fact, he had insisted. "Won't be doing me any good," he would say. Then he'd open his mouth to reveal the glittering bridge. it was all too morbid for Deano, though he was curious enough to shake the urn listening for the dull rattle of an ounce of gold.

Deano looked about, moving more of the camping gear, looking for a depression in the insulation that held his next objective. He scrambled backward, over a box with Christmas ornaments, squeezed through crates with tax documents, groaning at their weight, pushing aside those with dates older than seven years; those he could throw away. "Gotta clean up that mess if we ever want to sell," he whispered to no one.

"Sheila," he yelled down the stairs. "Are you sure it's up here?"

"Which one?" his wife returned.

"Moms! Found Dad's."

"Christ, I don't' know! It's a pigsty up there. We've got to clean up that mess if we ever want to sell," she said.

Deano rolled his eyes.

"Yeah, yeah, well maybe you could come up and help, huh?"

"It's your funeral!"

He winced at that and continued scrounging around for Mom, mouthing "bitch" under his breath. It wasn't his funeral. It wasn't a funeral at all. It was just that after years of his parents' ashes collecting dust, he thought it was time to let go of them. It wasn't emotional. It was a matter of convenience. He and Sheila were off to Provincetown for a romantic weekend. He remembered a rare moment of familial happiness there in the summer of 1965 and figured it was a fitting spot to finally dump his share of those ashes.

After having moved aside boxes with the kids' baby clothes, the china they'd gotten for their wedding and never used, various pieces of outdated luggage, and college papers he hadn't looked at in over thirty years, he found the wooden box containing his mother's last remains. He held that under his arm, tightly, and grabbed his dad's urn. When he stood to leave, his head banged a beam, jarring him to the side, where it hit a nail causing him to drop both parents. The box flipped open, and the plastic bag holding his mother's ashes tore while the top of the urn came off sifting some of his father's ashes on top of his mom's. "Oh, god-damn it," he said, wincing at the pain. There was no blood, to his relief.

He brushed the mingled ashes into the urn, stirring the mess with a finger as if looking for something, and swept the rest be-tween the cracks of the attic floor. He smiled, thinking that would have been the only time, since the divorce, that his father had gotten on top of his mother. Looking at the urn and the box with a now deflated bag of ashes, he said, "Time to say goodbye, guys."

※　　※　　※

Marion sat on the couch in her cramped Manhattan studio and stared teary-eyed at the urns that held her share of her par-ents' ashes. The urns were a matching set, touching each other, with a photo of a smiling couple holding a little girl, not more than four, pouting before the camera. The TV was on CNN—the TV was always on CNN—with the sound down low showing footage of the aftermath of a terrorist attack in Spain where a truck barreled down a busy shopping street killing half a dozen people and injuring twenty-three. Marion was wiping away tears as she picked up the phone.

Deano eyed the caller ID on his phone and squeezed his eyes tight. He hesitated before picking up.

"Deano?"

"Yeah, what's up?"

"I miss them so much."

"Who?"

"Mommy and Daddy."

"Mommy and Daddy? How old are you, exactly?"

"Fine. Mom and Dad then."

"Why today? Is it an anniversary or something?"

"No, I'm just thinking about their, you know, what you want to do."

"Oh, yeah. Right. Well, I think it's high time we let the genies out of their bottles. It's been, what, ten years for Dad or something, more for Mom. "

"Fourteen for Mom. Twelve for Dad. I can't believe you don't remember."

Deano rolled his eyes and was about to say, "What difference does it make?" but took the high road.

"Wow. Seems like yesterday. Fourteen years for Mom. The kids were, what, twelve and fifteen? Wow."

"Are they coming?"

"Coming? Coming where? "

"To the ceremony."

"Ceremony? What are you talking about?"

"When you put them to rest. On the Cape."

She'd called it a ceremony. Deano had said, made sure he was understood, that he was simply spreading their ashes. There would be no ceremony, no speeches, no priest even if they had been Catholic, and no fanfare. His very words to Sheila had been, "Just, you know, open up the box and let them go. It will be like a visit to the dump."

Apparently, Sheila hadn't delivered that message to Marion.

Deano tried to soften the words to Marion, but the line "like a visit to the dump" didn't go over well. There was silence at the other end of the phone, which meant tears would come, then blubbering, followed by a guilt trip, and they wouldn't speak for weeks until Marion contacted Sheila and Sheila then urged Deano to call her. Deano held the phone until he heard a click and put it away. He went to warn Sheila, who would give him a look, sigh, and then go back to whatever she was doing.

The phone rang again.

"I dropped the phone," said Marion with only a light blubbering.

"Oh, I was about to call you back."

"I think we should have a service, a ceremony. That's what I want."

"Well, you can have that. Sure. With your ashes, if that's what you want. I just don't think it's that big a deal. I mean, Dad didn't care. He did that Neptune Society thing until you intervened. And would you want, like, a rabbi, priest, minister? Druid, maybe? I mean, I wouldn't know."

"I intervened, as you put it, because that stupid Society was just so cold. They'd toss his ashes anywhere. They didn't care."

"No, not quite. The Society would take his ashes and distribute them over the ocean, which Dad thought was fine. He checked the 'Any ocean' box. That much I remember."

Marion started to cry, louder this time.

"He did it so not to burden us."

"Exactly, exactly. And I plan to honor that. Unscrew the top, pour him out, and voila, Dad's ashes are on their way. Better than hanging out in a cramped attic."

"And Mom?"

"Open the box and off she goes to wherever the winds may take her."

"The box? You still have her in a box? In the attic?"

Deano held the phone away from his ear, gritting his teeth, and took a breath through his nose, almost sensing the hairs being sucked down deep in his nostrils. Then he took another, more calming breath. Slowly, deliberately, with stressed calm, he said, "Marion, I gotta hop. Talk later. Let Sheila know you're going to have a ceremony for your ashes." He heard snuffles at the other end and a quick, controlled "fine" before his older sister hung up. He could breathe easily again.

He was up in the attic retrieving two suitcases before heading to the garage. He eyed his rods and tackle, deliberating over whether he'd need a surf rod of something lighter or maybe the fly rod. He took all three, just in case. Sheila yelled down the steps, telling him to take beach chairs and warning him it would be getting cool so he should bring a jacket. "It's the Cape in October, you know."

"Oh?" he replied. "It's not Boca in August?"

"What? I can't hear you."

"Nothing."

"WHAT?"

"NOTHING."

Sheila arranged a bag with snacks for the ride, and Deano suggested maybe they could stop for fried clams on the way. She said she'd already prepared food and didn't want it to go to waste. "We can get clams in P-town," she said.

"If anything's still open," he countered.

"Of course if anything's still open," she retorted.

When she opened the back of the SUV, she asked him to get a third chair. He looked up from organizing his box of lures. Confused, then worried, he asked, "Why?"

"For Marion. She won't want to sit on the sand, for goodness' sake. And can you move your rods? There's no room in the backseat."

"What? Why? Wait! She's coming? I didn't know. Really? Tell me you're joking, or I'll kill you!"

"I'm not joking. We're picking her up at the station."

"It's justifiable homicide then. I didn't know. God, she'll ruin everything."

"She said you told her to arrange it with me, so we did."

"Arrange what?"

"The ceremony."

"There's no ceremony! I'm just tossing their ashes in the water, finally, after a hundred years. What ceremony?"

"She wants to come and do it together. I think that's nice."

"She'll be there the whole time?"

"Of course. Why wouldn't she? It'll be fun. She can sleep on the pullout in the living room."

"She goes to bed at nine! I was hoping to watch stupid TV."

"There's Wi-Fi. You can watch on your computer. Hurry. Her train comes in soon."

Deano's life flashed before his eyes. He envisioned the last moments soon to come. The slurry of ashes in the sea coating his legs with a heavy, thick cement, in the cold water off Herring Cove Beach, dragging him out with the tide, his sister clinging to him like a drowning man, sobbing, taking him under the waves and Sheila filming it all with her iPhone 11+. "Ah, that's sweet," she'd say. "Ooh, this is really nice," then she'd swing the phone around to take in the lighthouse. "Oh, look, isn't that an osprey?"

He could feel himself prying his sister's arms and fingers from his now bruised shoulder, pushing her off as she grabbed for him, diving into the surf, swimming his best dog-paddle, then side-stroke out into the sea to the point of exhaustion, finally slipping beneath the waves as he hears the muffled cries of his sister and Sheila's enthused shouting about how much they love the Cape at this time of the year all while he takes into his lungs the mud of seawater and ashes, choking, smothering, in this final act of parental control. He could hear his mother's long-dead voice, "I told you you should take swimming lessons at the Y," and his father in rare agreement. "But nooo, you wanted to play guitar!"

"You okay? You look dazed."

"Fine, just fine. Like you said, it's my funeral."

Marion met them at the train station, with a very large suitcase in tow and a second one, larger, still on the platform waiting to be picked up. "You don't need your own mattress," said

Deano. Marion glowered at him, turned to Sheila, and said the second bag contained the urns. "They're heavy. Do you mind?"

She carried a bouquet under her arm that kept slipping out. "Flowers for us?" asked Sheila.

"Oh no. I thought we'd lay them in the water so the tide could carry them out with Mommy—er, Mom and Dad. Buddhists do that. Or Hindus. Maybe Hindus now that I think about it."

The drive to the Cape went surprisingly well—no fights, tears, or stirring up of a lifetime of family tensions—because Marion slept most of the way and only woke up as they crossed the Bourne Bridge, which was just in time for her to see the Clam Shack boasting of being the first or last fried-clam Mecca on the Cape, depending on whether you were coming or going. "Oooh, I love fried clams . . . let's stop, I'm hungry anyway."

Sheila said she was peckish, too, and might indulge in their onion rings. Deano glared at her, but she just smiled and said maybe they'd have a light dinner.

The sun was still below the horizon when he awoke to go fishing, tiptoeing past Marion, who asked him to keep it down. It was a long walk to the beach, but with rod in hand, he was happy. The tide was out, which was not the best time for fishing, and the wind was blowing hard, making for difficult casts. He managed to land just a handful of mackerel, which he threw back. Still, any fish were better than none. He looked into the morning sky and saw the night's final stars in the dark blue overhead giving way to a rising red from the east. "Red sky in morning . . ." he thought to himself.

After returning to breakfast at the rental, Deano said they should drive to Herring Cove Beach, where they used to go as kids, and do what they came to do, "Then we can head over to Wellfleet, catch the incoming tide, and, maybe, get some more fried clams." Marion said she'd be up for a cappuccino, maybe frozen custard, in Provincetown, and Sheila couldn't agree more.

"And then Wellfleet," said Deano.

"Maybe, let's see," said Sheila.

"No, not maybe. C'mon." It came out as a whine.

Marion looked at him with sympathetic eyes, leaned her head to one side like she did when she was trying to be helpful, and said, "It's hard, I know. You're upset."

"I'm not upset. It's not hard. It's easy. The hard part is doing what I'm here to do. Fish!!!"

"And the ceremony," said Marion.

"Not at all. I'm here to drop the ashes in the only place I remember them being happy together. How old was I? Seven? I probably didn't know any better. Let's go. And then cappuccinos."

"And ice cream. Daddy would have liked that. Pistachio with hot fudge was his favorite."

"God," said Deano.

There were only a handful of people on the beach, and they were already leaving as the wind picked up and clouds darkened. "No one's here," observed Sheila.

"Just as well," said Deano.

"Why just as well?" asked Marion.

"Because it's illegal to spread someone's ashes in a public place."

"You've got to be joking," Sheila said.

"Nope. It's illegal, and in federal waters it's seriously illegal unless you're three miles offshore. I looked it up."

"I don't believe you," said Marion. "They're clean organic matter. That's just not right."

"Yeah, well, whatever. I don't see any cops or undercover-looking people. Let's do it and get those coffees."

"Cappuccinos," corrected his sister.

"Honestly, they're still coffees."

"They're more espresso than coffee and I don't want you taking us to a coffee shop instead of a café, that's really—"

"Fine, fine, let's move it. Bring your ashes."'

261

"I'd rather not," said Marion.

"Do you want me to carry them, hon?" asked Sheila.

"No, I decided to keep them. I like having them near me."

"When did you decide that?" demanded Deano.

"On the train up. I just held those urns and couldn't let them go.

"So you didn't have to come up here?"

"Of course I did. You have Mommy and Daddy, too. Half of them anyway."

Deano turned to stare at Sheila, who put on a smile and said, "I think that's a very nice idea. Deano, maybe you want to keep them. Somewhere other than the attic."

"No, I don't. They were happy here. We were happy here. Once. I think. You know why?"

"Why?" they came back in unison.

"Because we didn't have to distribute anyone's goddamned ashes!"

"No," said Marion. "We buried Gramma and Papa."

"Let's get this done," said Deano.

They walked over the wet sand, Marion stumbling in her heels, finally leaning on Deano as she took them off. Sheila was smiling at the high waves driven by the wind. "Oh, it's like a storm," she said.

At the water's edge, Deano took out his mother's box from a large canvas beach bag and started to open it.

"Aren't you going to say anything?" said Marion.'

"What?"

"Aren't you going to say something, like a prayer or some words about Mom and Dad?"

Deano stared across the rough sea and wondered how far out he could swim. "The thought never crossed my mind. I'm up for a silent meditation."

"Well, I want to say something," said Marion.

"Be my guest!"

"Mommy and Daddy. I love you and miss you and now send you off to your rest."

"That's it?" said Deano.

"Yes," said Marion.

"Those are the words you wanted me to say?"

"Well, a bit more, a lot more. Like with God and everything, but I didn't prepare a speech, so, yes, that's it."

"Christ," he said.

Deano opened the lid of his mother's box, looked about again for the authorities, and, seeing none, undid the twist tie on its plastic bag, and poured the ashes into the shallow surf of the incoming tide. Marion came over to him, tears shedding, and held his arm in a vice grip. He threw the box back onto the sand and took a few steps into the water, the higher waves lapping over his thighs. Marion held on more tightly, sobbing now.

He unscrewed the urn and slowly poured out his dad's final remains. The slow stream of ashes made a soft whoosh as they hit the water. As the last dust fell into the sea, he heard the non-whoosh of a splash. Unwinding himself from Marion's clutches, he dove in, pushing her away. Sheila yelled, Marion screamed, and Deano rose, triumphant, his hand raised in the air.

"The sanitary pontic! A half-ounce if it weighs anything!"

He gulped in the ashy slurry after his sister pushed him into a particularly large incoming wave, still holding tightly onto his father's former dental work.

About the Author

DAVID ADER stumbled around after graduating from Tufts University and Columbia's School of International and Public Affairs. He was the #1 ranked strategist in his field, the government bond market, for twelve of that 30+ year career. He retired in 2019 believing that while bonds mature, he'd rather not. He's still stumbling, but gracefully so, pursuing long-held interests in fly fishing, archaeology, sailing, history, bushcraft, and the great outdoors. This work represents the first time his fiction has been collected into one volume. He lives in Westport, Connecticut with his wife of 38+ years.

CPSIA information can be obtained
at www.ICGtesting.com
Printed in the USA
BVHW081201161221
624197BV00005B/49